"What's the most important thing to you?"

Nick asked.

"Honesty," Mary Beth said, knowing it would have saved her so much.

"I'm a man who can't give you honesty."

She turned away, unwilling to let him see what she so desperately wanted to hide from herself. She'd fallen in love with him.

"I'm sorry." His words rumbled in the quiet of the room.

He'd tried to be kind, to give her some dignity to hold on to.

Whether he admitted it or not, he was an honest man.

Dear Reader,

Welcome to another month of excitingly romantic reading from Silhouette Intimate Moments. Ruth Langan starts things off with a bang in *Vendetta,* the third of her four DEVIL'S COVE titles. Blair Colby came back to town looking for a quiet summer. Instead he found danger, mystery—and love.

Fans of Sara Orwig's STALLION PASS miniseries will be glad to see it continued in *Bring On The Night,* part of STALLION PASS: TEXAS KNIGHTS, also a fixture in Silhouette Desire. Mix one tough agent, the ex-wife he's never forgotten and the son he never knew existed, and you have a recipe for high emotion. Whether you experienced our FAMILY SECRETS continuity or are new to it now, you won't want to miss our six FAMILY SECRETS: THE NEXT GENERATION titles, starting with Jenna Mills' *A Cry In The Dark.* Ana Leigh's *Face of Deception* is the first of her BISHOP'S HEROES stories, and your heart will beat faster with every step of Mike Bishop's mission to rescue Ann Hamilton and her adopted son from danger. Are you a fan of the paranormal? Don't miss *One Eye Open,* popular author Karen Whiddon's first book for the line, which features a shape-shifting heroine and a hero who's all man. Finally, go *To The Limit* with new author Virginia Kelly, who really knows how to write heart-pounding romantic adventure.

And come back next month, for more of the best and most exciting romance reading around, right here in Silhouette Intimate Moments.

Yours,

Leslie J. Wainger
Executive Editor

Please address questions and book requests to:
Silhouette Reader Service
U.S.: 3010 Walden Ave., P.O. Box 1325, Buffalo, NY 14269
Canadian: P.O. Box 609, Fort Erie, Ont. L2A 5X3

To the Limit
VIRGINIA KELLY

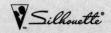

INTIMATE MOMENTS™

Published by Silhouette Books

America's Publisher of Contemporary Romance

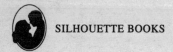 **SILHOUETTE BOOKS**

ISBN 0-373-27372-X

TO THE LIMIT

Copyright © 2004 by Virginia Kelly Vail

This edition published by arrangement with Harlequin Books S.A.

® and TM are trademarks of Harlequin Books S.A., used under license. Trademarks indicated with ® are registered in the United States Patent and Trademark Office, the Canadian Trade Marks Office and in other countries.

Visit Silhouette Books at www.eHarlequin.com

Printed in U.S.A.

VIRGINIA KELLY

Virginia Kelly lives in Florida with her husband of many years and the youngest of their three children. She loves reading and writing romantic adventure and romantic suspense stories, all with happy endings. A native of Peru, she loves to travel and enjoy new places. She can be reached on the Web at http://intimatemomentsauthors.com.

For Bruce.

With special thanks to: Susan Litman, Sheila Seabrook,
Linda Style, Susan Vaughan, Ann Voss Peterson
and RWA's Golden Heart contest.

Thanks to the following for getting me started
and keeping me motivated: Rita Fox, Cecile Cuevas,
Monica McLean, Sally Hawkes, the Gulf Breeze Group,
the Deadly Dames and the wonderful folks
at RW-L and CNN.

Chapter 1

Ciudad San Mateo
San Mateo, South America

She'd come armed.

The dress made a formidable weapon. Simple, sophisticated, tasteful. The kind of dress most women did not have the grace to wear. Another woman would have chosen a little black dress to show off a curvaceous figure. This woman's regal posture said she chose this little black dress to put off any man willing to approach her.

The thought made Nicholas Romero smile.

He knew all the other guests at his mother's formal fundraiser. That meant the interesting American had to be Mary Beth Williams. She'd telephoned this morning while he was busy trying to verify the rumors that had brought him home to San Mateo, rumors of something that could bring an end to what had torn at him for years. Annoyed at the intrusion, he'd listened politely, intending to hang up as quickly as possible. But her precise tone and insistent manner had made him curious to find out what she could want that demanded his immediate attention. Even though he'd wanted to avoid this evening's party, he decided to invite her. After a brief hesitation, she'd accepted.

She stood just inside the marble-floored foyer and looked into the formal dining room, as if searching for someone among the milling guests. A quick push at her short, stylish hair revealed nervousness, but almost before he saw it, a cool, composed mask fell into place. That type of control intrigued Nick.

He half listened to a new United States embassy official standing beside him as he watched the young woman. He'd always thought blondes were overrated by his countrymen, but this one was different. The black high-heeled sandals she'd chosen showed off her fantastic legs but contradicted her manner. It smacked of aristocracy, of grace and polish, and gave her a touch-me-not quality.

Not the sort of woman he normally found attractive.

But he was up to a challenge and, he admitted, excusing himself from the embassy official, he liked what he saw.

Standing inside the beautifully adorned foyer, Mary Beth hoped no one could tell she'd run in as if the hounds of hell were chasing her. Her relief at getting inside the huge, exquisite house in this elite neighborhood had been so profound, she'd wanted to hug Doña Elena Vargas, who'd greeted her. Now she tried to calm her jangled nerves while waiting for the middle-aged woman to announce Mary Beth's arrival to her son, Nicholas Romero.

If only the car she'd spotted across the street as she got out of the taxi had not looked exactly like the one that followed her from the airport earlier, she wouldn't have given it another thought. But it did, down to the muddy front plate.

Clutching her evening bag with a slightly shaky hand, she pushed the idea to the back of her mind. She couldn't afford fear. She had come here for one reason—to do whatever was necessary to save her brother.

She spotted Romero as he mingled with the guests. He was hard to miss. Even from across the room, Mary Beth couldn't help but notice his intense blue eyes, so at odds with his black hair. On the evening news he didn't seem as tall. Or as handsome. Or as…intimidating. But here, at this formal party, he was all that and more.

This was the man she had to convince to help her. She'd come prepared to pay him to take her into the San Matean jungle. One look at his home, at him, and she began to have doubts. But the Primero de Mayo terrorist group had given her no choice. If she did not take the hundred-thousand-dollar ransom to them, they would execute Mark.

At first she'd considered confiding in their father, but only momentarily. Spencer Williams, with his long history of issuing terse orders, would have placed his son at risk by arranging some sort of rescue. The only hope Mark had was for her to do as the terrorists dictated.

But her years of living as a foreign diplomat's daughter had taught her that she would need someone who knew how to mediate. And the only one who could do that in this country and make sure Mark was released was, according to everything she'd learned, Nicholas Romero.

She'd chosen him because her exhaustive though hasty research had told her he was the one who could see this through. Several magazine articles had praised his abilities as a successful negotiator. A newspaper article had reported that he'd even dealt with Primero de Mayo before.

Taking her eyes off him for a moment, she scanned the room, noticing the well-dressed guests, the uniformed waiters, the elegant buffet. A small band played a Latin ballad softly. Everything about the setting reminded her of the life she'd left behind ten years ago. She would never have guessed she'd have to participate in this sort of thing again. And certainly not in order to get Mark back safely.

Thank goodness for the shop just down the block from the hotel. She'd found an appropriate dress, though a bit low in the back for her taste, and skimpy sandals that were at this moment making her long for her tennis shoes.

She received appraising looks from several people and smiled politely in response. Sure her face would freeze in a sham of a smile if she didn't stop, she returned her concentration to Romero.

As she watched, several very attractive women stopped and spoke with him. Attentive, he shook hands and smiled, but treated them no differently than he had two elderly women he'd spoken with moments ago.

Now, standing beside a youngish man—American, she would guess—he listened courteously, until he looked up, his gaze seemingly drawn to her. He placed his drink on a nearby coffee table and crossed the room, politely greeting people. Dressed in formal black, he moved with confidence, his long strides bringing him closer and closer. The sounds of the party faded, and Mary Beth fought the overwhelming urge to bolt.

What was she going to say? Everything she'd rehearsed in her hotel room had evaporated. Her surroundings, his appearance, everything about this party told her that offering to pay for his services would be awkward, if not insulting. Wishing for some instant revelation, she scrambled to think of the right approach to get him to agree.

He had to agree. He was a man sworn to peace, to saving lives. He wouldn't refuse. He couldn't.

All she had to do was act confident. Schooling her features for the performance of her life, Mary Beth suppressed a nervous laugh and took a wineglass from a passing waiter's tray.

"Ms. Williams," he said over the sounds of other voices and clinking glasses. "You decided to attend after all." His English was perfect, his Spanish accent barely perceptible.

"It was kind of you to invite me." But from the cool reception she'd received on the telephone, she guessed it hadn't been kindness. He probably thought she wouldn't know how to deal with these surroundings. But then, he had no way of knowing that this was just the life she understood, the life she'd been raised in.

"You've made me curious," he replied, his voice quiet and too masculine. "It's not every day that urgent business brings someone to San Mateo to see me."

Probably not. He was the one to travel on urgent business. As a United Nations diplomat and special envoy to countless world trouble spots, he had pulled off some of the most spectacular feats of compromise in recent international relations.

But she hadn't chosen him because of his public reputation. That would be easy enough to manipulate—something she'd learned the hard way.

Never one to believe everything she read or heard, she'd checked with some friends who moved in the same diplomatic circles as Romero. They'd assured her that he was above reproach. But she had been careful not to tell anyone why she was asking. She couldn't afford to risk Mark's life in any way.

Before she could think of a suitable reply, she was jostled from behind. "Excuse me," she said and stepped forward, only to brush against Romero's chest. He smelled of some expensive but subtle cologne.

Steadying her with a hand to her upper arm, he smiled at the person behind her. It was a polite, professional smile, the same one he'd used with everyone she'd seen him with, the same one he'd used when greeting her.

And that reminded her that she had to get beyond his polite professionalism in order to get him to help her. She had to make him *want* to help her. Standing beside him with nothing to say was not the way to get what she needed.

Flattery, she'd learned years ago, generally worked. But the only flattering thing she could think of was that he was handsome. That didn't seem like the way to approach him.

"You have a beautiful home," she said finally, speaking over the music, which had become a bit louder.

"It's my mother's, although I live here when I'm in the city. It's perfect for fund-raisers such as this."

Before she had time for a response, he said, "Join me at the buffet." He indicated the long, elaborately set table on the other side of the room, directing her with a sweep of his arm.

As they made their way across the crowded room, Mary Beth felt the warmth of his hand against the skin of her back and silently cursed the low-cut back of the black dress. With the gentle unsettling brush of his fingers guiding her forward, she made her way around small groups of people. Behind her, he sounded confident as he greeted acquaintances, while she felt as if everyone in the room was staring at her.

As they reached the buffet, he stepped aside and looked down at her. "You're uncomfortable, Ms. Williams. You don't like parties?"

"I don't like formal parties, Mr. Romero." The words were out before she could call them back. It had been a rude thing to say, considering the setting and the fact that he'd invited her, graciously or not. She turned toward him, desperate to think of something to correct her faux pas, when her attention was suddenly fixed on the first genuine smile she'd seen on his face. He actually looked approachable. Human. And much too attractive.

"Don't look so surprised, Ms. Williams," he said, his eyes alight with mirth. "I don't like formal parties, either."

The young diplomat who'd caught the world's attention didn't like them? She wanted to ask why, to tell him he fit— had been born to fit—while she didn't. Not even after years of attending social gatherings just like this with her father. But she wouldn't think about that time now. Mark needed her. That's why she'd come.

"Mr. Romero—"

"Please, call me Nick."

Now she understood why the articles she'd read referred to him as charismatic. But he was beyond that. *People* magazine should have put him on their cover as the sexiest man alive.

He had incredible eyes. Bedroom eyes. Good God, she couldn't believe she'd had such a thought. She blurted out the first thing that came to mind. "My friends call me Mary Beth."

"Then, Mary Beth it is," he said with a smile.

"Nick," she said, feeling a resurgence of confidence. "I apologize for intruding on your party."

"Don't," he replied quickly, still smiling. Tiny crinkles formed at the corners of his eyes. "My mother will soon have your donation for a local orphanage. Before she tries to take your last dime for her good cause, she would want you to at least sample what she has prepared."

"Feed me before she turns me into a pauper," she replied, more at ease.

He laughed. "Exactly." Taking a plate from the table, he put a skewer of shrimp and a beautifully prepared tea sandwich on it. Farther down, he used tongs to lift a small semi-circular pastry, lightly sprinkled with powdered sugar. "These," he said, placing the confection on her plate, "are worth whatever she manages to get out of you."

"What are they?"

"*Empanadas de carne,* meat-filled pastries. You will never taste any better anywhere. My mother made these herself. The sugar makes them the perfect combination of salty and sweet."

"Ah, you found each other," Doña Elena said, taking her son's arm and looking at Mary Beth. "You must watch him. He will eat all the empanadas if we are not careful."

"Then I should eat mine before he takes it from me," Mary Beth replied, appreciating the woman's casual style.

"My Nicky is a gentleman," Doña Elena said with a laugh. "He will not take it—he will persuade you to give it to him."

"Mamá," he said. "I haven't found out why Ms. Williams is here and already you're scaring her off."

"*Vaya, hijo,* you have never scared away a beautiful woman. I am just alerting her to your methods," she said with a wink.

Nick laughed, and his mother reached up to give him a quick hug and a kiss on the cheek before turning away as another guest caught her attention.

"Now, tell me, why did you call?"

Caught off guard, she nearly said *frantic desperation*. Instead, she said, "I need your expertise."

"Expertise?" he replied, an amused smile on his perfect lips.

"Your diplomatic skills," she hurried to explain.

"I'm afraid I don't understand," he replied, his smile still too wicked for her comfort.

She was in way over her head. Somehow she managed not to take the deep cleansing breath she so desperately needed. "May we speak privately?"

He assessed her with a cool expression. The small band shifted easily into a Latin pop number she'd heard sung by Jennifer Lopez and another singer. Something about begging to be touched.

"My office is down the hall." With that, he placed the plate on a waiter's tray, took her elbow in his hand and led her away from the party, the sensual beat of the music mingling with the warmth of his hand on her arm.

The office was more of a library, the furniture rich and masculine. Three pictures, each framed in hand-worked silver, were the only softer touches on the massive wooden desk. One picture showed Mrs. Vargas, a younger Romero and another young man, a soldier, judging from the San Matean military uniform he wore. The other two pictures were of a small boy at different ages. If Mary Beth had to guess, she would say that the boy was under a year old in one, closer to three in the other.

"Please," he said, "have a seat."

She wanted to stand, but that would only show how nervous she was. She sat.

He walked behind the desk and eased into his chair, his posture relaxed. "Now, please explain why you need me."

She tried to think of how to begin, how to explain. But there was nothing except the truth.

"The Primero de Mayo terrorists are holding my brother for ransom. I need your help in dealing with them."

He made no reply, his expression suddenly closed.

''You have negotiated with them in the past,'' she said, his stillness making her feel as if she should justify her request. ''Successfully,'' she added in the lengthening silence.

He stared at her. The light from a table lamp accentuated his angular cheekbones and strong chin.

''It wouldn't take very long,'' she said, trying to maintain her composure. ''A few days at the most.''

What was he thinking? The oppressive silence grew. She couldn't look away from him, nor think of anything else to say.

''Have you contacted your State Department?'' he finally asked.

''No. I was warned not to. I won't risk Mark's life by doing anything like that.''

''Why not just pay the ransom, Ms. Williams? Primero de Mayo has released hostages when the ransom has been paid.''

He had reverted to the use of her last name, not a good sign. ''They insist that I must take the money to them. I want—need—an expert when I do this.''

''Where do you have to take the ransom?''

''To Los Desamparados, in the Upper Río Hermoso valley.''

Each tick of the large clock on the low bookcase to one side weighed heavily in the subtly lit room. She wished she could climb inside his mind, see what he was thinking.

''Do you know what *desamparados* means?'' he asked finally.

''That has nothing—''

''The forsaken. As in abandoned.'' He seemed to watch for her reaction. When she wouldn't give him that satisfaction, he continued. ''It's not a safe place. It's jungle.''

''That's *ceja de montaña* country, not jungle. The semitropical 'brow of the mountain' from what I've read.''

''Except for the slightly cooler climate, it's much the same.'' He stood, coming around the desk to lean one hip casually on the uncluttered top. ''It is dangerous country.''

''Which is why—''

"You need a mercenary, not me."

"A mercenary will get my brother killed."

"A mercenary will get you there and back in one piece."
He turned and picked up a sheet of paper and a pen. "I'll
give you the names of several men I consider to be trustwor-
thy. Tell them I referred you."

"I don't want or need one of those men," Mary Beth insisted. "You know how to deal with these people."

"Ms. Williams," he said with overwhelming patience,
"they are not people. They are animals."

"I'm prepared to pay—"

One look from him stopped her.

He put down the pen. "There isn't enough money in the
world to make me accompany you," he said simply.

"What can I offer—"

"What do you have to offer?" he asked, his expression
indecipherable.

For one second she didn't understand. "I—" Had he—
"No!"

The clock struck the quarter hour as their eyes held. Something fierce crossed his features, then he looked at her with
what she could have sworn was sadness. A sadness so profound that it gentled his features.

Embarrassed that she had assumed he meant anything sor-
did, she hurried to say, "I'm sor—"

"I will never deal with Primero de Mayo again." Handing
her the paper with its precise block letters, he added, "I apologize for any misunderstanding, Ms. Williams. Find yourself
a mercenary. You will need one."

Chapter 2

A sleepless night full of improbable scenarios and tangled dreams gave way to morning. As she dressed, Mary Beth replayed the evening before.

Nick Romero had refused.

Pride had made her thank him, struggling to hide her frustrated anger. Oh, she could have railed at him, begged, pleaded. But if there was one thing she'd inherited from her father, it was tenacity.

Tenacity and a good plan. That was all she needed.

Not that she had a plan.

Unbidden, part of their exchange replayed through her thoughts.

"What can I offer—"

"What do you have to offer?"

She'd been outraged, she'd wanted to slap him. But she remembered the look on his face. Emotions she couldn't read, followed by a fleeting sadness. And she realized she'd been wrong in guessing at what he'd meant. But he'd understood and, with an apology, she'd been dismissed.

But they weren't finished. This was a setback. Defeat was not an option. She had eight days left before time would run out for Mark. This was the beginning of the day she would get Nicholas Romero to help her save her brother's life.

The direct approach would be the best. She picked up the phone and dialed Nick's house. His mother answered and explained that he'd gone out and would not return until lunchtime. After thanking Doña Elena, Mary Beth decided she would not bother calling him again—she'd be there when he got back. It wasn't nine o'clock yet. She had hours to wait.

The newspaper didn't help her pass the time. Not until she saw a familiar name in an article on the front page. She scanned it quickly, then read and read again, trying to learn as much as she could, because she couldn't believe it.

Mark's friend, the one he'd told Mary Beth to contact if she couldn't reach him, was dead. Killed by the same group that held Mark. This man, Daniel Vargas, had been Nick's cousin, Doña Elena's only son. Nick was her nephew, not her son. None of the articles she'd read mentioned any of this, but she'd read only American magazines and newspapers. They had no reason to report such details.

No wonder Nick's response to her request was so overwhelmingly negative.

And thank God she hadn't known this before. She would never have dared approach him if she had.

She picked up the paper with the names of the mercenaries he'd recommended, and stared at it. Three choices. She'd have to interview them, decide which one would do.

No. She didn't have time. She wouldn't settle for a mercenary. She needed an expert, and Nicholas Romero was it.

She had to convince him to help her.

But if she told him that Mark knew his cousin, the cousin killed by Primero de Mayo, he would refuse again.

She couldn't tell him. Wouldn't.

As she finished a light breakfast in the hotel restaurant, that omission—that lie—did not sit well with her.

Rather than throw things at the walls in frustration, she decided to take a walk. The morning was pleasant, San Mateo's capital enjoying an early spring. She would take her time browsing the shop windows along the streets of the historic city. Then she'd take a taxi and wait in front of Nick's house.

Five minutes into her walk she became convinced she was being watched.

The small white car that had followed her the day before was no longer in sight. But that man standing on the corner by the newspaper stand, the bald one reading the paper, looked a little familiar. Where had she seen him? The party last night? Try as she might, she couldn't be sure.

Walking past a small jewelry store, she eyed the silver and gold trinkets on display in the window and worried about the small gold cross that hung from her neck. Mark had sent it three years earlier in a package that held a safety deposit box key along with a passbook to a San Matean bank account. He'd told her it was hers should something happen to him. She'd laughed off his disturbing words. But now, after selling her car and raiding her savings, she needed that money to help pay the ransom.

She turned, searching for the bald man. He'd moved and now stood looking down the street. Maybe he wasn't following her. Maybe, if she took her time, he'd leave and she'd know for sure.

She walked past the jewelry store and peered through the window of a craft shop. Colorful Andean blankets, ceramics and woodcarvings lay inside and atop sparkling glass cases. She stepped inside and picked up a wood carving of a jaguar, turning it over in her hands, her thoughts still outside with the bald man.

"It is perfect, yes?" a young male clerk said in accented English. "So much life, ready to spring for his prey."

"It is stunning," Mary Beth agreed, forcing herself to relax, to take advantage of the distraction. She felt some smoothly carved letters on the jaguar's belly. *J.M.*

"With four hundred fifty *soles,* it is yours." The clerk smiled.

"Three hundred." Mark, with his love of the wild and dangerous, would appreciate this.

"Señorita!" The clerk looked shocked and offended. "Can you not see the detail? The care that went into the making of this magnificent beast?" He continued. "Four hundred twenty-five, *señorita,* or we will wound the artist's pride."

"Three-fifty." She touched the stylized letters in the artist's signature again.

"Señorita, you have bargained before." He sighed. "I will explain to the artist that you are an expert at *el regateo,* no?"

Knowing she really hadn't bested the clerk in the haggling, Mary Beth paid the agreed-upon price, took her package and walked to the door.

He was still there. The bald man. Across the street, watching from the front of a coffee shop. She stepped back.

"Are you ill, *señorita?*" asked the clerk.

She couldn't answer for a moment. "No, I'm fine, just..." Scared. And becoming more so with each passing moment. The kidnappers had said she would be contacted once she arrived in Los Desamparados. Were they following her to be sure she did as she was told?

Stepping out into the bright sunlight, she walked quickly down the street in the direction of her hotel, throwing an occasional furtive look at the man who seemed to be strolling along behind her. She quickened her pace and bounced off a tourist's portly middle. Apologizing, she hurried on, concentrating on her destination, fighting the urge to look over her shoulder.

One block down, in front of a pharmacy, she turned, trying to avoid the moving crowd. Rising up on tiptoes, she scanned the sea of faces for her pursuer.

He was gone.

Nick folded the newspaper he'd been reading and placed it on his cousin's desk. Staring outside, he pushed aside the memories evoked by the paper's lead story. He wouldn't dwell on the past. He would remedy the future.

Carlos worked on San Matean time, so their eight-o'clock appointment would probably turn into a nine-o'clock appointment. He stood and stretched, wondering if Mary Beth Williams had called one of the men he'd recommended.

He couldn't forget their encounter. She was a woman armed with more determination than most people he knew. She'd guessed he meant something unbelievably crude. He hadn't, but that she would think such a thing made him wonder about himself, wonder what she'd seen in him. Still, in the clear light of day, he was as surprised at what he'd said as she had been.

He'd apologized because he sincerely regretted the misunderstanding. He lived his life so that he rarely regretted anything, let alone apologized for anything.

Had he meant it as a subconscious way of testing her? Her character? Her motives? If so, she'd passed with flying colors. When he should have been kind, he'd been cruel. After all, her brother was in terrible danger, something he understood too well.

Still, he found himself attracted, surprisingly so. She wasn't really beautiful, not in the way the women he normally wanted were. She didn't calculate or flaunt her femininity. She had that elusive something so many women worked a lifetime to achieve—presence.

A regal air, refined manners—those were traits the lovely Ms. Williams had learned. Dignity and integrity were hers, deeply ingrained.

"Nicholas." Carlos Montoya greeted him, coming through the open door. "*Buenos días.* I thought to talk to you at your mother's, but you had left."

"I should have called this morning."

"You thought I was late," Carlos said, smiling. "You are much too Americanized. I had breakfast with Elena. She gave me two cups of *café con leche* strong enough to keep me awake all day.''

Nick laughed. ''Be glad it's warm or she would have forced you to eat oatmeal.''

''Elena is priceless,'' Carlos said, closing the door behind him. ''Even after her charity work last night, she was up early.''

''I'm sure you've piqued her interest, stopping by so early.''

''Your mother sees too much, no?'' Carlos commented, sitting.

''What can you tell me about my evening visitor?''

''You did not give me much time, Nick. I am not a magician.''

No, but sometimes Nick thought he was. The oldest of Elena Vargas's nephews, he had been a mentor and surrogate father. Now, at the age of sixty, he was a friend and, since Nick had taken the reins of the Romero empire, his greatest asset. Carlos, with his enormous web of contacts, could find out anything.

''What have you learned so far?''

''The only information I have is very basic. Your Miss Williams is a university librarian. She is twenty-eight years old and lives in Atlanta, Georgia. Her father was a diplomat, ambassador to Spain a few years ago. I can find no mention of a brother, but we should know more by this evening. You say someone is following her?'' Carlos asked, his eyebrow creased.

''From what my man tells me.''

''And you refuse to help her. Have you lost your sense of chivalry?''

Four years ago, before Nick took over the Romero estate, there would have been reprimand in the words. But Carlos had willingly—eagerly—given over his responsibilities, wanting only to provide guidance to Nick, the only male who still carried the Romero name. Now Nick heard the censure in Carlos's tone.

He met his older cousin's eyes across the expanse of the desk. The morning sun slanted in through the open window, brightening the office. "She'll be safe until she makes contact with one of the men I recommended."

"It would have been a simple thing for you to go with her."

"I never want to deal with the Primero de Mayo again, you know that."

"It did not stop you last year when you—" Carlos cut off his sentence abruptly and picked up the newspaper Nick had left folded on the desk. "This is why you came back from New York so suddenly."

Nick said nothing as Carlos opened the paper to the headline, which read "General Vargas to Lead Gunrunning Probe." The photo beneath the caption was of an older man in a military uniform. Beside that was one of another soldier, younger.

"This is why you refused her," Carlos continued. "You think you can get him this time."

"You're jumping to conclusions."

"It is true," Carlos said, tossing the paper back on the desk, "or you would not be home." He shook his head. "When are you going to stop, Nicholas? When will you let it rest?"

"When he burns in hell."

The sudden opening of the door interrupted the silence of the office.

"*Perdón, Señor* Montoya—" Carlos's secretary said, her voice agitated.

"Carlos, Nicholas," a male voice said from behind her.

"I did not—" the secretary began.

"It is okay, Isabel. Let him in." Carlos stood.

Nick stood, too. Mario Gomez, from the Ministry of Justice, pushed past the secretary. She looked the man up and down and closed the door as she left, indignation in every line of her body. The heavy, graying man paid her no attention.

After brief, formal greetings, Mario took the seat Carlos offered.

"What brings you to my office?" Carlos asked.

"I owe a favor to the Romeros," Mario said. "I have come to pay Nicholas back for helping my son." He looked from Carlos to Nick. "It is better for you to stay away from this woman."

Neither Nick nor Carlos said anything.

Mario continued. "This Miss Williams, her brother, a Mark Williams, is a known gunrunner. He jeopardizes the safety of many. It would do no good for you to become involved in the situation in the Río Hermoso."

"Situation?" Nick repeated.

"Our Rangers—Daniel's old outfit—have an operation with the Americans." Mario sat forward in his chair. "Mistakes were made years ago. Serious mistakes. There is an investigation. It has become political."

Nick picked up the newspaper Carlos had thrown down.

"Stay out of it, Nicholas," Mario said, glancing pointedly at the paper. He stood. "I talk reason, no, *amigo?* Diplomacy, you would call it." He looked from Nick to Carlos, then at his watch. "I have a meeting."

"You can tell us nothing more?"

"There is no more to tell, Carlos." With that, Mario Gomez shook hands with both men and left.

Once the door closed, Carlos shook his head. "No, Nicholas."

"You wanted me to help Miss Williams."

"For her, for her brother. Not for this. You cannot bring Vargas down. He is too powerful."

"He'll make another mistake, and this time I'll be able to take advantage of it."

Carlos was silent for a moment. Nick could tell he was

looking for another approach. "It is dangerous. This is Primero de Mayo, Nick—"

"I know that I have failed with them before."

"Not your failure," Carlos said with an angry shake of his head. "What about this brother? What if he is a gunrunner?"

Nick shrugged. He would not think of Mary Beth—the loss of a brother would be devastating. "Find out what you can about him, but it makes no difference. Our Rangers will probably kill him, if Primero de Mayo doesn't."

"As they did Daniel."

Nick stood and walked to the window. He didn't like to think about it, or remember it. Primero de Mayo might have pulled the trigger that ended Daniel's life, but it was Antonio Vargas who was responsible.

Outside, the sun shone, lives moved on. But Daniel, the man Nick considered a brother, the man who was Elena Vargas's only son, was dead. Nick, the infant she'd taken in and raised, was alive. During that first year after Daniel's death, Nick had wished it had been he who died. Sometimes he still did.

"Elena would not want this."

"She knows what her husband is capable of. It's why she hasn't lived with him since before Daniel was born."

"Daniel would not want this vendetta," Carlos argued.

"He has no voice now. No one but me to stop his father. No one but me to keep Vargas from hurting our mother."

"Your death will hurt her. Do not do this thing."

"He nearly destroyed her when he killed his own son."

"Primero de Mayo killed him, Nick."

"If Vargas hadn't refused to ransom him, if—"

"Do not think of ifs, Nicholas. You cannot live your life that way."

"I don't need to concern myself with ifs. I know with certainty that Vargas will hurt the family again. He will hurt us, he will hurt San Mateo. He has to be stopped."

"And you believe you are the one to do it?"

"I'm the only one who can," Nick said with quick assurance.

Because I'm the one most like him.

Mary Beth pushed through the heavy glass doors of her hotel. The cool interior felt soothing. The amiable concierge greeted her, smiling oddly as she passed him. She understood why when she caught sight of her reflection in the lobby's large mirrors. If she'd felt like the hounds of hell had chased her the night before, today in bright daylight, she looked like it. Her hair was windblown, her face pale, her hands shaky. She appeared nothing like the elegant, charming woman she'd wanted to be at eighteen when she so desperately tried to fit into her father's life. She looked more like she had when she discovered how miserably she'd failed, how easily she'd been fooled by charm and looks.

She walked through the sparsely decorated lobby toward the elevators, her breath coming a little easier now that she was back. After pressing the call button, she scrambled in her purse, digging impatiently for the plastic key card—

Glancing at the two elevator doors, she noticed an out-of-order sign on one. The other elevator was taking too long. She punched the button again.

"Having trouble?"

The card flew from her fingers as she turned. Her gaze took in the enigmatic smile on Nick's face. "You scared me half to death!" She bent to pick up the card just as he plucked it from the floor.

His expression changed to one of concern as he handed her the card. "I'm sorry." Worn jeans and a dark-blue polo made him less intimidating than had the formal attire of the evening before. But the casual clothes only made him more attractive.

"I didn't hear you walk up," she said, embarrassed at her reaction.

A little niggling thought crept into her mind. Had he been

waiting for her, or had he followed her? That was ridiculous. A bald man had been behind her. But had Nick ordered—

Surely not. She was letting her fears get the better of her. And letting the lies of the past cloud her judgment, when she was the one holding back something he should know.

He looked up at the floor indicator, then at the sign. "It looks like you're in for a long wait."

"Why are you here?" She put the card back in her purse, wishing her jittery nerves would calm down, wishing she hadn't sounded so abrupt. He'd come to her. This was her second chance to convince him. She couldn't afford to sound waspish.

He smiled. God, he had a smile that could stop even the most cold-blooded woman dead in her tracks. And Mary Beth wasn't cold-blooded.

"I wanted to apologize again, for any misunderstanding last night."

She didn't want his apology. She wanted his help. She would get it, even if she choked trying to be polite. "Apology accepted."

"Have you called one of the men I recommended?"

"I told you, I don't want or need—"

"What plans have you made?"

None. She'd made no plans except to convince him to go along, no matter what it took. "Plans?"

"How are you going to get there?"

"Drive," she said with much more conviction than she felt. She hadn't thought at all about how she'd get there. She'd figured he would know how to do that.

He arched a brow. "What sort of deadline did they give you?"

"Ten days. I have eight left if you count today."

"With no complications, it should only take two days at most."

She didn't like this. He'd refused outright. Now he was asking questions, being too...nice. Such a bland word. *Nice* was not a word she would ever use to describe Nick. Common sense was sending her the strong message to tread carefully. But that was silly. He was Nicholas Romero, trusted by world leaders.

So why couldn't she just accept that he was being nice?

Because he's a handsome, worldly man. Because he operates in a world where nice people are nothing more than casualties, a world that nearly destroyed you. She knew better than to tangle with this stranger standing beside her.

"Why are you here?"

"I think it's time we talked about your predicament."

"I told you—"

"You simply asked me to accompany you because you believe I can be of help. That is not a discussion."

"What is there to discuss? I have to pay the ransom for my brother. He will be killed if I don't."

He seemed to study her for a moment before saying, "Tell me about him."

"Tell you what?" her guilty conscience prodded her to ask too sharply.

"What does he do? Why is he in San Mateo?"

"Will you go with me?"

He looked at her, his expression unreadable. "This isn't a good place to talk. Join me for coffee. There's a café around the block."

Coffee? She didn't want coffee. She wanted an opportunity. That was all she needed. He wanted to discuss her predicament? She would convince, not discuss. She just needed a moment to step back, to compose herself. To decide what she would say without telling him that Mark knew his cousin.

The cousin Primero de Mayo killed.

The elevator chimed and the doors swept open. Two men in business suits stepped out.

"I'd like to put my package away and change first," she said. "Can you wait for me?"

* * *

Fifteen minutes later, Nick was still waiting on one of the uncomfortable couches in the modern, marble-floored lobby. The two men who'd stepped off the elevator when Mary Beth got on had long ago given up waiting for it and had taken the stairs, apparently having gotten off on the wrong floor.

An embassy official he'd met months earlier walked in from the street and looked around. Nick couldn't remember his name or title. The dark-haired man spoke with the desk clerk, then the elevator door opened and Nick forgot everything else.

She'd done it again. The Mary Beth who stepped out of the elevator was no longer the harried woman he'd surprised minutes earlier, but a beautiful and poised woman. She wasn't wearing the little black dress, but it didn't matter. Her armor—green blouse and cream slacks—was in place, and she was ready for battle. Nick smiled in appreciation and wondered what she'd think if he did what every male instinct told him to do—walk up to her, run his fingers through that wild, honey-colored hair and pull her against him.

Distracted by his musing, he'd barely gotten to his feet when he heard the embassy man call out, "Miss Williams?"

Eyebrows raised in surprise, Mary Beth turned. "Yes?"

"I'm Elliot Smith," he said, handing her a business card, "from the American embassy. Your father and I worked together in Madrid. May I have a few moments of your time?"

"Is something wrong, Mr. Smith?"

"Yes. In a way." The short man looked around the lobby, let his eyes meet Nick's for a moment, then straightened his tie.

Mary Beth excused herself from Nick and led Smith a few feet away, stopping beside a replica of an Incan urn. Nick made himself comfortable by leaning on a nearby column. He'd be able to hear their conversation, which, judging from the man's pointed stare, Smith didn't want.

Mary Beth gave Nick a cursory look, then dismissed him with a slight turn of her head. "What is this about?"

"We are warning Americans visiting San Mateo about the dangers here."

"I'm not aware of any dangers," she said.

"There have been problems with terrorists. It's not a good time to be here. Especially not for an American woman."

"Your concern is appreciated." Mary Beth studied him with cool regard. "I still don't see why you're here."

Nick smiled as she deliberately ignored the man's condescending look.

"The ambassador is always worried about Americans who put themselves in jeopardy in San Mateo. He's limited in what he can do to help, especially in dealing with the San Matean bureaucracy."

"I certainly hope he doesn't have to intervene in anything because of me."

"Since you're Spencer Williams's daughter, we thought we'd speak with you about reconsidering your…visit to San Mateo and going home. We are concerned that you're on your own."

"Thank you, and—" Mary Beth moved away slightly "—please thank the ambassador. But I'm not alone. I'm visiting with Mr. Romero."

Nick fought the urge to smile as Smith turned toward him, then focused on Mary Beth again.

"Mr. Romero?"

"Is that a problem?"

Nick pushed away from the column, feeling an odd sense of satisfaction. If Smith had hoped to find a woman susceptible to intimidation, he'd been wrong.

Smith straightened his tie again. "No. Of course not."

"Is that all, then?" Mary Beth asked.

"One last thing." He buttoned his suit jacket. "How is your brother?"

"My brother?"

"I met him in Barranquilla a few years ago."

She paused before answering. "I'll tell Mark you asked about him."

"Please do." Smith shook her extended hand, nodded at Nick and made his way to the front entrance.

Nick felt an unexpected respect for Mary Beth Williams. She was a force to contend with.

"Do you know that man?" She stood with her back ramrod straight, her polished manners perfect.

She reacted to difficult situations with studied decorum. For one wayward moment, he wondered what it would take to rattle her composure, then his better nature took over.

"I've met him," he replied.

"Is he really the military attaché?" She looked up from Smith's business card, which she held in her hand.

"As far as I know."

"Why would he tell me to leave?"

"He's probably worried about your safety." But Nick didn't think so. Smith might have found out she was here through regular channels, but there was no reason why he'd make the effort. It was time to find out exactly what was going on with her brother, what he was about to get himself involved in.

She took a few more steps toward the doors, then turned quickly, her short hair swinging around her face. "Do you think he would have someone follow me?"

Nick masked his expression carefully. "You believe you're being followed?"

"A car followed me from the airport, then again to your house last night. I also saw a man earlier, when I was shopping." She pushed her hair back with the same gesture he'd noticed the night before.

This time Nick recognized it for what it was. Beneath the designer clothes and the cool exterior beat the heart of a frightened woman. Ingrained protective instincts rose to the surface and made him reassess the situation.

Time for the truth. At least part of it. "The man you saw this morning is mine."

It took Mary Beth a moment to fully understand what Nick had said. In that moment, she finally realized how far out of her league she was. "Having me followed doesn't seem like the kind of thing a man of your reputation would do."

"I meant nothing sinister by it." He kept his voice low. Skeptical, she met his gaze.

"Last night," he explained, "my neighbor told me he suspected you were followed. I had my man verify it."

"Does the Primero de Mayo have people in the city?"

"Probably," he replied. "Did you tell anyone about your brother?"

"No. I was told not to." She took a quick breath. "Why would you have me followed?"

"For some reason, I thought you might need protection."

His eyes, intense in the sun-washed lobby, flashed a combination of humor and something that puzzled her.

"Although I've come to the conclusion that there are areas in which you don't need protecting."

She felt the warmth of his steady perusal as he continued.

"That cool demeanor, the ability to brush off all questions, serves you well." He looked her up and down with some degree of admiration. And something warmer. "Where did you learn to handle yourself like this?"

"My life is not at issue. My brother's is." She hoped she sounded more confident than she felt.

"You've made it my concern by involving me." He stepped closer.

For an instant she had the unsettling feeling that he might touch her. The thought confused her, made her aware of the fleeting notion that she didn't know whether to move toward him or step back. Insanity warred with common sense.

"I only want to save my brother," she finally said, as calmly as possible.

"Then we have to come to an agreement."

Heart pounding in her chest, she asked, "Does that mean you will go with me?"

"It means you have to tell me about your brother. Why would terrorists kidnap him? Why would the embassy care enough about you to warn you out of the country?"

Did he know about Mark and his cousin? Had he known all along?

No. If he knew, he would tell her. No need to play this game unless he was at least considering helping her.

"I don't have time for this. Mark is in danger and you're the only one who can help. I would have thought you, of all people, someone whose profession it is to deal with hostage takers, would know this."

"I'm sure I deserve the subtle insult." His lips twitched up in a half smile. "But the ice-maiden act doesn't work with me. You can't dismiss me and my questions the way you did Smith and his." With that, he directed a silent challenge to her, walked back to the plush couch and sat down.

Mary Beth told herself only necessity made her follow and sit down opposite him.

When she did, Nicholas Romero, well-known diplomat, world-class negotiator, looked at her and said, "You're all alone in this, Mary Beth. You don't like it, but you need me. And to get me to cooperate, you'll have to answer my questions."

Chapter 3

Nick had to hand it to her. Mary Beth didn't allow that studied poise to slip even though they both knew he had her.

Instead, she asked, "What do you want to know about Mark?"

She was hiding something. It was obvious from the defensive tone of her question.

He found his gaze drawn to the spot where her silk blouse parted slightly to reveal a tiny gold cross. Maybe it was the sight of the religious symbol, or the fact she was such a fascinating woman. Either way, he realized he was surprisingly tempted to go easy on her.

And that made no sense. No matter what protective instincts he might possess, he had one goal and one goal only. Antonio Vargas would pay. Mary Beth Williams was nothing more than a means to an end. He would not abandon the promise he'd made to himself, what he owed his family.

"What was he—"

"*Señorita* Williams," the concierge interrupted.

Mary Beth looked up.

''The chief of hotel security would like for you to meet him in your room.'' The older man wrung his hands.

Nick rose. ''What's wrong?''

The man's gaze shot from Mary Beth to Nick. ''The cleaning woman has discovered a break-in. *Por favor,* you will come?'' He led the way to the elevator, which opened immediately when he depressed the call button.

Once in the elevator, Mary Beth's eyes remained focused on the display indicating the passing floors. Her stillness made Nick wonder if he would finally see a crack in her composure. But he didn't. She stepped quickly, but calmly, out of the elevator.

A security man waited for them in the hallway, hands behind his stiff back. ''The cleaning woman interrupted two men going through the closet.''

''Was she hurt?'' Mary Beth asked.

''No, no. They ran away,'' replied the security man. As Mary Beth walked past him, he added, ''*Señorita.* I am very sorry.''

The room was a shambles—the dresser drawers flung open, the contents of the closet tossed on the floor. Mary Beth's suitcase had been opened, her clothing thrown aside. Even her cosmetics had been dumped on the bathroom floor, lotions splattered on the tile.

Nick watched her move around slowly, taking in the chaos.

Suddenly, she walked toward the closet and looked down at the overturned suitcase. Her back to him, she crouched and began straightening the mess.

''*Señor,*'' the security man said. ''We cannot find who did this.''

''How did they get in?''

''They broke the lock.''

''Do you have a lot of break-ins?''

''No. We are very careful. This is the first in years.'' He looked around at the room. ''*Señorita,* if you will check your belongings. The cleaning woman will help you.''

Mary Beth, now kneeling on the floor, nodded and put her shoes back into her suitcase.

"Señor," the security man said. "These men. It is not usual. The maid says they were not dressed as common thieves. They have masks to cover their faces and they wear business suits."

The men in the lobby. Nick wished he could remember something besides what they wore. Definitely San Matean, going on what he could remember. The way they stood said they were military, not civilians, despite their clothing.

"Mary Beth, did they take your passport or your money?" Nick asked when the security officer stepped into the hall to talk to his assistant.

She looked over her shoulder, her face pale. "I keep that in my purse." She sounded bewildered. "I don't understand." Standing, she turned and pocketed something.

"You have nothing in here anyone could want?"

A flush crept over her cheeks. Her arm muscles tensed, as if she were fisting the hand in her pocket.

"Nothing anyone would break in here for?"

She slid her hands out of her pants pockets and looked around the room, her eyes stopping first on the stripped bed, then on the overturned dresser drawers. "I don't see any reason why the kidnappers would do this. I don't have the ransom money here. I put it in the hotel safe."

She was scared. The catch in her voice betrayed her.

Nick closed the distance between them, put one hand on her shoulder, trying to keep his touch impersonal, and felt her tremble slightly. "Who else, besides the embassy, knows you're in San Mateo?"

"No one." She met his gaze, the golden brown of her eyes dark.

But something was going on. The kidnappers wanted the money, but they wouldn't steal it from her. If he believed Mario, and he had no reason not to do so, the San Matean government was interested in Mark Williams in this gunrunning investigation. If the men who broke in were military, they were San Matean Rangers. And if they were Rangers, Vargas was behind the whole thing.

But why take an interest in the gunrunner's sister? Unless she was involved in the business. Instinct told him to discard that possibility, but Carlos would find out more and he'd know for sure. Still, the Rangers were looking for something.

The fear on her face nearly made him reach up to push a stray strand of her hair behind her ear. "Tell me about your brother. What he does. Maybe we can figure out what's going on."

Mary Beth saw Nick's hand move up, anticipated his touch and felt oddly bereft when he lowered it. She stepped back.

She was scared. Scared for Mark. For herself. She didn't understand why the embassy was warning her out of San Mateo, why a military attaché found it necessary to talk to her. Unless they knew about the kidnapping. But how could they? None of it made any sense—not Mark's kidnapping, not anything that had happened since she'd arrived in this country. And certainly not the single connection Mark had to Nick.

"There's something you have to know," she said, praying she wasn't about to make the one mistake that would guarantee Mark's death. "Something I didn't know until I read it in this morning's paper."

"What's that?"

"Mark knew your cousin, Daniel Vargas."

She felt the silence of the wrecked room around her, felt him close everything out, then continued. "I had no idea, not of your relationship, not that he was killed. It's not the kind of thing that makes the news in the States."

"What did your brother have to do with Daniel?"

"I don't know. But Mark gave me his name and phone number, here in San Mateo, in case I ever tried to get in touch with him and couldn't."

"Do you have that number with you?"

"I called it when I heard from the kidnappers. There was no answer."

"What's the number?" he insisted.

Grabbing her purse from the floor, she pulled out a tiny address book. "Here," she said, handing him the open book. "Was it really his number?"

"Yes," he replied, handing the book back to her.

She thought she saw his fingers tremble slightly.

"His private number," he added.

"The paper said your cousin was a San Matean Ranger. Mark's work had nothing to do with the military."

"Maybe they met outside of their work," Nick replied. "What does your brother do?"

"He's a civil engineer with a Miami-based firm. They do a lot of road construction, bridges, that sort of thing."

"Did you contact the engineering company when you got the ransom demand?"

"No. I was told not to. They told me not to tell anyone." She took a deep breath in an effort to keep her voice steady.

Nick nodded and turned away. "We'll find out what's going on. What he was doing for the company." Picking up the phone, he asked her, "Mark Williams, right?"

"John Mark Williams," she corrected.

He dialed a number. "Carlos, Nick. I need information on *John* Mark Williams, an American, born—" He looked at her and waited while she told him Mark's birth date. "Yes, that's right." He listened for a moment, then spoke into the phone again. *"Sí, muy bien. Gracias."*

Then he turned to her. That darker, fiercer look, which she'd seen as he spoke about his dead cousin, was gone. "What did you put in your pocket?"

One tiny doubt, probably a remnant of her past, remained, but she had to get the rest of the money she needed to ransom Mark. "The passbook to a bank here in San Mateo. It's where Mark keeps some money."

"Which bank is it?"

She took a small red booklet out of her pocket and handed it to him. He touched the key Mary Beth had taped inside and looked up at her.

"That's a safety deposit box key. Mark told me he kept his papers there."

With strong, deft fingers he opened the booklet. "This is a branch of a large bank in San Mateo. It's in an Andean town near the Romero family *estancia*." He examined the booklet for several moments, then handed it back to her.

Hands shaking, she put it back in her pocket as he studied the mess in the room.

"We can be there by tonight," he said finally.

He'd agreed. Her relief was so profound, her knees felt weak. It was what she'd wanted, the only way to save Mark. She should be thrilled.

But she'd seen something beyond the darkness of grief in Nick's eyes. Something...cold. It made her question herself and her reliance on him.

Nick drove through the gate of his mother's house, still unsure why he'd told Mary Beth he'd take her to her brother's bank. He didn't need her with him to accomplish his goal. Maybe he wasn't as hard-hearted as he'd thought. Maybe Carlos's admonitions of helping a woman in distress had gotten to him. *She* certainly had.

He'd left Mary Beth here earlier. No doubt by now Doña Elena had given her a room and made her feel welcome. He could always count on his mother.

It had taken him two hours to clear his schedule, freeing himself for at least ten days. Plenty of time to deal with this sudden turn of events, this opportunity to ruin Antonio Vargas.

No one was in the house when he went in. Mary Beth was either upstairs or with his mother, wherever she was. He walked to the foot of the stairs and picked up the framed photograph that his mother had placed there so many years ago.

He remembered the joy of the day Doña Elena had taken this snapshot, remembered it and so many other moments shared with Daniel.

"Hi," Mary Beth said from the landing.

He hadn't heard her, he'd been so caught up in his memories.

She came down the rest of the way and looked at the picture he held. "Is that Daniel?" she asked.

"Yes. We'd just finished a soccer game."

They'd been eleven or twelve years old. Daniel on the left, his arm causally thrown over Nick's shoulder, laughed into the camera. They were both dirty, dressed in shorts, knee socks and jerseys.

"*Fútbol*. The national sport," he explained.

Mary Beth seemed to study his face, then looked back at the picture. "Did you win the game?"

"I don't remember." He couldn't. Funny. Winning had seemed so important then. "All I remember is my mother taking the picture, then telling us we were filthy."

"You miss him."

He looked up, wondering if she'd seen what he tried so hard to hide from everyone. "His mother misses him more."

"She has you."

"I'm not really her son. She took me in as an infant. I claim the Romero name by way of her only brother. The Romero heir, who happened to have an American mother who died in childbirth."

"I wasn't—"

"Prying? I know. But you must have wondered why I call Doña Elena 'mother.' She raised me. She became my mother. And Daniel was more than a cousin to me."

"You're lucky to have such a family," she said after a moment's silence.

Nick put the picture down. The recitation had cost him.

He'd never had to explain. He never expected parentage, or the lack thereof, to matter one way or the other. It bothered him that it did. With this woman.

"Is my mother home?"

"I think so, but I haven't seen her."

"I've told her we are going north to the wildlife preserve, on a sightseeing visit. If I told her the truth, she would try to talk us out of going."

"Why?"

"How much do you know about recent San Matean history?"

"Only that there was a big problem with terrorism."

"It was war. Terrorists would invade parts of the country and take over, killing all opposition. The government finally seemed to have it all under control, but then a group took over the Italian embassy, here in the city. It took over two months for San Matean Rangers to free the hostages. The terrorists were killed. After that, there was some sporadic activity." He chose his next words carefully, trying to remain objective. "Terrorists involved themselves in drug trafficking and gunrunning in Los Desamparados and the rest of the Río Hermoso valley. Daniel's Ranger unit was assigned to stop them. He and three of his fellow Rangers were taken from his house outside of Los Desamparados."

Nick paused, remembering the helplessness he'd felt, how his chance to get Daniel out had been sabotaged by Antonio Vargas. The general had done it in order to save his own career, and Nick had failed to deliver on the childhood promise he'd made to Daniel. "Demands for ransom were sent to the families. Hard-liners in the Army would allow only one attempt at negotiations before a military attack. Daniel and the others were shot and killed. The terrorists got away." Anger threatened to smother him. Fists clenched, he fought back against the rolling tide. "Doña Elena has nothing good to say of the place."

Mary Beth felt a sudden need to reach out and comfort him,

but there was nothing she could say or do that would take
away such pain. And pain was the one thing she had sensed
in him from the moment she'd seen him staring at the picture
of his dead cousin.

"Nicky?" Doña Elena called as she rushed into the living
room. The interruption saved Mary Beth from trying to find
something to say to Nick.

"*Sí, Mamá.*" Nick kissed her cheek.

"Will you go by Dr. Rousseau's clinic?"

"Not this time, no."

"Oh." She looked a bit disappointed, but continued.
"There are many things he will soon need. I will talk with
Carlos about finding someone to take them."

"He has several people he could send."

"Antonio came by today. He wanted to know why you are
home."

"What did you tell him?" Nick asked.

"That this is your vacation." Doña Elena touched Nick's
cheek as she spoke. "*Hijo,* perhaps you should—"

"*Papi!*" A child's voice broke in.

Nick turned as a small boy dashed toward them. The dark-
haired child, no more than three, threw himself at Nick, un-
balancing him. He bent and lifted the boy.

"Daniel Alejandro Romero, you must not jump on your
father," Doña Elena scolded with mock ferocity, her hands
on her hips.

The child in the pictures on Nick's desk. A son. No reports
she'd read about the San Matean diplomat mentioned a child.

"Papi," the boy giggled breathlessly, undaunted by his
grandmother's reproof. "Mami is taking me to Miami. Can
you come, too?"

Nick shifted the child from one arm to the other. "No,
Alex, I have to stay here for a few weeks. But I'll come to
Miami as soon as I can."

"Will you take me to Disney World?"

"Yes, I'll take you and your cousin, okay?" Nick eased

Alex to the floor. "Now, remember your manners and meet my guest."

"Mary Beth, this is Alex. Alex, this is Miss Williams."

The little boy seemed to consider what he should do, lifting first his left hand, then his right. Finally, mind made up, he stretched out his left hand. Mary Beth quickly compensated by extending her left hand. From the corner of her eye she could see Nick's smiling approval.

"How old are you, Alex?" she asked.

"Three," he replied, holding up three chubby fingers. "Papi is taking me to Disney World." A single dimple appeared on Alex's left cheek. Black eyes flashed mischief as he looked back at his father. "Can your friend come, too?"

Mary Beth couldn't help but grin. While the little boy's eyes weren't blue, the resemblance was there.

"We'll see," Nick replied. "Where is your mother?"

"Here, Nicholas."

The woman who spoke these words stood in the living room entryway, her gaze lovingly fixed on the small boy. Alex's mother was gorgeous. Lustrous dark hair fell to her shoulders. Her designer clothing emphasized her height and voluptuousness.

Nick looked up. "Laura, it is good to see you."

"You also, Nick."

Mary Beth's gaze moved from one to the other, curious about the formality.

"Laura, this is Mary Beth Williams. I'm taking her to the wildlife preserve."

Laura smiled and walked across the room toward her.

"Mary Beth, this is Alex's mother, Laura Morales."

"Ms. Morales," Mary Beth said, shaking the woman's hand.

"Laura, please. It is good to meet you," she said, then turned toward Nick. "I will take Alex upstairs to get his ball. Your mother has asked us to stay for lunch since we are going away for a few weeks."

Nick nodded and Alex ran from the room; his mother and grandmother followed.

A thick silence enveloped the room.

"He's a beautiful child," Mary Beth said, eager to break the awkwardness of the moment.

"Thank you." Nick smiled, pride in his expression.

She struggled to push aside half-formed ideas about him. She'd obviously been wrong to think he showed any interest in her. "His English is very good, especially at his age."

"I've chosen to speak English to him. His mother and mine speak Spanish to him."

"He doesn't get confused?"

"No." Nick stood and moved behind a wingback chair, his hands on the back. "Alex is very important in my life—"

"There is no need to explain—"

"His mother and I are divorced."

But there was a need, Mary Beth acknowledged. She hadn't misunderstood Nick Romero's interest. The expression on his face had given way to a look of very masculine regard, to eyes too hot for her. She felt pinned by his intensity.

"We share custody of Alex."

She tried to unjumble her thoughts. He had a child. A child not mentioned in any article she'd read. A child they had named after his cousin. She wanted to ask why they hadn't named him after Nick, but she couldn't figure out how to ask, then realized she was fixating on something inconsequential. Why did his child surprise her so much?

Alex bounded down the stairs ahead of his mother. "Papi, let's play *fútbol*."

Nick turned toward his son, smiling with genuine pleasure. "Let's go, then, Alex."

Mary Beth sighed, relieved at the interruption, and watched Alex pull Nick away. She wasn't ready for this. For Nick.

He's not why you're here.

She was here for Mark. She would have to depend on Nick to help her save him. That was all that mattered. Nicholas

Romero and his family were of no concern to her, never would be.

She began walking through the living room into the dining room, intent on asking Doña Elena if she could help, when Laura came down the steps. What was she supposed to say to this woman? *You have a beautiful child and your ex-husband is the most attractive man I've ever met?*

"Nicholas is a good man," Laura said with an unassuming smile, coming to stand a few feet away from her.

"Yes, he is," Mary Beth hurried to say, uncomfortable and not sure where this conversation was going.

Laura looked out the window into the backyard where Nick played with Alex, then back at her. "He deserves much happiness. His mother and I, we want him to find someone who will take the darkness from him."

Was this woman giving her blessing to a future relationship? That was insane. "I—"

"Because of Alex, he tells me that he is taking you to Los Desamparados."

Surprised, Mary Beth nodded. "Yes, he is."

Laura shook her head slightly, glanced out the window again, then said, "He has taken responsibility for the family. He has put the Romeros, all of them, before himself." Her voice tightened, turned into a whisper. "Daniel would not want this for him." She caught an unsteady breath.

Confused that Daniel Vargas featured so prominently in Laura's words, Mary Beth could only listen as this beautiful woman, her eyes dark and lost, continued.

"Be very careful, Mary Beth. Make Nicholas be very careful. Alex cannot be without a father. The Río Hermoso is a killing place."

Chapter 4

A killing place. The words still echoed in Mary Beth's mind hours later as Nick shifted an older-model Land Rover into third gear. They were on the ascent into the Andes, en route to the town where Mark kept his bank account. The fact that he'd chosen an Andean town instead of the capital was odd, but then Mark often shunned the city in favor of the mountains and jungles. He'd always craved adventure. Mary Beth prayed that this one didn't kill him.

The road was dangerous, with tight curves and a precipitous drop that had her initially clinging to the armrest. But she'd relaxed after the first few miles, surprised at her trust of Nick's driving despite the endless switchbacks. She hadn't expected the dry, chilly temperatures that made his suggestion of jeans and a light sweatshirt a good one. He'd explained that their route would take them over the Andes Mountains before they reached the semitropical slopes of the *ceja de montaña*. She should have known, should have thought of that but hadn't. She'd been too surprised to discover he had a son, and was puzzled by the formal and cordial relationship between Nick and his ex-wife. And their dedication to Daniel Vargas.

But there was no point in dwelling on something she would never understand, never needed to understand.

Patterns of shadow and light, formed by the immense boulders and afternoon sun, played against the steadily climbing car.

"This is incredible." Mary Beth pitched her voice to be heard over the heavy drone of the vehicle's engine.

"This canyon is called Infiernillo." Nick kept his gaze straight ahead. "Little Hell."

"A demon had to have built this road."

"Civil engineers with tons of dynamite," Nick corrected. "Nothing else would have cut through solid rock."

"It looks like a cubist's fantasy," she said in wonder.

Nick smiled and shifted yet again. Around the next bend, he pulled the Rover into an overlook.

"Let's get out and stretch," he said once he'd secured the emergency brake.

Mary Beth did, but waited for him before stepping away from the car. While she appreciated the geometric beauty of the Infiernillo, she held tightly to the guardrail. She'd never been fond of heights. This was the highest she'd ever been, other than in an airplane.

"How much farther?" she shouted against the wind that whipped up in swirls.

"Probably another twenty miles to the top, but it'll take us about an hour."

She took a small step back toward the Rover before asking, "Then what?"

"Then we head for the Romero *estancia*. We can stay at— I have a house there. We'll spend the night and go to your brother's bank in the morning."

Once back in the Rover, Nick asked, "Have you ever had *soroche?* Altitude sickness?"

"No. I've never been above ten thousand feet."

"When we reach the top, we'll be at around fifteen thousand feet. There's a thermos of tea in the back seat. Drink some of it. It should help."

Minutes later, Mary Beth choked on the first swallow of tea. "What is this stuff?"

"It's what you'd call a traditional remedy. It'll keep you from having *soroche*." Nick drank from the mug he'd prepared for himself.

"It tastes awful."

"Drink it anyway."

She didn't want to, it was so bad, but she realized he wouldn't be drinking it if there wasn't a reason to do so. They drove on, only the steady drone of the engine breaking the silence. Mary Beth's ears popped several times.

"Is that the top?"

"Yes. Finish the tea or you'll get sick."

A half-hour later they drove through a jagged break in stone and onto the level plateau. At fifteen thousand feet, the air seemed rarified. If the road had been spectacular, the plateau was eerie. Quiet, flat, not a thing in sight but blue sky and brown grass broken by white boulders. Higher mountains loomed in the distance.

"Wow," Mary Beth whispered.

"As flat as the sky. And as cold."

Mary Beth rolled her window down a fraction of an inch and inhaled the crisp, cold air. "Fifteen thousand feet, you said?"

"Yes."

"I'm not sick," she said, turning the cup slightly, watching the last of the now-tepid liquid swirl around and around. "What's in this tea?"

His answer proved to her that she really didn't know what she'd gotten herself into.

"Coca leaves."

* * *

"Here we are," Nick said finally, as the sun dipped below the faraway horizon and twilight settled over them.

Mary Beth stretched, tired from the drive across the dusty plateau and back down to around ten thousand feet. Here the terrain was not so desolate, with some conifers and other vegetation visible along the sides of the rocky dirt road. While not as cold as the area five thousand feet higher, the temperature seemed to drop as the sun set.

They turned onto a track that led to a surprisingly modern single-story house nestled among the trees. The roof angled down low over the huge windows of the facade. Nick drove the Rover around to the side and parked.

"Wait here," he said, getting out but leaving the door ajar. Glancing from side to side, he moved toward the rear of the house, his back against the aged cedar siding, and peered around the corner. Turning, he looked around, as if making sure no one was watching.

She saw it then. Or perhaps she'd seen it all along.

This was not the Nicholas Romero she'd met in the city. This was another man. Not Alex's father, not Doña Elena's son and certainly not the man she'd read about. He looked…harder. Capable of taking care of himself in the isolated interior of San Mateo. He'd said she needed a mercenary to find Mark. All she needed was Nicholas Romero.

"This way," he said, once he'd walked around to her side. He led her to the front door and inserted a key into the lock. It clicked loudly when he opened the door. A clean, white marbled foyer held the cold of the unoccupied house.

Stepping inside, she could see a small living room-dining room combination with ultramodern furniture. The room was austere, with only a single painting on the wall, a panel of black splashed with white. Nothing about the house fit what she'd seen of Nick.

Surprised at the decor, she asked, "This is yours?"

"I have some calls to make," he said. "Bathroom's down the hall. You can freshen up."

Wincing from so obvious and abrupt a dismissal, Mary Beth took her bag and walked down the short hall, past a baby's bedroom. There was, indeed, a bathroom. A woman's bathroom, with stockings hanging on the shower curtain.

Nick hadn't been in Daniel's house since his death. Neither he nor Laura had been able to face it, so they'd just closed it up. He would not dwell on that now. Instead, he would concentrate on what he had to do.

He waited until Mary Beth closed the bathroom door before picking up the phone. Mario Gomez was too scared to speak freely, but Nick had other contacts, friends who'd take a chance.

A woman answered on the third ring.

"Colonel Vidal, *por favor?*" he asked, and waited while the woman called Roberto Vidal to the phone. In the background, he heard the sounds of computer keyboards clicking and people talking. The Ministry of Defense was not a quiet place.

"*Sí,*" he heard Roberto say.

"Roberto, Nicholas Romero. *¿Qué tal?*"

"*Un momento.* Let me take this call in my office," Roberto said without any undue inflection. But once he was on the other phone, Nick could hear the tension in the man's voice. "What are you doing calling here?"

"What's going on, Roberto?"

"A disaster" was his quick reply. "You need to get out of the city. Fast."

Nick saw no point in telling Roberto he'd already left.

"You have stumbled into a joint operation between the Americans and our Rangers. The woman you have been seen with is wanted. The Rangers are after her."

He'd been right about the men in the hotel. "What do they want with her?"

"Her brother is running guns across the border. I saw the

report. I hear that the Americans tried to get her to leave the country. They do not want a woman on trial here.''

"Why didn't the Americans make her leave?''

"I do not know, but the gunrunning is an old case.'' Roberto paused. "One of Daniel's.''

So that was the connection between Mark Williams and Daniel. But why would Williams give Daniel's name and number to his sister? That made no sense.

"Who is our liaison with the Americans?''

"Francisco Arenales. You remember him. He is a colonel now, in Daniel's old outfit.''

"What about on the American side?''

"A man named Elliot Smith. They have him listed as the military attaché, but I think he's CIA. Who else would take on such a common name?''

Nick smiled. "So what do you know about the woman?''

"Nothing. I have been kept out of it,'' Roberto replied.

"Did the brother sell guns to Primero de Mayo?''

"That is what the report said. I do not think the man is alive, personally,'' Roberto continued. "The last time anyone saw him, he was up along the northern *frontera* about two or three weeks ago—then he vanished.''

That sort of timeline coincided with the kidnapping. Could Mark Williams be so unlucky as to have been kidnapped by the terrorists he did business with while San Matean Rangers and the American CIA looked for him?

"If there's been nothing for so long, why all the sudden interest in him?''

"I do not know. The report I read is more than a month old. A friend told me that Williams was seen, but I cannot verify that.'' Roberto paused. "According to what I read, Williams worked the area for years. I think the Rangers found some proof against him and he ran. Maybe they killed him and now they are left with no one to arrest. You know the political climate.''

"Vargas has to have a public victory,'' Nick filled in.

"If he is to make a run for the presidency."

The general had lived his whole life, even allowed his own son to be killed, for the sake of his dream of the power of the presidency.

"Did Daniel ever report on the original operation?"

"I am not sure. I think so, but it would have been at the very beginning. He died before he made more than cursory contact with his American counterpart."

"Do you know who that was?"

"No. Those records were removed, so I cannot check. I thought the investigation died with Daniel."

"*Gracias,* Roberto."

"Nicholas, be careful. Vargas knows this is his last chance for a public victory. He will go after Williams and the sister with everything." The phone clicked off.

Nick knew that meant shoot first, ask questions later. Whether a terrorist hostage or gun merchant or both, Mark Williams, if he wasn't already dead, soon would be.

And his sister was likely to meet the same fate. They hadn't taken her, as Roberto thought they would, as made sense. They'd followed her, searched her hotel room. For what? To frighten her? To what end?

To get her to contact her brother.

That meant that the Rangers didn't know about the ransom demand.

Or the ransom demand was a ruse. One designed to get at Williams through his sister.

If that was true, Vargas was behind it, he had to be. There was something he was hiding. Something that could end his political aspirations. Something Nick knew he'd be able to use. He just had to figure out what it was.

The sound of Mary Beth coming out of the bathroom interrupted his thoughts.

"Were you talking about me or Mark?" She delivered the line with no more inflection than if she'd asked a stranger about the weather. She stood in front of the awful abstract, her chin high, her body language screaming displeasure.

Even in jeans, sweatshirt and tennis shoes, she had whatever it was that made her appear to be in complete control at all times. He knew her better now than he had on the evening she'd worn that devastating little black dress. The beautiful Mary Beth of the sweet name and the high fashion hid a vulnerability that packed an emotional wallop he had not expected. One he couldn't afford.

"I had to make a phone call."

"So you told me," she replied, barely inclining her head in his direction.

"It was private."

She nodded. Absently.

That was enough. Getting up from the hard sofa, he stepped around the glass coffee table and came to stand only a few feet from her and the stark abstract, forcing her attention onto him. "There are some things I can't discuss with anyone."

"I understand perfectly." Her tone said the exact opposite.

He thought about telling her what he knew about her brother, but only for a second. He needed her trust. He had to know how she figured in the big picture. How Vargas did. Without her trust, he'd never get the truth. And the truth would help him ruin the general.

"I was talking about Romero family business." He soothed his conscience by reminding himself there was truth in that.

The general had always been his business, and would be until one of them was dead.

She'd been put in her place, Mary Beth acknowledged later. Hopelessly caught up in her concern for Mark, in the pull she felt toward Nick, she'd ignored who he was—the head of a wealthy and powerful family, a world-renowned diplomat. There would be dozens of things he couldn't discuss in front of others.

Just as her father had been unable to discuss the details of his diplomatic posts and his banking business, secrets that could be innocently spoken and used by others, so, too, would Nick be unable to discuss the details of his. It made her wonder how different his home life was from the way hers had been.

Yes, she'd been raised by her parents, or at least one of them, while Nick's real parents were dead. But there was an undeniable closeness between him and Doña Elena. With Daniel Vargas, they had been a family. She wasn't sure how Laura fit into that picture, but a marriage between her and Nick seemed oddly off-kilter, despite the existence of Alex.

Except for her relationship with Mark, there had been no sense of family in her life. From the best she could tell, her parents married because it would advance them individually and as a couple. When her mother decided she'd done her duty, the year Mary Beth was twelve, she'd calmly announced she was getting a divorce. Her father, even more of a stranger to Mary Beth and Mark than their mother, had been thrust into the role of single parent. But the relationship between father and children had been nothing like the relationship between Doña Elena and her two sons, nor Nick's with young Alex. Spencer Williams had used his role as father to his own advantage, pushing his children into the limelight while pretending it was the last thing he wanted.

Mary Beth's gullibility in the face of a man who promised her the love and family she so craved proved to be her, and her father's, undoing.

Mark had saved her, kept her sane. She could not help but wonder if Nick and Daniel had been thrown together because of family problems.

But when she and Nick joined his mother's family, less than an hour's drive from the modern house, it didn't appear that the Romeros, Doña Elena's sisters and their families, had any problems. They welcomed her with open arms into a huge, rambling Spanish-style house. The family made it difficult to keep her distance and easy to momentarily forget why she was here, what she had to do in the coming days. It didn't make any difference to them that she and Nick had arrived unannounced; they were simply absorbed into the moment.

"Pero, Tía," Nick was saying to the elderly lady sitting on the couch. The hum of several conversations didn't cover the fast beat of a San Matean band pouring from a high-tech CD system. "Manuel is doing fine at the university."

"Nicholas," replied the lady, whom Mary Beth knew to be his aunt Rosa. "He needs your influence. Please, talk with him." *Tía* Rosa squeezed his hand as another aunt pulled him away.

This family was so different from the cool, polished exterior of her own. They doted on Nick. She laughed quietly to herself. Of course, aunts could dote on a saint or a sinner. She had a feeling there was a lot of both in him.

"What's so funny?" he said, his voice deep and amused as he approached her.

"You, your aunts, your family." She couldn't help sounding wistful.

"We're funny?" There was a teasing tone about his statement, indicating he knew she wasn't laughing at them.

"No, not at all. It's just that your family is so…normal."

He stepped closer, a half-grin on his lips, a twinkle in his eye. "Did you expect us to be abnormal?"

She laughed. "I think I can almost picture you eating meat loaf and potatoes, with all your aunts encouraging you to eat your spinach."

"They encouraged me to eat everything." He smiled, then added, "But it was *anticuchos* I balked at, not spinach."

The difference between barbecued beef hearts and spinach illustrated their differences so well and so humorously that she reflexively reached out and put one hand on his forearm as she laughed. His flesh felt warm, the silky hair of his arm smooth against her palm. She jerked back.

He grabbed her hand and held it. The deep blue of his

eyes revealed something that made her want to move away from him.

Heat.

That was the only word for it. She suddenly wanted him to be more aloof, less the man who attracted her despite herself. Not the son, the father, the nephew. Not a fascinating man.

"I'm not going to bite you," Nick said with a smile, releasing her hand. But she'd seen the truth again, if only fleetingly.

She wasn't ready.

The attraction was reciprocal. And, for her, dangerous because she wasn't able to take that sort of risk. She'd promised herself never to fall into anything like that again. And certainly never with a man as complex as this one.

"Your taste in women has improved," a man's deep voice interrupted.

Nick released her hand and turned so quickly that Mary Beth nearly missed his surprise at recognizing who spoke.

"Introduce us," the older man commanded, as if daring Nick to refuse. Slightly shorter, with jet-black hair, he wore a shirt, tie and expensive sports jacket.

"This is Mary Beth Williams," Nick said, his tone so fiercely cold that it seemed to bring a hush to the room. "Mary Beth, this is General Antonio Vargas, my mother's husband."

The general extended his hand to her, his eyes hard. "Another beautiful American," he said, looking her over before turning his gaze toward Nick.

He ignored whatever implication his uncle's statement seemed to have. Around them, the Romeros began talking again.

"I must speak with you. Privately."

"In the library," Nick replied.

"It is always a pleasure to meet such a lovely woman, Miss

Williams.'' The general shook her hand again and walked toward a hallway.

''He's Doña Elena's husband?'' Mary Beth asked quietly, when General Vargas was out of hearing range.

''Yes,'' Nick replied, his attention on the man.

''They seem so ill-suited.''

''That's probably why they haven't lived together since before Daniel was born.''

''Why didn't they just get a divorce?'' The question burst from Mary Beth before she could recall it. ''I'm sorry,'' she hastened to add. ''It's really none of my business.''

''But an astute observation, just the same.'' Then Nick excused himself, an unreadable mask firmly in place.

She could have kicked herself for asking such a thing. She had always found explaining her parents' relationship difficult, almost impossible. The only one who ever understood was Mark, because he lived the experiences with her.

And Nick had lost *his* confidant when Daniel Vargas was killed.

''The perfect Romero,'' Antonio Vargas said when Nick joined him, ''in the Romero inner sanctum.'' The general glanced around the library.

''Who let you in?'' Nick leaned back against the heavy Spanish desk. Dim lamplight threw their shadows across one wall of books that stretched from floor to ceiling. The portrait of the Romero patriarch stared down at them.

''Elena's sisters dare not stop me.'' The general took a book from a shelf and flipped it open. ''I hear you are going to the Río Hermoso.''

Nick placed his palms flat on the desktop behind him and waited for the general to continue.

''Burn the house.'' Vargas closed the book and looked up.

Nick had to struggle not to show surprise. ''Burning the house won't cleanse you of the sin of Daniel's death.''

The old man didn't flinch. "Daniel is dead. The house holds secrets."

At Nick's silence, the general continued. "I believe you would want him to be remembered as a hero. Daniel was, after all, half Romero. The family must be protected. That is your role. If you hope to do that, you must be certain nothing will come out to destroy his military record."

"His military record is spotless."

"How sure are you, Nicholas?" He opened another book, his attention seemingly on the pages. "If anything exists that could ruin his name, it would be in the Río Hermoso hacienda. Much easier for you to burn the house and its secrets than to have the dilemma of another lie."

"Why don't you burn it?"

"There should be no accidental fires, no reason for anyone to question such a thing. You could do it openly as an act of…cleansing." He closed the book and looked up. "Burn the house."

Nick forced himself to remain focused, to concentrate on this conversation, not on the implication that Daniel could have done something wrong. "Did you mourn him at all?"

"You know I am not a sentimentalist."

"The Vargas pragmatism."

"It is in the blood—"

The old man's answer shouldn't have surprised Nick.

"Do not make me wait for you to do what you know must be done."

"Wait forever." Nick's reply took him back years to a time when he'd heard the exact words from this man's mouth, the one and only time he'd demanded anything from him.

Vargas put the book back carefully. "Boys do not wait patiently. Men—ah, Nicholas—what can I say? Boys who learn patience are men of rare character. You should know that."

Character. But good or bad? That was the question. He looked into the face of the man responsible for Daniel's death and said, "Character is not a subject you and I should discuss."

The general straightened, his black eyes fixed on him. "Deny it all you will, Nicholas. You are a Vargas. My son, my blood. Only Elena's desperation gave you the Romero name. Protect your brother." With that, he turned and walked out of the library.

The acknowledgment came twenty years too late.

As a thirteen-year-old boy, Nick had wanted this recognition from the general, whom he knew to be his biological father, but the general had refused. Nick had never again asked, never regretted not getting it.

As if waking from a surreal dream, Nick remembered the boy he'd been, devastated by a lie, loved by a mother not his, by a brother he could not claim publicly. Denied by the man who'd begotten him.

Until now. When the last thing in the world he wanted was to concede that Antonio Vargas was his real father.

He opened the door that led to the tiled patio with its soothing water fountain. This small piece of southern Spain served as a reminder of the origins of the Romero family. The family that had taken him in based on Elena Vargas's lie—a lie designed to give her another child to love. One that trapped her in marriage to a man who refused her a divorce with threats of exposing that lie.

Nick looked up at the sky, remembering nights when he'd looked up and wondered how the woman who bore him had been so foolish as to give herself to a man like that. But he'd never known Angela Crosby. All he knew were the few things Doña Elena had been able to tell him. He carried a picture of her, one Doña Elena insisted he carry.

And he kept the secret of his paternity, just as Daniel had.

It wasn't something Nick dwelled on. As a matter of fact, after over thirty years of living with the name, he considered himself a Romero. He'd done well with the family fortune.

All of his "aunts" and assorted relatives lived very well. It was only when he had to deal with the general that Nick wondered what it meant to have the blood of Antonio Vargas flowing through his veins. As it had through Daniel's, who had lived life heroically but always under the shadow of the corrupting influence of a man unwilling to bend even for the life of his son. A man who implied Daniel had something to hide.

Nick was the son of that same man. Not a good gene pool.

"Your aunt said you'd come outside. Are you okay?" Mary Beth's voice floated over the musical sounds of the fountain.

Turning, he saw her, silhouetted against the inside lights, holding his jacket over her arm. A woman of impeccable pedigree, facing a man with a claim to nothing but secrets. Why had he brought her here, to the Romeros? He'd never wanted to introduce any woman to his aunts.

"I'm fine. Why do you ask?"

"You were talking to the general. You don't like him."

"Nobody likes the general."

She moved toward him, her footsteps quiet on the tiles. "Was he a good father?"

Surprise nearly made him jump. "What?" Surely she wasn't that astute. Nobody was.

"Was he a good father to your cousin? Separation can make it difficult."

"No."

"That was a quick answer."

"I wouldn't consider the man responsible for his son's death a good father."

In the silence that followed, he heard music and laughter from inside.

"You hold him responsible for your cousin's death?"

"He didn't shoot Daniel, but he is responsible." The old man's impatience, his need for a quick victory, had ended Daniel's life before Nick could save it. "And not just for

Daniel's death. For the deaths of Daniel's companions. His decision to attack the compound where they were held amounted to murder.'' Nick had worn out his rage on the topic, but he could still taste the bitterness of what had happened.

''You assign him an awful lot of power,'' she commented.

He did. And he didn't like it. ''It's a reflex. Left over from my youth.'' He ran a hand absently through his hair.

''What was it like, growing up with Doña Elena and Daniel?'' She put her arms into the sweater she had thrown over her shoulders.

She seemed genuinely interested in a response, not simply making idle conversation. He found himself answering with more candor than he would have thought possible. ''Doña Elena is one of those women who's a natural mother. She could have been handed any child and she would have loved it.''

''But you weren't any child. You were her brother's son.''

But he wasn't.

Nick looked toward the horizon, then straight up to the sky. All traces of sunset were gone now. ''You can see the stars clearly here, away from the city lights.''

Mary Beth stepped closer and held out his jacket. He had the oddest need to hold on to her. To anchor himself against the shock waves of the general's admission. But she had no way of knowing that, no way of knowing he wasn't who he pretended to be. He was already using her—too much of a Vargas trait.

He shrugged into the jacket and tried distracting them both. ''When we were boys, *Mamá* would take us higher into the mountains. The Romeros have another farm there. Her father was still alive. A fantastic man. He would take us out on horseback and tell us stories about the stars, about Indian legends.'' He looked past her, lost in thought. ''Daniel and I were hellions. When our girl cousins went with us, we pulled their hair and scared their horses.''

"Did your grandfather punish you?"

He quickly looked back down at her, catching a bit of light as it reflected off her eyes. "Who?"

"Your grandfather."

"Oh, yes. He made us walk back once. We'd heard all the stories of the *wamanis.*"

"The whats?"

"Wamanis," he repeated. "The Indians of the region believe them to be spirits that live on the mountain peaks. They're in charge of the herds of llamas and sheep. During certain parts of the year, the *wamanis* roam the earth searching for offerings. Sometimes they eat the hearts of men who walk alone or show them no respect."

"That's a scary legend."

"Very," Nick agreed. "And for two thirteen-year-olds, absolutely frightening." He laughed, remembering. "After the first few minutes of the walk, I couldn't tell if I was shaking because of Daniel, or if he was because of me. We were locked together. We promised, then and there, that each would protect and defend the other forever, no matter the cost." He fell silent, unwilling to talk about how he'd failed Daniel. *"Mamá* was angry with her father, but he said we had to learn to be understanding of those weaker. We deserved the punishment." It was a lesson neither he nor Daniel would have learned from the general.

"I don't think Mark and I were ever punished. It's amazing to me that either of us has a conscience." She paused. "That makes it sound like we had a horrible childhood."

"Did you?"

"It was…not traditional. Not the close family you seem to have."

"Are you close to your brother?"

"We were. He's been traveling for so long, we don't see each other often. But we grew up close. Sort of like two musketeers. We did everything together, including fight." She hugged herself against the cold and let him put his jacket over her shoulders. "Our parents divorced when we were young. We went to live with Dad, which meant private schools, socially and politically correct acquaintances. Dad was a diplomat, like you. When he was given the ambassadorship of Spain, Mark and I went with him. It was difficult having to deal with that…social life."

"And you don't like formal parties," Nick interjected.

"Oh, I liked them at first." Mary Beth bowed her head. "It was sort of a challenge, to see if I could be sophisticated enough to fit into those circumstances."

"You learned your lessons well."

In the dark, her hair cast a shadow across her face. He reached out tentatively, his fingers aching for the feel of her. Then she looked up, her eyes glittering.

"Mark was always there for me. He stayed close, when he should have gone on."

Nick pulled his hand away and rubbed his forehead. "You said he's an engineer. Where did he study?"

"In Spain, while we were there. Then, when I came back to the States, he came with me and made sure I…got my life in order."

"That was very loyal of him."

"And very foolish. He should have gotten on with his life, instead of waiting for me to decide what to do."

"He sounds like a good brother, Mary Beth." But good brothers, good men, could make mistakes. Nick knew that firsthand.

"He's the best. Which is why I have to help him now."

"Did Primero de Mayo contact your father?"

"No, which surprises me."

It was odd, but fit nicely with the possibility that the kidnapping, the ransom demand, were a ruse arranged by the general to cover up something.

"Nick," said a voice from the house. *"¡Teléfono!"*

"I'd better get it," he said, stepping toward the door that led to the library. "Why don't you come inside. It's cold."

After letting Mary Beth into the living room, Nick closed the door of the library and picked up the phone.

"Do you remember Paul Martens?" Carlos Montoya asked over the crackling connection.

"Vaguely. I met him years ago, at the Hague, when I was still a Ranger. There was a problem. Some sort of trouble in England, wasn't it?" Nick sat down behind the ornate desk. The sound of music seeped into the room.

"Spain. It was a scandal, Nick. He was spying for the Russians."

"What does he have to do with Mark Williams?"

"His sister was engaged to him."

Nick got up and pulled the phone with him until he could move around to the front of the desk. "What happened?"

"She was never implicated. She called off her engagement before the news broke, but it didn't save her the humiliation or the questions. Her father's position as ambassador was compromised, and he was forced to resign. No one knows how the Americans found out about Martens, but our ambassador in Madrid during that time says rumors were flying that it was Mark Williams who trapped Martens."

That explained so much of what she'd told him about how he'd helped her. "Anything on the brother?"

"I am waiting on an American contact, but so far there is very little beyond the basics. It is as if the man barely exists in any American file."

Not a good sign, Nick thought as he hung up the phone. If Mark Williams did not register on the American's very efficient and computerized systems, what was going on?

Opening the door to the living room, he found an impromptu dance. His aunts, uncles and cousins were all doing a *marinera*. White handkerchiefs and colored scarves flipped with the turn of each dancer. Over to one side, clapping with enthusiasm, stood Mary Beth. The dance ended and one of his uncles started an old record. The music was slow, a *vals*, or waltz, with a regional, Latin rhythm.

"¡Nicholas, *baila con la niña!*" shouted *Tía* Rosa. For a tiny little woman, she had the voice of a lumberjack. Soon everyone was shouting at him to dance with Mary Beth. Never one to be stopped, *Tía* Rosa grabbed Mary Beth's hand and dragged her across the living room to Nick. *"Baila, pues, hijo,"* she ordered, her voice booming over the music.

He laughed. He loved this family—pushy, meddlesome, annoying. A family not really his. But the man who *was* his family was beyond contempt. Nick deliberately pushed aside the general's acknowledgment of paternity.

This was his family.

When he saw that Mary Beth wasn't upset by *Tía* Rosa's bossiness, he pulled her into his arms and began to move to the steady beat of the *vals.*

She fit him perfectly. The realization almost made him miss a step. Unable to resist his other curiosity, he gently touched her hair. Soft, thick, lustrous.

"Your family is really something," he heard her say against his shoulder.

"They're usually not this boisterous. I think I've been away too long." He was fighting the urge to pull her closer. He could feel one of her hands, high on his arm. He held the other against his chest.

"How long do these get-togethers go on?" She sounded breathless.

"They're wound up tonight. We'll be lucky to get away by midnight." And then they'd go back to Daniel's house. Alone.

Damn.

"What?" she asked, turning her head slightly to one side.

"I didn't say anything."

She stepped closer, her breath a whisper in his ear as she tried to keep her words between them. "I thought you said 'damn.'"

He slid his left hand up her back toward the nape of her neck. "I never swear in English."

"I wondered about that. I don't think I've heard you swear at all." She pulled back marginally when his hand touched her neck. "Nick, I don't—"

"It's just a dance, nothing more."

"It feels like something more," she said, so softly that he knew she hadn't intended him to hear.

She was right. It felt like something more.

Damn.

Chapter 5

Cool off, Mary Beth told herself. Turning into the cold, crisp breeze, she raised her arms high. She should be freezing out here in the cold Andean night. The soft rhythmic sounds of the tiled courtyard's fountain competed with the music drifting from inside, where Nick's family was still at it, pulling him into their gaiety.

She'd laughed and danced and had too much wine. It felt wonderful. Nick felt wonderful. Everything was wonderful.

No, she scolded herself, dropping her arms. *Look at him,* an inner voice whispered. *You're being a fool again. Didn't you learn?*

Nothing is ever what it seems.

It's not the same, she argued back. But she knew it was. She could never again go starry-eyed into any relationship. Appearances were deceiving. Her childhood would seem picture-perfect to anyone—money, the best schools, the best social contacts.

But devoid of love.

Except for Mark. The reason she was here. Infatuation had

made her forget about the one person she trusted, the one person she could depend on. Tomorrow morning would give her seven days to save him.

"Mary Beth?"

She spun around at the sound of Nick's voice.

"Are you okay?"

No, she wanted to shout, *I'm not okay.* Instead, she said, "I'm just cooling off." She fanned herself ineffectively with one hand to prove her point. "Don't your aunts get tired?"

He walked up to her, blocking the breeze, tantalizing her with his presence. "They're asking for you."

"I just needed some air," she said, trying to step around him.

"Don't rush in. Stay here for a minute," he said.

"I don't think—"

"Stay." He touched her shoulder, holding her gently, turning her toward him. "Please." The outside light flickered on and glanced off his cheekbones, casting his eyes in shadows.

Move away, the inner voice shouted. But it was too late. She was trapped by indecision, by his nearness. By her own curiosity.

With exquisite care, Nick touched her cheek with one finger. Mary Beth felt the breath leave her body. He stepped closer and moved his caressing finger to her chin. With the barest minimum of pressure, he tilted her face up. She shifted, restless at the contact, unable to move or look away.

The heat of his hand ran down her neck to her shoulder and shimmered to her arm. Twining his fingers with hers, he tugged.

Helpless to resist, she swayed forward, and he held her as he had earlier when they danced. With her senses swallowed by his solid presence, she finally heard the soft strains of a ballad pouring from the house. Nick adjusted his legs to hers as they began moving to the music.

Endless, breathless seconds later, he released her hand and tangled his fingers in her hair at the back of her head, holding her still. His face drew nearer until Mary Beth closed her eyes to block out anything that might interfere with this moment. His breath, so gentle, brushed her lips before she felt the tenuous contact.

The barest touch, a soft meeting of lips.

Floating on a sea of warmth, she heard something calling her back to reality.

She released her hold on Nick's neck, using her hands to push against his chest. She felt a rumble in his chest just before he spoke.

"It's just—"

"This isn't—"

"Nicky!" a woman called out. *"¡Teléfono de nuevo!"*

Dazed, glad for the faint light so he couldn't see her face, Mary Beth stepped back quickly. She could feel his eyes on her, even though it was too dark to see his expression. He didn't release her arms.

"¿Quién es?"

"¡Carlos!" came the feminine reply from the French doors.

"Carlos is on the phone." Nick stepped back.

"I—"

"Be right back."

He walked away, his powerful strides taking him away from a moment suspended in time. A moment that should not have happened. Mary Beth wanted to groan. He walked past his cousin. What was her name? Maria, that was it. She was coming out to join her. Great, just what she needed.

"We are all so happy, Mary Beth," she said, squeezing her arm lightly.

"Happy?"

"That Nicholas has found someone."

"You don't understand—"

"We were so worried, no?" Maria's English was heavily accented. "He never brings any woman to the family. My mother and his other aunts all despair for him. He is so handsome, so smart. *Tía* Rosa has tried for years to find someone for him, but he has shown no interest.''

''You don't—''

''Now you are here.'' She paused only a moment to gather a breath. ''*Las tías* are so happy. They have wanted a big wedding for Nicholas. We, the girls, we have big weddings, but this will be a Romero wedding.''

''I don't understand,'' Mary Beth said, giving up on trying to explain away what Maria had seen.

''It is clear, no? You marry our Nicky, the Romero family will have a celebration, no?''

''What about his wedding to Alex's mother?''

''Laura Morales?'' Maria took a step back. ''He did not tell you?''

''Tell me what?''

''I don't think—''

''Tell me what?''

''It is for him to—''

''What?'' Mary Beth insisted.

''Little Alex is his, how do you say?'' She paused. ''*Hijo natural,* his natural child. He married Laura quickly because she has the baby. Is okay, really,'' Maria continued, in rolling English. ''We did not know about her. One day here is Nicky telling us he has a child. The boy is six months old. *No es posible,* we all say, but he says yes, the child is his. A Romero. *Las tías* call Alex *la inmaculada concepción.*'' She paused, searching for the words. ''Ah, *sí,* immaculate conception.''

This should be funny. Mary Beth wanted it to be funny. ''I don't understand,'' she murmured.

''The only time we have seen him with the baby's mother, they behave like strangers. No one can imagine how they…'' She shrugged, helpless to explain. ''You know.'' She paused, obviously hoping Mary Beth would catch on. ''Nicky would not act that way with a woman who had his child. *No es posible,* but the child is a Romero,'' Maria continued. ''He married because of duty. Now he will marry because he is...*enamorado?*''

"In love," Mary Beth translated automatically.

Maria grabbed her hand in a reassuring squeeze. "All will be okay. You will see. Nicky will explain."

She wanted to say, *Nicky doesn't have to,* but she didn't. Instead, she watched Maria go back into the house.

She'd learned nothing from her life or her mistakes.

Nicholas Romero kept his secrets well.

"What?" Nick asked, loud enough for one of his aunts to open the library door and ask if he was all right. Explaining that he was, he closed the door again and listened as Carlos told him what he'd learned.

There was no doubt that Mark Williams was being hunted down as a gunrunner. Not only were San Matean Rangers trying to capture him, but Carlos had verified that both the American CIA and the Secret Service were involved. But his contacts had told him to stop asking questions, so he had no information as to the man's whereabouts.

"Where was he last seen?"

"Along the northern frontier," Carlos replied. "As far away from the Río Hermoso and the Primero de Mayo as he could possibly be."

That information matched what Roberto Vidal had told him. "So why does the government think he's the one selling arms to them?"

"There is a report that details his activities."

Again Nick asked himself, Would terrorists hold their source of weapons hostage? To what end? Money? The desire for international attention? Possibly, yes, but Mark Williams and Daniel knew each other. Was that the reason the old man wanted Daniel's house burned? Because there was a connection between a gunrunner and his son?

Or because there was a connection between a gunrunner

and himself? Vargas had the power to create and destroy reports, to make things happen, to—

"Nick," Carlos said, "I have been told by one source that he has heard that the Americans have a dossier on the sister. According to this, she is heavily involved as the one who handles the money. According to another source who cannot verify such an allegation, the Americans wanted her out of the country, but when she refused, they washed their hands of her. They will let Vargas and the Rangers take her because they believe her as guilty as her brother."

Mary Beth was expendable. Had he been wrong about her? Had he been fooled by an attraction he didn't understand?

"Nick, do you want me to ask more questions?"

"*Sí, por favor,* find what you can on this Elliot Smith. Don't ask more about the brother, but let me know about anything you hear. I will take care of the rest of it," Nick replied, and hung up the telephone.

Now, to see if he'd been right about Mary Beth Williams.

Because if Antonio Vargas was manipulating the situation, the pretty woman so determined to save her brother could be nothing more than the general's pawn—or guilty as sin.

Or both.

Mary Beth stood uncertainly against one of the living room walls. The Romeros were still dancing, even though the older aunts were sitting down. She'd walked in just in time to see one of Nick's aunts open the door to the library. Through the slightly open door she'd seen Nick, his expression at first surprised, then tense. Something was up and it wasn't good.

She didn't know what to say to him. Should she ask what was wrong first? Or should she tell him that the kiss had been nothing more than the result of too much wine and a beautiful night?

She'd let herself be tempted by a man when she knew better. The kind of man she would never understand, nor trust, who moved in a world she'd deliberately left behind. One she could never deal with again.

Looking around at the Romeros, she reminded herself that Nick's world was also made up of family. And he demonstrated a deep-rooted sense of responsibility to that family. He'd fathered a child and he'd given that child his name and his love. She knew of several men who had refused to take on such responsibility. Based on what did she think she could claim any of that caring for herself? A kiss under a dark, star-spangled sky? She was being as childish as she'd been before. Worse, because she couldn't excuse herself with a claim of innocence anymore. She knew the realities of the world, knew how people used others. If he saw no need for explanations for a brief kiss, she wouldn't bring up her foolishness.

He came out of the library, paused to speak with one of his male cousins, then moved around the dancers. He scanned the room, finally settling his gaze on her.

Mary Beth's breath caught. This was not the man who'd touched her so sweetly. Here was a man who did the expedient, like her parents. Like Paul Martens.

Angered at how easily she had succumbed to his charm, how impressed she'd been with his accomplishments, she put on her best cosmopolitan smile, joined her hands behind her back to steady a slight tremor and faced the stranger Nick Romero had once again become.

"What did Carlos have to say?" she asked, hoping he hadn't heard the tiny quiver in her voice.

"When was the last time you saw your brother?" He nodded absently at Maria, who passed by, then grasped Mary Beth's elbow and led her into the library.

"Three years ago," she replied, knowing now that the telephone call had dealt with Mark.

He closed the door behind them. "Where?"

The room felt small, stuffy, the sounds of the party still clear through the closed door. She turned to look at him. "At my father's, in Washington."

''When was the last time you spoke?'' The question was smooth, the bite behind it sharp.

''We haven't. He writes.'' As she struggled for patience, she clenched her fists so tightly she felt her nails bite into her palms. ''Has something happened to Mark? Do you know something?''

''What does he say to you?''

Gnashing her teeth, perilously close to tears, Mary Beth replied, ''That he's okay, that he might be home in a few months.''

''When did he give you Daniel's name?''

''A little over two years ago. He told me he'd be in touch, on and off, told me not to worry. He said not to contact the engineering company he works for.''

''So you didn't.''

''No.''

''Did you call and tell them about the ransom demand?''

''No, of course not! The kidnappers told me not to.''

''You came straight to San Mateo?''

''I called the number Mark gave me. I told you that. Remember? Then I called *you*.'' Mary Beth's hands felt frozen from clasping them so tightly.

''Why me?''

''I'm a librarian. I started researching the Primero de Mayo and I read that you had negotiated the release of some Argentinian oil field workers. I thought you would be able to make sure that Mark got out of this alive.''

''What if I hadn't been home? What would you have done?''

''I would have hired someone.''

''Who do you know in the country? Who would you have asked?''

''My college roommate's husband is Enrique Norton.''

He paused, surprise evident on his face. ''The OAS chairman?''

''Yes.''

He rolled his shoulders back, then asked. "Does he know about this?"

"No. I found you. There was no need to say anything further to him."

"Anything further?"

"I asked him if he knew you. He said he did, that you are a close friend."

Nick looked down at her. She could see nothing of the man who'd kissed her so sweetly.

"You're doing all of this for a brother you haven't seen in three years." It was more statement than question.

"Wouldn't you do anything for your brother?" she asked more sharply than she'd intended.

His response, completely unexpected after their exchange, almost broke her heart with its sincerity.

"Yes."

Mary Beth obviously knew nothing about her brother's activities. All Carlos had learned about her was hearsay. Misinformation. There probably was no dossier, certainly not one that proved her guilty of anything. She would never have considered contacting anyone else on behalf of her brother if she knew he was running guns, certainly not Enrique Norton, who was above reproach. She couldn't know Vargas. Nick had been insane to think it, even for a moment.

Insane because he'd let the general's admission push him into reaching for something fine, just to prove that they weren't as alike as he knew they were.

But they were. The proof lay in the fact that he would use Mary Beth to get to the general. Use her and her brother to get the answers he needed about his, to avenge his.

Williams and Daniel knew each other—well. The gunrunner and the Ranger captain. Nick could not allow Daniel's name to be dragged through the mud. It would destroy his mother.

They drove back to Daniel's house in silence, Mary Beth

stiff and staring out the window into the dark of night. Nick composed a hundred different ways to tell her what he'd learned, but discarded each one.

She would be devastated when she learned of her brother's actions.

And he could offer no consolation. He couldn't touch her again. Wouldn't. Because he liked her. Admired her courage. Yes, he wanted her, but hearing about her family and knowing she'd been used by Martens reinforced the knowledge that she would be cautious with anyone, especially a man. She would expect loyalty and honesty after that nightmare.

His loyalty to family precluded honesty to anyone else.

Arriving at the silent house, he led the way into the kitchen and offered Mary Beth a cup of coffee. He was stalling, trying to think of the right words to tell her about her brother. He fumbled with the coffeepot.

"You did an excellent job of lulling me into compliance. I'm surprised you're trusted by anyone, let alone governments." Her quietly spoken words carried the force of her repressed anger.

"I'm sorry—"

"What did you expect to gain from that little show in the courtyard? Butter me up, then trick me somehow? Why? I've told you all I know."

"I'm not trying to trick you." Nick turned, forgetting the coffee. He wished he could call back the tone of his questions. Wished he didn't have to tell this woman her brother was in deep trouble, if he wasn't already dead. "Carlos had some information about your brother."

She spun toward him, her hair swinging around her face. But behind the eagerness lurked fear.

"He's involved in some criminal activities."

"Not Mark" came the instant reply.

"San Matean Rangers are after him for gunrunning."

"Not Mark," she repeated, her eyes angry.

"The CIA and the Secret Service are investigating him."

"Not Mark." Shaking her head, she drew in a quick breath. "Why are you saying this?"

"I'm not making this up, Mary Beth," he said quietly.

"You don't understand. Mark is…good."

She turned away from him. But what he saw in her eyes before she retreated would remain with him for a long time. There had been a tiny instant when she'd doubted her own defense.

"Maybe there's been a mistake." That sounded lame. Except when dealing with family, Nick had never tried to soften any news. That he was trying to do so now should tell him to back away from her.

Spinning around to him, she said, "Yes, that's it. Mark would never do anything illegal." She paused, staring beyond him. "You just don't know him."

Nick could think of nothing to say in response.

"Your cousin—" she rushed to say. "Your cousin knew him. Mark trusted him. If Mark was this gunrunner, this criminal, why would he tell me to contact your cousin?"

Why indeed? Nick wondered. "The only way to know is to find Mark," he said.

"How long will it take from here?"

"We're one day's drive, two if the weather turns ugly."

"Then we should be there the day after tomorrow. That still gives me five days to get the ransom to the kidnappers."

There probably weren't any kidnappers, but Nick didn't say anything. "There are San Matean Rangers, American CIA and Secret Service agents all looking for Mark, and now for you, because they believe you're conspiring with your brother. It's too dangerous for you to go."

"I have to go. You agreed to take me," she said.

"It's rough country. I'll have to stay away from the main roads. It will be difficult—"

"You agreed to take me. That was our deal. I stick with mine. Do you stick with yours?"

He wanted to shout at her, had to force himself to speak

softly. "Remember the men who ransacked your hotel?" He watched for her grudging nod. "They weren't common thieves. They were Rangers. They won't ask you politely for anything. They play for keeps. According to Carlos, not even the Americans will give you a chance."

She bit her bottom lip and stared back at him. Finally, she let out a sigh and said firmly, "We haven't seen them again."

"Just because we haven't seen them doesn't mean they haven't followed you," he shot back. "It doesn't mean they aren't behind us somewhere or ahead, in Los Desamparados or in the Río Hermoso Valley."

"You don't understand. I can't let Mark die."

"It's dangerous for you."

Her eyes narrowed. "You're trying to get out of our deal," she accused. "That's typical, isn't it."

"Typical? What are you talking about?" A hot tide of anger threatened to engulf him. He never lost his temper.

"You're just as big a double-dealing, double-talker as—" She cut herself off so quickly, Nick barely had time to react.

"As who?" He bit back his own answer. *Paul Martens.*

"Nobody. Nothing." Anger flushed her cheeks. "Bear this in mind—if you leave without me, there will be no ransom and my brother will die. You'll never know what he had to do with your cousin. You'll always wonder if *he* was a criminal."

He watched her walk away, regal in her bearing. He found his gaze drawn to the angry sway of her hips beneath the blue jeans. He hoped she'd given Paul Martens a real good dose of her cool-as-ice act, because the thought of that son of a—

When had he started swearing in English?

Oh, Mark, what have you done?

Mary Beth believed in her brother with every ounce of her being. Mark was good—there was no argument there. But she remembered how frightened Paul Martens had been when faced with Mark. She hadn't thought about that in ten years except in terms of how lucky she'd been to learn the truth. She had deliberately pushed aside the menacing, dangerous Mark who'd forced the truth from Paul with a single look.

Eighteen-year-olds should not be allowed out of their rooms, Mary Beth concluded as she recalled the past. That was how old she'd been when Paul had swept her off her feet. They had met at an embassy party. Older, sophisticated, elegant, Paul was at home in his surroundings. Mary Beth had been awed by him. The awe lasted until the moment he'd been confronted by Mark and two Marine embassy guards. Mark had been the one who'd saved her.

As she stripped and stepped into the shower, she was determined to remember everything he'd said to her in his letters. It was her turn to save him.

Frantic pounding on his bedroom door made Nick stop undressing. He'd been about to take a shower. Instead, he pulled his jeans back on and opened the door. Mary Beth walked in, clad in jeans and a bulky T-shirt, her hair wrapped turban-style in a towel.

"When we see his safety deposit box, you'll believe me. Mark hasn't done anything wrong." She flashed him a grin, then held up the bankbook he'd seen at the hotel. "Otherwise, why would he tell me about it?"

"Mary Beth—"

"Don't you understand?" Her brown eyes were alive with excitement. "Mark must have left something there that he wanted me to see."

"Mary Beth," he said patiently, afraid she was getting her hopes up. "What do you hope to find?"

The excitement drained from her. "Something. Anything." The words left her lips on a whisper. "My brother?" With a small shaky voice, she added, "Alive?"

It was that questioning inflection that got to him. He opened his arms, inviting her to take what comfort he could provide.

With a quick breath, her golden eyes locked to his, and he took the few steps necessary to bring her within reach.

Her arms wrapped around his waist. Her head, still in the towel, rested on his shoulder. She didn't make a sound, but he could feel the wetness of her tears rolling down his bare chest and the soft strength of her woman's body, so warm against him.

He wished he didn't remember how well she'd fit before, didn't know how well she fit now. He wanted to relish the feel of her, but her quiet sobs stopped him. He recognized the pain. They had no idea whether her brother was dead or alive. He knew the finality of a death. Because of that, he couldn't give in to his need.

The towel tumbled off her head. Her hair, wet and tangled, felt cool against his neck. She allowed a single sob to escape, her cheek still resting on his shoulder. When she pulled away, just enough to swipe at the tears that had wet his skin, Nick came perilously close to groaning.

"I'm sorry," she sniffed, still wiping wet droplets from his collarbone and chest. Her lashes were spiked, her nose a little red.

How he ever managed to get any words past the lump in his throat, Nick would never know. Empathy and passion warred inside him. "You can cry on my shoulder anytime," he said gently, feeling the lopsidedness of his own smile. He'd never had a smile hurt.

Mary Beth realized what she was doing when she felt the springy hair beneath her fingers.

She'd walked—stormed—into his room and hadn't noticed the way he was dressed. Half dressed. Too stunned to move, she looked at him, knowing she had never seen anything quite like Nicholas Romero. Broad shoulders tapered to lean hips. The jeans he wore hugged his thighs gently, emphasizing his maleness. And his chest—it was perfect. Not overdeveloped, just firmly muscled with a perfect sprinkling of dark hair.

Dark hair that arrowed down to a lean waist and disappeared beneath unfastened jeans.

"I'm so sorry." The words rushed from her lips. But she couldn't quit looking at him. Her palms still tingled from the feel of resilient, well-muscled flesh.

He blinked several times, then opened heavy-lidded eyes to stare back at her. She sensed more than felt the movement of his right hand leaving her waist and moving up to cradle the back of her head. The room was suddenly small, lacking in oxygen. She licked dry lips moments before she saw his face descend toward her.

Time stood still. It seemed as if they were again on that patio, before Maria had interrupted them. But where that had been an experiment, one not carried to fruition, this was the promise kept. A sensual feast of taste and sensation, the only contact their lips, and his hand gripping her hair. Her own hands, hanging at her sides, were useless to her.

He was heat and male and solidity. She was waking up slowly. Waking up to the sensuality radiating from the hunger of his mouth on hers. Suddenly, her hands were no longer useless. Beneath her fingertips she felt the long, solid muscles of his back, the belt loops on his jeans and the gap between the waistband and the indentation of his backbone.

But his mouth was her undoing. Her thumbs caught the material of his jeans at the waist for support and she leaned into him. Want spun out of control, into eroticism and need. Feeding the sensations were his hands, cupping her bottom, pulling her against his wonderfully aroused body.

Nick was going to lose what little control he still had. Right here, right now. He couldn't stop clutching her to him, wanting to meld their bodies. The kiss wasn't enough, fiery as it was. Her heat beckoned him with a promise he had never thought possible. A promise he couldn't imagine. Even now, with the soft delectable feel of her unbound breasts beneath the worn cotton of the shirt she wore, the emotion of that promise was just out of reach.

But she'd come into his room to talk about her missing brother. He couldn't—shouldn't—do this. Because he cared about her. About the regal grace she used to handle situations she didn't like. About that hidden vulnerability. Because she loved her brother and would do anything for him.

He released his grip on her hips, moving with great care to cup her face, and slowly withdrew from the heat of her mouth. Staring down at her closed eyes, her lashes dark fans against the smoothness of her cheeks, her lips slightly damp and still parted from his kiss, he felt a sensation that was so close to an electric current running down the length of his body that he groaned.

She stared up at him, her eyes half open, her hair wild and still damp, forming a halo around her head. An instant later she was withdrawing from him, both physically and emotionally. The Mary Beth Williams of the high-fashioned, expensive dresses and cool, polite manners stood before him dressed in a cotton T-shirt and dark jeans. The only thing to give away the fact that she'd been touched was a tiny shiver he felt just before she stepped completely away from him.

"I didn't mean for that—"

"There's no need to explain," she interrupted.

"I—"

"Please." She looked down at the floor.

He put his index finger under her chin and gently raised it. He could see a turmoil of emotions in her clear brown eyes. "I was going to say, I didn't mean for that to get so out of hand so quickly. There's nothing for you to be ashamed of. If anyone lost it, it was me. I apologize." *And desperately hope this whole mess is resolved before I hurt you the way Martens did.*

"I didn't mean to burst in here like that."

He shook his head, smiling, knowing when she'd realized he was only barely dressed. "It's okay."

"I'll go to bed now." She was all frantic energy, eager to get away.

"We'll go to the bank—"

The telephone broke in, sharp and shrill, ringing from the nightstand next to the bed. Reluctant to let her go, he grabbed her hand just as she made the move to turn away. With his other hand he reached for the receiver.

Laura's voice, so late at night, alarmed him momentarily. Then she explained why she was calling and put Alex on the phone. The little boy's nightmare poured out in jumbled sentences as Nick listened. He did his best to soothe the momentary fears.

"Papi, when will you come to Miami?" The small voice, the loving term for *Father,* so easily spoken after a night of so much emotion, weighed heavily on Nick's heart.

"Very soon, Alex. As soon as possible. But you must let your mother go to sleep. Okay?"

"Okay. I love you."

"I love you, too," he replied. Then he spoke with Laura, telling her everything was fine, and hung up.

"Is he okay?" Mary Beth asked.

"He had a bad dream."

She nodded. "You're a very patient father." But he could sense she wanted to say more.

She'd probably heard about the hurried marriage. He had always been able to count on his cousins to talk too much. "I love him."

She looked at him, really looked, as if she was trying to figure something out. He wanted to explain, but there was no way to do that. He was still trying to come up with what to say, when she spoke.

"You don't parade him before the media," she said with a bit of surprise in her tone.

"I would never do that—"

"But you're there for him. He was six months old when—" She stopped herself, turned her head just slightly, then continued. "You named him after your cousin."

Where was she going with this? Had he given something away? "Laura and I agreed—"

"Because he's not yours, is he? He's Daniel's son."

No one had ever guessed. No one had questioned. Well, no one but his mother. Why had Mary Beth? It was as if she'd seen something no one else had. She'd surprised him so much, he couldn't think of what he would do. What he would say to prevent the looming disaster.

"Yes, he's Daniel's." He'd never intended to say it aloud.

She nodded, apparently satisfied, and quietly asked, "This is their house, isn't it."

"Yes."

"Why?"

He understood what she was asking. It was so simple, yet so complicated. And the real answer could not be spoken. "No child should be without a name. Laura and I wanted him to have at least part of Daniel's heritage. Daniel's maternal last name was Romero, so his son's will be Romero." He'd said way too much. "No matter what happens, Alex is the one important thing in my life."

"You're lucky to have him, then."

Her words didn't disappoint him. Any other woman would have mouthed an insincere platitude.

"As I'm sure you realize after hearing my cousins gossip to you, no one knows. Laura and I want it kept that way."

"Why did you admit it to me?"

He paused, trying to answer honestly, even though he really didn't understand why. "Because I trust you to never hurt a child by revealing the truth." But it was more than that, and he knew it.

She freed her hand from his grasp. She had more questions, he could sense them. In the muted light of the bedroom, he could see the ripeness of her figure beneath the bulky shirt. He'd made a terrible mistake, much worse than using her to get Antonio Vargas.

He'd confided in her. He'd tasted something he couldn't

have. Something that would haunt him forever. He had to stop this. Stop before he hurt her. And himself.

"We'll go to the bank in the morning," he said.

Her expression said she expected more, but understood he would say nothing else. "When do they open?"

"Nine o'clock," he replied.

"I'll be ready," she said, then walked to the open door. "And Nick—" She stood in the hallway, looking back at him. "Thank you for being honest about Alex."

She couldn't guess how he felt when she said that. Because by the time it hit him, she'd turned away. He stood in somber silence, knowing he hadn't been honest. Honesty about some things was a luxury he could not afford.

Ever.

Chapter 6

The bank didn't match Mary Beth's expectations. She'd envisioned one of the old banks she'd seen in San Mateo—high ceilings, marble floors, bars on the teller windows. Instead, it boasted yellow brick, glass doors—though security bars were visible—and beige carpet. A little disappointed that it looked so American, except for the guard armed with a machine gun, she followed Nick as he approached a receptionist positioned in the lobby.

She had not slept well. The idea that Mark could have done anything wrong, that American agents thought she had something to do with gunrunning, of all things, colored everything, especially her response to Nick. His honesty about Alex had touched her, made her more susceptible to him. Still, there was too much unknown about him, too much she couldn't trust.

Hoping to find some measure of peace of mind in the contents of Mark's safety deposit box, she followed Nick as they were led through a side door and into the room where a huge steel gate barred the entrance to the boxes. A guard opened the gate-like door, stepped in and returned with the small metal drawer. Moments later, he excused himself, leaving Nick and her alone, the box on a table in front of them.

With shaky fingers, Mary Beth took her key and opened the box. The hinged top swung open. Inside were stacks of papers in stiff letter-sized folders marked to indicate they contained Mark's life insurance policy and will.

Mary Beth opened the folder that held the will and found a single one-hundred-dollar bill. "I wonder why he kept this in here?"

"Maybe it's the first money he ever made." Nick took the bill from Mary Beth and put it on the table as she investigated the will.

"Mark's not a sentimentalist. He wouldn't do that." She scanned the brief document and almost sobbed in frustration. Mark hadn't left her any sort of message. This was nothing more than the disposition of his belongings, what few there were. She would be using Mark's money, part of their grandmother's bequeath, to help pay the ransom. She turned the page. "There are numbers penned into the margins. See?"

"They're dates. Do these mean anything to you?" Nick turned the page so he could read it.

"No," she replied, and took back the will. "I don't understand why there's not more in here. Something that would explain what's going on."

"Don't be disappointed. This is probably a good sign," Nick said, restacking the papers into the folder.

"I was sure—" She stopped, her hand reaching into the box again. A small manila envelope, no more than two inches square, lay on the bottom.

"What is it?" Nick asked.

When she lifted the tiny envelope, something metallic jingled inside. She ripped it open and poured out the contents.

A chain fell into her palm. A chain with a metal tag about one inch long, three-quarters of an inch wide.

Nick's quickly inhaled breath made Mary Beth look up at

him in confusion. He reached for the chain and held it up, letting the tag hang from his fingers. There hung what appeared to be a military dog tag. Nick's fingers trembled slightly as he held it steady.

She didn't understand until he passed it back to her.

Embossed in square businesslike type were a date and a number, followed by a name: Daniel Vargas Romero, *Capitán.*

Nick drove away from the bank in silence. Finding Daniel's dog tag in Mark Williams's safety deposit box had been startling. It had not been on his body when Nick found him after the general's assault on the terrorists' compound. Had Daniel given it to Williams? Or had Williams taken it? Did it mean that Williams was with the Primero de Mayo when Daniel was killed? Or did it mean that Daniel had been running guns with him? Or both?

If Williams was suspected of being involved with the terrorists, the CIA might be involved. But what about the Secret Service? Daniel had worked with both the American CIA and DEA on a number of cases. Nick couldn't recall mention of the Secret Service. Maybe, as with every other bit of confusing information having to do with Williams, Carlos's contacts had simply added another American agency.

But there was a connection between Daniel and Williams. The general had to have known what it was. The request to burn the house had a purpose. He must believe it contained something incriminating. The question remained: Did it incriminate the general? Or Daniel?

The key was Mark Williams.

"Was your brother ever in the military?" Nick asked Mary Beth.

"No, he finished college and immediately got the job he holds now."

"Does the company he works for contract with the military?"

"I wouldn't know that." She looked at him curiously. "What are you thinking?"

Carlos could find out more about the company. There was a connection between his brother and hers. Some connection...

They pulled up in front of the house, both deep in thought. Nick checked the perimeter, aware that by now anyone following them could have guessed they'd be here. But he saw nothing out of the ordinary.

"Mark hasn't done anything wrong," Mary Beth said. "I know that. There has to be an explanation for this insane accusation, for his involvement with your cousin."

The phone began ringing in the house. Nick ignored it, choosing instead to follow through on his thoughts. "What if we find out it's true?"

She shook her head vigorously. "It's not."

So she'd lost whatever doubts had haunted her. Mark Williams was the type of man who inspired loyalty. Nick hoped it was well deserved. And wished desperately that the general had not shaken his faith in Daniel.

He got out of the car and came around for her, the phone still ringing. As he opened the front door, it quit, only to begin again immediately.

The house, dark because of the closed shades, felt odd.

Pushing Mary Beth behind him, he turned on the lights.

The house had been ransacked, the couch cushions overturned, every drawer in the dining room and living room upended.

Keeping her behind him, he eased down the hall. The phone quit ringing. The room she'd used looked much the same as her hotel room had looked the day before. Clothing tossed everywhere, drawers open, the contents torn apart.

"What do they want?" she whispered.

The phone started ringing again. Nick dragged her with him toward the room he'd used, alert to any noise in case someone was still in the house. This room looked the same as hers. He grabbed the phone.

"*Sí,*" he said, his gaze on Mary Beth.

"Nicholas!"

He recognized the voice despite the panicky quality of it.

"Mario?"

"Nicholas, you must leave. Quickly."

"What are you talking about?"

"Rangers will take you. You must leave the country. Quickly!"

Even over the phone, Nick could hear the man's uneven breathing.

"Many hands are involved. Leave, Nicholas. I am doing you a favor. Believe me. Your family name cannot save you."

"Save me from what?"

"The woman. *La americana. Los gringos,* our Rangers, they are in competition to get her. If they find you, they will take you also."

"What—"

"*¡Escucha,* Nicholas! I am warning you because I owe the Romeros. You. There is a fabricated story of a ransom demand by Primero de Mayo. I can say no more. You must leave," he repeated.

"Mario—"

But Mario had hung up.

"What's happening?" Mary Beth stood staring at him.

"I don't know." He wasn't yet convinced that the ransom demand was a hoax, but someone still thought she had something of value. If Mario was right, having her things ransacked was nothing. If both Americans and Rangers were trying to arrest her, the game had changed. Nick preferred to believe that the Americans would treat her fairly, despite what Carlos had said. He had no doubt what the Rangers would do. Especially as led by Vargas.

Nick reached up into the closet and pulled out a box. From

it, he took two handguns, a Glock and a .357, along with several boxes of ammunition.

"Guns?" Mary Beth asked, her voice catching.

He met her gaze steadily. "Do you know how to shoot?"

She glanced at the guns, then at him. "Sort of."

"Can you hit anything?"

"I could ten years ago," she said, "if the can held still."

He smiled. Grabbing the guns and boxes, he put them into a small duffle bag. Next, he pulled two sweaters and two raincoats from the closet and handed them to her. "Take these. We're going on and may not have shelter from the rain and the cold. Pack only what you'll need for two to three days."

Two hours of riding in the lurching Rover over a non-existent road gave Mary Beth plenty of time to think. She'd exhausted herself with possible explanations for Mark's predicament and had turned her attention to Nick.

The peacemaker wasn't necessarily a peaceful man. He knew how to use a gun. Well, that wasn't so odd. Diplomatic security took care of American diplomats overseas. Surely all diplomats were trained in self-defense. Nick had been sent all over the world, not only by San Mateo but by the UN. It stood to reason he should know how to take care of himself.

But it didn't explain that sense she'd gotten when they first arrived at his mountain home. Daniel's home. She'd sensed...well, a predator.

Now that was fanciful.

"Here we are."

Ahead, cast against the brilliant blue of a sunny sky and the barren Andean plateau, stood a single-story wooden house, smoke pouring from its chimney. A ramshackle old barn was off to the left.

Nick pulled up to the barn, got out to open the huge sliding door, then drove the Rover in. Hay stacked to the ceiling left little room for the car. Two stalls held what appeared to be milk cows.

"Why are we stopping?"

"I want to ask a question or two."

"Do you know the owners?"

"Of course. I wouldn't come in here if I didn't." He stepped out of the car. "I'm going to walk over to the house and tell César we're here."

She didn't want to be left alone. The barn, with the door shut and its tiny window covered with dust, was dim and cold despite the midday sun. She climbed back in the car, shivering.

Minutes later, the grinding sound of the barn door startled her, as did Nick's voice. "Mary Beth? Come give me a hand."

When she got out, she saw a short heavy man holding a bundle, standing next to Nick, who held another, smaller bundle.

"Blankets, *señorita*," the man said in Spanish. "And food."

Nick made the introductions in the same language. "This is César Gonzalez."

"Gracias," she said, taking the blankets from César and putting them inside the Rover.

"I will leave you, *señor*."

"César," Nick said, stopping him as he reached the open barn door. "When was the last time you saw Capitán Daniel?"

"Oh, *señor*. Let me see." César scratched his head. "It was a week or two before he was taken. *Sí*, that is when it was. He came with the man he met here."

"What man?"

"Tall. He spoke like a city man."

"San Matean?"

"I do not think so. Many here called him *el rubio* because of the color of his hair."

"A blonde?"

Mary Beth stepped closer, her attention fixed on what César was saying.

"Like *la señorita,* maybe. Hair the color of straw."

Mark. It had to be Mark.

"How often did he meet this man?"

"Maybe once, twice a month." César paused. "*Sí,* almost every two weeks. Chabuca, my niece, she spent time with *el rubio.* She claimed he was a carpenter, from *la montaña.* She said he worked for Padre Franco at the mission."

"Is your niece here?"

"Yes, she stays with us because she teaches here."

"May we talk to her?"

"I will go for her. She cannot come until after her school. Eat, rest. I will bring her."

After César left, Mary Beth voiced her question. "It's Mark, isn't it? Mark meeting your cousin."

"It's possible."

"But Mark's not a carpenter."

"Would you rather believe he's a gunrunner?"

She had no reply.

"Do you have a picture of Mark with you?"

"It's small," she hedged.

"We'll see if she recognizes him."

A few minutes later, after they'd eaten the bread and ham César had brought them, Nick spread a blanket on the hay. He wanted to ask Mary Beth what she would do when she found answers that destroyed her faith in her brother. As he might find answers that would destroy Daniel's professional reputation—the one thing Daniel had left that he could claim with pride as his own. Nick had taken everything else.

Mary Beth wrapped herself in the other blanket Carlos had supplied, and huddled, shivering next to a bale of hay. She arranged and rearranged the cover around her shoulders until he couldn't watch anymore.

Smiling, he said, "You could sit next to me."

She stopped fiddling with the blanket and looked up.

"We could even share the blankets." He couldn't really see her face in the dimly lit barn, but he could feel her tension.

"It's cold, Mary Beth."

"It's not that cold."

Nick almost laughed at her quick retort. "Do you think I'm so desperate I'll assault you in your sleep?"

She shifted, as if uncomfortable with what he'd said.

"Look." He paused. "We're going to be spending a lot of time together. We both have reasons to continue—obligations, promises, if you will. We are adults. There is an attraction, but you set the limits."

"That's rather generous of you."

"Not really. I know what I want. The real question is what do *you* want?" He could tell he had her undivided attention. He did know what he wanted, that was true. It was something he couldn't have.

"I want to find my brother."

"That's not what we're talking about."

"That's what's important, what matters."

He felt compelled to make her acknowledge the passion that had flared between them. He refused to be alone in his wants. He stepped toward her, squatted down close enough to touch her and gently traced her cheek with his fingers.

"Is that all?"

Confusion seethed in her eyes. And yearning. He could see it as clearly as he felt the same pull in himself.

She took a deep shaky breath and pulled away. "I won't let anything interfere with finding Mark."

Mary Beth woke to the sound of a cow mooing. Heat encompassed her back from her neck to her legs. A heavy weight curled beneath her arm and against her breast. She revelled in the heat, then suddenly remembered where she was. And with whom.

Pushing the hair away from her face, she looked down to

see Nick's strong arm curved around her. A stab of desire, so quick it startled her, speared her senses. He was wrapped around her, spoon fashion. The picture she conjured at the single sight of his arm would have made her blush if she'd thought he was awake. But she felt his steady breath against her neck and calmed herself.

He'd given her the power to decide where their "attraction," as he called it, would go. Nothing about him, nothing he'd said indicated any interest in permanence. He was simply being a gentleman and letting her decide. Or was he? As a diplomat, he knew better than most what it would take to get what he wanted. Even Doña Elena said he knew how to be persuasive. She didn't kid herself that he was here only to help her and Mark. He was here because his cousin was somehow involved. Practically, he was using her as much as she was using him.

But what did it really matter? She knew what kind of life he led. The kind of life she'd left behind ten years ago because she could not deal with half-truths and secrets. If she had the misfortune to find Nicholas Romero a lure too great to withstand, why worry where it went? She wouldn't get hurt as long as she didn't let herself expect anything from him. He'd do only what served his purposes. As long as he saw a need to save Mark, she'd get what she came for. She had to remain in control of her emotions.

She should kick herself for coming to such a simple conclusion. Nothing about this was simple.

She tried to move away. His arm tightened around her and his breathing altered.

"Did you sleep well?" His voice rumbled against her neck, sending shivers to her toes.

With gentle pressure he turned her onto her back so that she gazed directly into his eyes. He had no right to look so good. A shadow of beard roughened his features. Those blue eyes, so deep, pulled at her.

"Yes," she managed to say, and felt him stretch against her.

"Warm enough?"

Hot enough to sizzle. "Oh, yes." Was that her voice?

"Chabuca should be here shortly," he said softly. "We should get up." It sounded like he was trying to convince himself.

And then she knew he was doing just that, and not doing a very good job. Because he lowered his face to hers and, eyes fastened to her mouth, kissed her.

The contact, so soft and fiery, made her gasp. He caught the soft sound in his mouth and settled one strong thigh across her hips. She was melting against the blankets rumpled on the hay. His mouth, fierce and enticing, feasted on hers. The scratchy feel of his unshaven chin added texture to the fires of passion and woke her to what she was doing.

He was too complicated a man for her. She wished, desperately, that she could separate the physical from the emotional.

He pulled away, still close enough for her to see the curl of his lashes.

"Stop me now." His words reverberated against her tingling nerves.

She nodded slowly, unable to utter a word with the delicious feel of his body crushing her to the hay.

"Don't look at me that way," he ordered, then moved a hand to touch her lips. Suddenly, he sprang from their coarse bed.

When she'd composed herself enough to look at him, she saw arousal in the taut lines of his body.

"I'm sorry," she said softly. She was, but she wasn't sure if it was because she hadn't made up her mind or because he'd stopped so easily.

He looked down at her, the lips that had scalded her turned

up slightly. He raised his arms over his head and stretched, his body sleek and perfect and enticing. With something akin to regret, he said, "So am I."

Chabuca was a pretty woman of around thirty. She did recognize Mark's picture. After looking at it, she stepped close to Mary Beth and examined her face.

"You are his sister, no?"

Mary Beth stood quietly, afraid to ask her million questions, afraid not to.

Nick asked his. "This is the man your uncle spoke of?"

"*Sí, por cierto.* Hair the color of honey. Is he well?"

"When was the last time you saw him?"

"He came looking for *Capitán* Daniel. I told Juan—that is his name, Juan Marco—the news. That he had been taken by the terrorists."

"What did he do?"

Chabuca blushed. "He stayed only a few hours, not for the night."

"Why was he looking for *Capitán* Daniel?"

"He did not say. But he…"

"What?" Nick prompted.

"It is a feeling only, *señor,* but I thought he would go after *el Capitán.*"

"What made you think that?" Nick's voice sounded oddly tight.

"He asked for a radio and listened to the news about the Primero de Mayo. The reports spoke of ransom demands. He was very quiet. Very intense. Not the same."

Mary Beth remembered that same Mark, the Mark who had intimidated Paul Martens all those years ago.

"Did you hear from him again?" Nick asked.

"No. He said I probably would not."

"*Gracias,* Chabuca," Nick said.

Chabuca turned to walk away, then swung back quickly. "*Señorita,* the cross you wear—it is a family thing?"

"My brother sent it to me." Mary Beth touched the warm gold.

"Juan had one like it, but in silver. For luck, he said. He wore it always."

Mary Beth prayed he still wore it and that his luck would hold out.

Nick closed the barn door after Chabuca left.

"So Mark and your cousin met here. Often." Mary Beth sat on a bale of hay.

He shook the blanket they had slept on and put it in the back of the Rover. "Twice a month."

"Twice a month," she repeated.

He turned to meet her gaze, the sudden knowledge clear.

"That's it, isn't it?" she asked, grabbing her bag off the floor and rummaging until she pulled the papers they'd taken from Mark's safety deposit box. She unfolded the will, turning the document toward what little light came through the small window. "Every two weeks," she said, handing it to him.

Nick took the papers. Next to some dates were check marks. The last entry was dated a week before Daniel was captured.

"They're the dates of their meetings," she said.

He turned the will over, and a small piece of paper fluttered to the ground. "What's that?"

Grabbing it off the scattered hay, she held it up. "More numbers," she said quietly. "Different numbers."

Nick took the paper, an off-white carbon, from her fingers and held it up to the light. "Anything you recognize? Telephone numbers?"

She examined it again. "No."

"They have letters and they're too long anyway," Nick said, wondering if the numbers were a code. He handed back the will. "Anything else in there? Any more notes in the margins of the pages?"

"No."

"Are the dates in Mark's handwriting?"

"Yes." She sounded sure.

He held the carbon for her to see. "What about these numbers—are these Mark's writing?"

She held the will up once again. "I don't... No. That's not his handwriting. Mark makes his eights upside down."

Nick touched her hand gently, angling the carbon so he could see it better. What he saw shook him. "That's Daniel's handwriting."

"If these dates are the dates of their meetings, then the numbers must mean something too." She took the carbon, studying the paper intently.

He agreed—but what? What could Daniel Vargas, special agent of the San Matean government, Ranger captain, have to do with Mark Williams, engineer, living in rural San Mateo pretending to be Juan Marco, carpenter? "Yes, they must."

The only explanation Nick could come up with was not a reassuring one: serial numbers. Guns.

"Where is this place Chabuca talked about? This mission?"

"It's about a two-hour drive, if we stay off the main road. North of here."

"On the way to the Río Hermoso Valley?"

"Yes."

"We could stop there, see if it really was Mark, find the proof that will make everyone quit accusing him of things he didn't do. Otherwise, once I pay the terrorists the ransom, he'll be running from the Rangers and the Americans."

If he's still alive, Nick thought. If terrorists really were holding him. But he didn't voice this. He had to know what Daniel had been up to. There would be no way to protect him from this unless he did. No way to keep a childhood promise he'd broken once.

Nick stopped himself. Did he really have so little faith in Daniel that he'd already found him guilty of gunrunning? Was he projecting what he knew of the general onto his brother?

Nick stretched his neck, his hands steady on the steering wheel. How he'd managed to keep himself from taking what both he and Mary Beth wanted hours earlier made him wonder at the emotions he felt tangled deep inside. He knew exactly what to do to entice a woman. He'd done it countless times. But Mary Beth was different.

This woman was grace and polish and vulnerability. Something a man like him couldn't hope to touch because he could offer nothing but a life based on a lie. He cursed the fates for allowing him to see her, taste her, because he would go to his grave wanting her. He'd selfishly told her she had the final say in their relationship because he couldn't fight the want or the need. The only way to fight it was to empower her. She'd already been able to guess too much about him. He'd too easily admitted the truth about Alex. God help him if she somehow got any closer.

In that instant, driving across the flat, cold Andean plateau in search of her brother and his mysterious connection to Daniel, Nick realized the enormity of his mistake. Should she decide to take their relationship further, he wouldn't be able to walk away. Because if she took his body in passion, Mary Beth Williams would want more. And more was something he didn't have to give.

"What's this place like, this mission?" she asked.

"It's run by a priest. I suppose it's like your Peace Corps. He runs a sawmill and helps the people farm. There's a school, run by an order of nuns."

An hour later, they stopped beside a large lake. A small herd of llamas grazed in the distance while a local shepherd, dressed in typical Andean clothing, kept watch close by. Deep, dark, reflecting the blue of the sky, the lake was freezing cold, something Mary Beth learned when she washed her hands. But it felt so good that she washed her face, too, only to realize she didn't have a towel.

"Use this," Nick said, holding out a large white handkerchief.

She took it and dried her face, then her hands, and folded it again.

"You missed a spot." He took the kerchief from her and blotted at her temple.

Mary Beth felt a shiver that had nothing to do with cold, everything to do with Nick. She closed her eyes in an attempt to shut out his face. It did no good, only brought home how inept she was at handling the physical draw he represented.

The next thing she realized, she was encompassed in his warm embrace, a sob of frustration bursting for release.

"It's okay." Nick's soothing tone rumbled against her ear. "We'll find your brother. We'll do what it takes."

She looked up into eyes the color of the bright highlands sky and realized she was doing something she hadn't done in years.

She was risking her heart.

Chapter 7

Mary Beth adjusted the outback hat Nick had insisted she wear, saying her blond hair looked too out of place in this rural part of San Mateo. They'd left the lake and driven on. After about an hour, they stopped. He left the Rover in a thick grove of trees, positioned between boulders in an attempt to hide the vehicle before beginning their walk to the mission.

The temperature on this eastern descent of the Andes, at around six thousand feet, was warm and dry with a blazing sun and a nice breeze. All around were cattle and horse farms. As they approached the mission, Mary Beth could see a small market spread out in disorder from the church.

Dusty and tired from the long afternoon walk, she wanted a drink of water—and answers about Mark. A young nun, habit stiffly in place, directed them to the sawmill, down by a fast-flowing river no wider than twenty-five yards across. A priest, dressed in black, waved them over.

"*Dios mío*, Nicholas. *¿Qué haces aquí? Te están buscando.*" He looked at Mary Beth and nodded. "They are looking for you also, *señorita.*"

Nick embraced the priest. "Who's looking for us?"

"Americans and a group of our Rangers. The Americans say they are here to save Miss Williams from danger."

"What about the Rangers?"

"Do you remember Francisco Arenales?"

"Yes. Why is he looking for us?"

"Nonsense about our great diplomat and the terrible mistake you have made by trusting a *gringa* gunrunner." He glanced apologetically at Mary Beth. "A million pardons, *señorita.*"

"What did you tell them?"

"The truth, of course, Nick. That I have not seen you. Now I must think of another truth." He winked at Mary Beth. "The Americans are searching the area. Yesterday, the Rangers go to the Río Hermoso Valley."

"We are looking for someone. A man named Juan Marco."

"Oh?"

"We think he worked here as a carpenter."

"Would you remove your hat, *señorita?*"

The priest's polite words made Mary Beth glance quickly at Nick. When he nodded, she removed the hat.

"Ah, Juan Marco," the priest said. "A very good man. You look very much alike."

"Where is he?" Mary Beth interjected.

"He is gone. He left without a word...oh, a little more than two weeks ago. This is not like him at all. He always tells me he is going."

"You have no idea where he went?" Mary Beth jammed the hat back on her head.

"No. And the man who buys his work looks for him often."

"Man who buys his work?" Nick echoed.

"*Sí*, Nick. Juan carves animals. Beautiful animals. He sells them to a man who deals in *artesanía,* then he gives the money to the mission."

"He carves animals?" Mary Beth echoed.

Padre Franco nodded.

"Not my brother." She was sure of it. Mark couldn't sit still long enough to do anything like that.

"I will show you, yes?" He led them into the dark interior of the sawmill.

Mary Beth's shoes kicked up sawdust as they wound their way through machinery and lumber on their way to a small office. Inside, on a rough wooden table, stood three figures, each no more than four inches long. One was a llama, one a *vicuña* and the last, a jaguar much like the one she'd bought.

She grabbed it and turned it over, looking for the artist's signature. And there it was, exactly like the one she'd seen on her jaguar. *J.M.* Juan Marco. John Mark.

Could Mark really have carved those exquisite figures?

"You recognize his work?"

Staggered by learning she knew her brother so little, Mary Beth put down the jaguar and picked up the *vicuña*. "They're beautiful."

"Mary Beth," Nick said, "is this his work?"

"No." She looked from the *vicuña* to both men. "Yes. I mean, I don't— I didn't know he did work like this. I bought a jaguar the other day, in the city. It's a lot like this, with the same signature."

"*Señorita,*" Padre Franco said, his voice kind, "Juan has many talents."

"Talents I didn't know about." *Oh, Mark. What else do I not know about you?*

"It is difficult to know one's brother, no?" He looked from Mary Beth to Nick. "You should be proud to be his sister." Padre Franco nodded. "You look very much alike."

"You said that before," Nick commented.

"Very much alike," the priest repeated.

Mary Beth started to explain, but Nick had picked up the figure of the llama.

"This is good work."

"I tell you, Nick, this man has a gift."

"How long have you known him?"

"He has come to the mission, on and off, for...oh, maybe two, three years."

"Is he politically involved?"

"Politically?"

"Any strong opinions?"

"No, not that I know. Juan is restless. Very capable, works very hard. Then he disappears. But he always tells me he is going."

"Was he here at the time Daniel died?"

Franco looked at him sharply. "No. He was not. He had been gone, maybe a week. He was here when I got back from Daniel's funeral."

"Did he say where he'd been?"

"No."

"Did he stay?"

"Only one day. He said he had business. I did not see him until I went to Daniel's house to get his things for you."

"He was in the valley?"

"He was in Daniel's house," the priest answered.

Nick shook his head. "Did he say why?"

"He said he thought someone else lived there, then he helped me gather Daniel's things."

Mary Beth put her hand on Nick's arm. "We have to go there."

"You cannot go now. The rains. They are very strong. There are *huaycos*—how do you say, Nick?"

"Mud slides."

"Yes, mud slides. The only road to Los Desamparados is blocked. You cannot go until this is cleared. The Rangers, they are trapped on the other side."

"Can we stay here until the road opens?"

"We must hide you well, no?" He smiled at Mary Beth and clasped Nick's arm, leading them both out into the sunlight again. "You will stay in the small house, downriver. No one will look there. Where is your car?"

"I left it hidden. It's an hour's walk away."

"Good. Good. You must do something to look less like yourself, no? Perhaps do not shave?"

"What about Mary Beth? What do we do about her?"

Mary Beth had listened to the exchange in silence. Now, she felt compelled to talk. "I'll keep the hat on."

"Not good enough," Nick said. "They'll spot you in a minute." He pulled her hat off her head and looked up at the sun, shading his eyes. "Does Rosario still work for you?"

"*Sí,* yes, of course."

"Ask her for her hair coloring."

"What?" Mary Beth said, trying to stop such a crazy idea. "I'm not dying my hair."

"Would you rather the Rangers find you?"

She looked at him. His beard wouldn't take long to grow out. Not having shaved in two days he already looked like an outlaw, not like Nicholas Romero.

But he was right. She was too easily identifiable.

"Yes, ask her for the dye."

Black hair made Mary Beth look wanton.

It was the last look Nick wanted for her.

Against the black of her hair, her light brown eyes looked golden green. Rosario had also provided a long bright-blue skirt and a white peasant blouse that belonged to her daughter. When Mary Beth put those on, Nick wanted to groan.

He'd felt her breasts when he'd held her, seen their shape when he'd looked—a temptation he'd been unable to fight. But in the stark white of the simple peasant blouse, a single tie closure at her cleavage, Mary Beth's breasts were perfect. With the fabric too thick for him to see through, he caught himself thinking like a teenager. Did she wear a bra?

"No, I don't," she said, shaking her head.

"What?" He nearly jumped up from the chair where he sat.

"I don't want to wear the sandals."

"Oh." He'd asked if she wanted to wear the sandals Rosario had given him. Embarrassed by his juvenile thoughts, he struggled to clear his mind.

"Tennis shoes are more comfortable." She gave him a puzzled look. "Are you okay?"

Never better. "Fine, I'm fine." He had to control his mind. His body. Parts of his body.

"What can we do about your eyes?"

"My eyes?" That wasn't where the problem was.

"They're blue."

It took him two full beats to understand. To tamp down desires that were wreaking havoc with his mind. "Yes, they are."

She put her hands on her hips and looked up at him, a frown on her face. "You thought my hair was too light. Well, your eyes are too blue."

"I'll keep the sunglasses on."

"Better wear a hat, too."

"Why not a bag over my head?"

"Good thinking." She smiled, on the verge of laughter, until she saw his frown. "What is wrong with you?"

For one improbable moment he felt tempted to grab her hand and make her feel what was wrong, but Franco opened the door of his own kitchen and came inside.

"Very good, *señorita*," Franco said, admiring her hair.

"Mary Beth, please."

"Oh, that will not do. You must answer to Maria, now."

"It's too close to her own name." Nick's cross words surprised even him.

Franco frowned at him. "There are so many Marias, one more will not matter."

"What about Nick?" Mary Beth asked.

"He will be Manuel."

"Okay. So we're Maria and Manuel," Nick said.

"You are my new carpenter." Franco beamed.

Mary Beth looked at Franco. "But Nick can't—"

"You would be surprised at what Nick can do—no, Nick?" Franco laughed.

"You start now." Franco opened the door, letting in bright sunlight. "We are building another sawmill across the river."

"What about me?" Mary Beth asked.

"Maria, you are the new *lavandera,* the...washerwoman."

By six o'clock that afternoon, Mary Beth vowed to never wear blue jeans again. They were heavy and hard to wash by hand. Especially since she had to do the washing squatted down, ankle deep in the river.

She watched some of the local women wash, amazed at their ingenuity. They used low flat boulders as washboards and lay the clothes to dry on larger boulders. Of course, they only had to wash their own family's clothes, while she had to wash the clothes worn by the five men who worked at the sawmill. It was one of their perks.

On the other side of the river, the men were framing in the new sawmill. Padre Franco directed the effort from below, while two workmen, one of them Nick, hammered in huge cross beams. Men's laughter filled the air as they struggled under the weight of the lumber. Nick fit in as if he were born to the effort.

Mary Beth stood, rubbing her lower back, then bent down again to pull up the eighth pair of jeans she'd washed this afternoon. That's when she saw the Jeep.

It splashed across the shallowest part of the river. Inside were four men, three of them in camouflage fatigues. The fourth man looked vaguely familiar, but at this distance, Mary Beth couldn't see his features, only that he wore khaki slacks and a white shirt. When the driver pulled to a stop next to Padre Franco, the civilian got out of the Jeep to shake his hand. Nick and one other workman continued hammering at an upper beam while the priest and the man talked. The driver held a short rifle across his lap. Heart in her throat, she shielded her eyes from the sun and stared.

Then as suddenly as they'd come, they left, splashing back across the river, never even glancing her way. She'd grabbed the wet jeans she'd been washing, before the silt stirred up by the Jeep could reach her. Now she wrung them out and placed them alongside the other seven pairs to dry. She stretched her back muscles again.

"Need a back rub?" Nick's voice startled her. He'd waded across the river, boots in hand. From the knees down, his jeans were soaked. He raised his sunglasses to his head.

"I hope you don't expect me to wash those now. Clothes should be outlawed."

He laughed, his eyes flashing, his face shadowed by the stubble of his beard. "Lack of clothes would certainly change a lot of things."

He was teasing, of course, but a delicious vision crept into her head anyway. She knew what he looked like beneath his shirt. "That's not what I mean," she replied as primly as possible.

"Come here, *niña.*"

He'd never used any term of endearment with her before. The use of "girl" didn't do much for her, until she realized the tone he'd used. That made her shiver. And made her gravitate toward him despite his teasing. He stepped behind her and rubbed her shoulders, gently massaging away the stiffness. Then he anchored her in place by putting one arm across her collarbone before his other hand slipped to her lower back.

His breath, warm against the back of her neck, the weight of his arm around her, his fingers working their magic on her overused muscles, made her want to lean against him.

Minutes later, he stopped, the hand on her back caressed instead of rubbed, and she felt more of his body heat as he seemed to get closer. Then he broke the contact.

"Come on, let's go to the house." His voice sounded rougher than usual.

It took a moment for Mary Beth to come back to reality.

When she did, she remembered what she'd intended to ask. "Who were those men? What did they want?"

"That was your friend, Elliot Smith, from the American embassy."

"The one who wanted me to leave San Mateo?"

"One and the same."

"What did he want?"

"To find out if Juan Marco had come back. And to find you."

"What does he have to do with Mark?"

"He claims he's trying to stop a gunrunning operation."

"Does he have the authority to do that? I thought that was the San Matean government's job."

"Normally, yes. But the Americans are very involved in trying to stop the drug trafficking in South America. Part of your war on drugs. Smith is investigating what he calls an offshoot of that, with soldiers he says are part of a small advisory U.S. Army unit stationed here."

"When he asked about Mark he was really checking to see what I knew," she speculated.

"Franco said that my old Ranger friend Francisco Arenales is looking for both you and Mark. With Smith out here and Arenales in the Río Hermoso, we are between the two interested groups."

She shivered at the use of "we," though they had been in this together for a while now. "Why aren't they working together?"

"That's what I'd like to know. Smith shouldn't be out here without a San Matean escort."

"They're both looking for Mark. Can they have such bad intelligence that they really don't know about the kidnapping?" What if, in their rush to capture Mark, they caused his death? They had to be stopped. Proof of Mark's innocence would force them to help her. "Since we can't go on until the rain lets up and they open the road, we could ask around. See if we can find some information that will clear Mark."

"Play investigator?"

"It's not a game," she argued.

"No, it's not," he agreed. "We'll start in the morning. Let's go eat."

"Wait—my clothes."

"It won't rain tonight. They'll be safe. You can get them tomorrow."

They walked away from the sawmill, past the market and into the woods. Nick seemed to know his way down the small trail that wound next to the river. The sound of rushing water echoed through the thick growth.

"You've lived here before, haven't you."

"My mother used to bring Daniel and me during school vacations. We lived with the laborers and did what they do."

"That must have been rough for two city boys," Mary Beth said, stepping over a huge tree root.

Nick held a branch away from her. "We hated it when we were sixteen. We wanted to go to parties—"

"Meet girls," she interjected, and immediately regretted her words.

He looked back at her with a smile. "Yes." He let go of the branch as she passed. "At the end of two weeks, we were exhausted. It was hard work. We swore we'd never come back, but we did, every year until we finished college."

"Where did you go to college?"

"Boston."

At her lifted eyebrow, he added, "Harvard."

She should have known. "What about Daniel?"

"Daniel stayed here." He stopped, looking up a straight, tall tree, and pointed. "We used to climb up trees like this to see who would get to the top first. I'm surprised we didn't break our necks." His gaze traced the length of the tree back down. "University made us grow apart." He started walking again. "No, it wasn't that. We made different choices, had different influences."

"The general."

"Yes, the general." He sounded tired.

"And the fact that Daniel became a soldier while you became a peacemaker."

"No, that didn't change anything. We both know—knew— the need for soldiers. Daniel knew how to negotiate. I was a Ranger, too, for a while. A long time ago."

Just how much had those news wire articles left out about Nick? Mary Beth wondered.

The tiny, wood-framed house—a bungalow—sat back about fifty yards from the river. Thick forest surrounded it, isolating it from any passersby. This was where they would spend the night. Inside, the unfinished wooden floor seemed clean and well cared for, as did the kitchen with its small table draped in red vinyl.

"Do you know how to light this thing?" she asked, walking toward the kerosene stove.

"Yes, but I'll have to go back for food. I don't think there's anything in the cabinets." He opened the cupboard above the sink, revealing cans of vegetables and tuna. "How's your tuna casserole?"

"Not too good. What else is there?"

He opened another cabinet. "Nothing. I'll go back and get some other things. I'll cook tonight."

"What's the rest of the house like?"

"There's a bedroom over here, with an adjoining bath."

There was. A single bedroom with one double bed. Mary Beth stood in the doorway, staring at the mosquito netting, wondering how she was going to survive this. "I'll sleep out here." She pointed to the rather disreputable-looking two-seater couch.

"I can—"

"I insist." She looked up at Nick. "It's too small for you."

"It's too small for anybody."

It was too small for a gnat.

Mary Beth twisted uncomfortably on the monstrous little

couch. Her back hurt and the tea she'd had with the dinner Nick had cooked had gone right through her. She had to go to the bathroom.

The one inside the bedroom where Nick now slept.

She sat up and stretched, rubbing her lower back. The moon shone through the single window, a silver surge of light in the darkness. She stood and looked out into the night forest. A cool breeze blew around her and she hugged herself, slightly chilled.

She really had to go to the bathroom.

She looked around but couldn't see her skirt, so she retied the closure on a clean, borrowed blouse that hung to her hips, identical to the one she'd worn all day, and hoped for the best.

With extra care, she tiptoed to the open bedroom door and looked in. Moonlight pooled in a white glow on the bed in the center of the room. Nick lay sprawled on his back, behind the gauze of the mosquito netting, his arms open. Darker shadows centered on his broad chest and beneath his arms. She couldn't bring herself to look past his flat stomach.

She stepped into the room, prepared to leave if he woke. Another step brought her closer to him. Behind the netting, his chest rose and fell with his steady breathing, the white sheet stark against the bronze of his skin.

She walked past the bed, trying to keep from looking at him, and made her way quietly into the bathroom. Somehow, she managed to close the door.

When she came out, he'd moved—rolled to his side toward her, the sheet tangled across his hips, the outline of his legs shadowed in the moonlit room.

She couldn't help herself. She stopped and stared.

His black hair shone blue in the ethereal light. His lashes cast shadows on his angular cheeks. And his chest. Oh, his chest…

Embarrassed, she walked out quickly, eager to push aside the butterflies she felt.

She just needed sleep.

She didn't need Nick Romero.

Nick took a deep breath and tried not to move. She didn't wear a bra beneath the blouse. At least, not when she slept. The erotic sight of Mary Beth walking out of his room, her body bathed in moonlight, the cotton translucent, went beyond any fantasy he'd ever had.

What was he going to do about Mary Beth Williams?

Stay the hell away from her, he told himself.

Damn.

Mary Beth stretched and rubbed her back. Rolling to her side, she adjusted the pillow beneath her head and caught the fresh scent of Nick. Sleepily, she remembered how he'd looked beneath the white mosquito netting. Those thoughts let her doze off.

She shifted her legs against the cool sheets.

Cool sheets!

Her eyes flew open and she cringed at the brightness of the morning. The brightness beyond the mosquito netting of Nick's bed.

A surge of adrenaline brought her up off the mattress. But she was alone in the room, the bed a tousled mess, the netting pushed aside. Glancing outside, she realized it was light.

How had she gotten here? The last thing she remembered was tossing on the tiny couch, fighting the image of Nick sprawled on the bed.

Had she crawled into bed with him? Had he left when he'd discovered her next to him? She felt the hot flush of embarrassment.

She walked to the bedroom window and saw Nick walking toward the house through the huge trees. Shirtless, he wore the same black jeans and heavy boots he'd worn the day before. His hair was wet, a towel slung over one shoulder. Over the other, he carried a leather holster that held one of the guns he'd brought. His chest, the chest that had so tempted her the night before, glistened with droplets of water. She swallowed. Hard.

She ran into the living room, grabbed her skirt and managed to pull it up to her waist just as Nick opened the door.

"You're awake," he said, closing the door behind him.

"Yes." She wanted to run and hide.

"I hoped you'd sleep longer. I can't believe you were comfortable on the couch." His eyes lingered on her face before drifting down, leaving a trail of heat over every inch of her skin.

"Uh…no, I wasn't." She shifted her weight from one bare foot to the other.

He smiled. "I went down to the river to wash up so I wouldn't wake you."

She nodded and tugged at her blouse. "Thanks."

"Are you okay?" He pulled the towel off his shoulder and stared at her, a twinkle in his eyes.

He had combed his hair back with his hands and trimmed his short beard neatly. He looked older, more powerful. Less civilized.

A bigger temptation.

"Mary Beth?"

"Oh—" she tried to gather her wits "—yes, I'm fine." Sort of.

He put the towel down on a chair and stood in front of her. "Do you remember getting into my bed?"

"I—I got into your bed?" she stammered.

"Not exactly." Casually, he pushed her hair behind her ear. "I got up and found you mashed to fit the couch, so I transferred you."

"I didn't—"

"You probably had a couple of hours of sleep there."

He'd carried her. She hadn't acted on her desires.

"There should be hot water in the shower," he said.

He wasn't even aware of her desires.

* * *

Nick pounded out his frustration on the nails he was driving into the frame of the sawmill. In his mind, he saw Mary Beth's relief when he told her he'd carried her to bed. Didn't she have any idea what picking her up and putting her down on his bed had cost him?

Even as he mechanically hammered another nail in place, the only things he could see were her long bare legs and the softness of her stomach where the cotton blouse had bunched as he'd lowered her onto white sheets. The way she'd curled to her side, smiling in comfort as her head rested where his had only moments before. He'd been overwhelmed with the need to lay down next to her, gather her close and find relief from the ache he felt.

"You are going to pound a hole in that board."

Nick came back to reality with a resounding *thump*.

Franco was looking at him with a mixture of curiosity and laughter. "Did you sleep well?"

"Very well," he answered, grabbing another nail.

"You look like hell."

"Such an unpriestly thing to say."

"She is a beautiful woman."

He gave Franco an accusatory look. "Why couldn't I stay where her brother lived?"

"And leave her alone? You know better than that." Franco smiled broadly. "Who slept in the bed?"

"I did," he replied gruffly.

Franco smiled. "You are losing your touch, Nicholas."

"And you're not acting like a priest."

"Relax, Nick. I can see you—"

"You can see nothing."

"No?" Franco shook his head. "You have feelings for her."

"We're looking for her brother."

"What does he have to do with Daniel?"

He dropped the hammer to his side and looked at the man who'd helped him bury his brother. "I don't know."

"Juan—Mark—is a good man."

"How can you be sure he wasn't involved in something illegal? How sure can you be of any man's character?"

"You should know," Franco said. "You've seen the best and the worst."

"Most men fall in the middle." And the scales were tipped by unseen factors. Daniel's character depended on the ever-present fact that Antonio Vargas was his father.

As did his own.

Mary Beth sat on a dry boulder and turned the wooden figurine of a *vicuña* in her hands. Padre Franco had given it to her when she'd taken the dry clothes to his house.

Mark had made this carving. He'd taken time and care to create something beautiful. He'd never shown any indication of an artistic nature. Why had she never known he had this talent? It was fine to tell herself she hadn't seen him often in the ten years since they'd left their father's home, but that didn't answer all her questions.

What did he have to do with Daniel Vargas? Why were all these people looking for him? He wasn't a gunrunner, no way.

Was he?

She remembered how he'd looked that day with Paul. A stranger, not her brother. They'd never talked about it, about the things he hadn't told her about the man she intended to marry. In hindsight, she wondered how he'd discovered the truth about Paul.

"Maria," Rosario, the middle-aged cook, called to her from the edge of the river.

"*¿Sí?*" Mary Beth had surprised herself with her ability to speak Spanish again so quickly. She knew she had an accent, but Rosario didn't question that she was Juan's sister, come from Argentina to find him.

"It is time to eat."

Mary Beth put the *vicuña* in her skirt pocket and walked toward Rosario.

"Tu hermano es un artista," Rosario said. "He makes beautiful things."

"Did he have any close friends here?"

"He and *el Padre* play chess often."

"I mean…"

"Women?" Rosario shook her head. "No, I do not think so."

"Did he meet anyone here?"

"I do not know. He comes and goes many years now. But always he tells us he is leaving. That is why I worry, no? It is not like him to go away with no word."

"He didn't seem anxious before he left?"

"No. But Juan is the kind of man no one knows. He hides behind good looks and charm. There is much below the surface."

And that was precisely what Mary Beth worried about as she made her way to the sawmill for lunch.

She found the priest and Nick already seated at the coarse tables located under the protective overhang of the mill. One of Rosario's assistants served the workers as they lined up before her. Mary Beth queued up and waited her turn.

When she finally got to the table where Nick sat talking to Padre Franco, the priest said, "I hoped you would join us. I was afraid you were not hungry."

She laughed at that. "I'm starving."

"Didn't Nick feed you?"

She looked from the priest to Nick, who seemed to be boring holes into Franco with his eyes. "Yes, he did. But breakfast wasn't enough. I guess I'm not used to physical labor."

Padre Franco leveled his gaze at Nick as Mary Beth sat down. "You must take better care of her."

Nick shifted on the bench and stared at his food.

"He cooks very well," she said.

"Of course he does. Doña Elena insisted the boys learn to

cook. They came here and worked like *peones* and learned to cook for the workers.''

So that was why Nick's cooking was so good and effortless. And abundant. She'd eaten every bite of the chicken stew he'd made last night, surprised at her appetite.

''Your mother is an unusual person,'' Mary Beth said to Nick, hoping he'd look up.

He shifted on the bench. ''I know.'' He took another bite of food.

''Have you heard how Doña Elena came to raise Nick?'' Franco asked, his eyes moving from Nick to Mary Beth.

Nick's head jerked up.

''Nick mentioned some things.''

Franco put down his fork. ''Elena's brother, Enrique, married an American girl. But he died in a mud slide in Cien Fuegos. The girl, already pregnant, went to Elena's house when she learned of this. Of course, the child she carried was the Romero heir, Enrique being the only son. She gave birth to Nick, but died shortly after,'' the priest crossed himself. ''Elena, her own son only two months old, chose to raise the boy.''

Nick pushed his food around the plate, his jaw tense. Mary Beth couldn't understand why he objected to Padre Franco elaborating on what she already knew.

''Nick and Daniel were more brothers than cousins,'' the priest continued.

Mary Beth caught a flash of some deeper emotion in Nick's eyes.

''Of course, Daniel was a Vargas and had very little to do with the Romero fortune. That has been Nick's to deal with.''

''That's enough, Franco,'' Nick said, putting down his fork.

The priest's smile didn't quite reach his eyes. ''Nick has too many responsibilities.''

Mary Beth felt the tension between the two men. Laura had said something similar about Nick and the Romeros. That had made sense once she learned that he had claimed Daniel's son. But this seemed like more. She felt like she was in-truding.

"I don't think—"

"I apologize," Padre Franco said, his gaze still fixed on Nick. "Nick knows I want him to find his own life. One that does not entail the duties he has accepted. One that will give him satisfaction."

"Duty is a part of life. You should know." Nick looked directly at the priest. "You could have had a carefree life in the city. Your family is wealthy, you could have married, had children. Instead you chose this."

"Ah, but Nicholas, this is my choice. Has your life been your choice?"

Chapter 8

Nick didn't like to think of choices. He'd never questioned the roles handed him. Everything he was, everything he'd become, was predicated by the circumstances of his birth.

He picked up a small pebble and skipped it across a deep pool in the river. Somehow, he'd managed to turn the conversation away from Franco's attempts to analyze his life. Mary Beth had excused herself and spent the heat of midday helping Rosario. Nick walked upriver, away from the mission, thinking, remembering.

Doña Elena had taken in her husband's bastard child and treated him like a son. Everything she'd done for Daniel, every ounce of her love for her child had been equally dispersed to Nick. He had no doubts he was loved. But she could not take away the stigma of a boy with no father.

For thirteen years he'd believed the fairy tale Elena Vargas had told him: that he was Enrique Romero's son. Then he'd overheard a particularly bitter argument between General Vargas and Doña Elena. Elena wanted a divorce. She wanted out of the sham of her marriage, wanted to raise her sons her

way. The general had told her she could do as she wanted
with Nick. The general would never acknowledge him as his
own, she should be glad he'd provided a Romero heir for her
useless family. And before leaving the house, the general had
told his wife that if she persisted in asking for a divorce, he
would tell the whole world that Enrique Romero had no child,
that the boy living as a Romero was nothing more than a street
urchin. The general's words had turned Nick into a man.

Confused, he had run to the boy he considered his cousin.
Daniel told him he was glad to have him as a brother and
urged a confrontation with the general, one that had broken
whatever tenuous connection existed between Daniel and his
father. Nick and Daniel had grown even closer then, their
everyday rivalries played out more for the joy of brotherhood
than out of any competitiveness. Doña Elena sensed the
change in both boys and, when they confessed they knew the
truth, swore them to secrecy. She refused to insist on a divorce, claiming that the Romeros needed Nick. Now, clearer
than before, he saw her decision for what it was: protection
and a future for the boy she raised and loved. The only people
who knew about his parentage were Doña Elena and the general.

Daniel had carried the secret to his grave. Unable to handle
his grief and anger, Nick had told Franco the truth on the day
they buried Daniel.

From that day on, Franco did not shy away from giving
him the benefit of his opinion. He should step back, the priest
said, from the obligations imposed on him by the name he'd
been given. When challenged, Franco reminded Nick that he
owed him the courtesy of listening. Owed him because it had
been Franco who'd stopped him from killing the general that
day.

He squatted down and splashed water on his face. It was
time to go back to work. Back to pretending he was Manuel,

the carpenter, married to Maria, the washerwoman. If only it were that simple—that these were the only pretenses in his life.

Hours later, Nick felt hot and miserable. He'd bashed his thumb. Twice. He opened the front door of the cabin and found Mary Beth sound asleep. Her head rested against the back of the faded couch, her hands lay lax in her lap. She'd pulled her skirt up to her thighs to allow her to bend her legs under her and untie the blouse closure, barely exposing the white lace of her bra. The top swells of her breasts moved with every breath she took. Each of his breaths forced heavy heat through his body.

He wanted to laugh in frustration. With one last long look at her, he stalked to the small bathroom and stripped off his shirt. Tossing the thing to one side, he turned on the shower. It gurgled and spit water out onto the metal floor. He turned it off and tried again. Nothing.

"It's not working?" Mary Beth's voice surprised him.

He turned to see her standing behind him, clutching her blouse closed and peering over his shoulder.

"No."

She looked so forlorn. He understood the feeling. He really needed a cold shower. A very cold one.

"We can bathe in the river."

"The river?"

"There's a waterfall a few hundred feet downriver. I'll show you."

"I'll get soap and a towel."

This was a mistake. Mary Beth had been so eager for a bath, she hadn't thought beyond the cool water. Now she stood on the banks of the river, near a deep, clear pool. On the other side, a five-foot-high waterfall poured over Nick's head and bare back. She could see the flexing of his muscles as he scrubbed with the bar of soap.

Only a few minutes earlier, she'd watched him put aside

the leather holster he'd brought with him as he sat to pull off his boots. She'd turned her back then, knowing if she continued to watch, he'd notice her mouth hanging open.

"Where's the shampoo?" he yelled over the roar of the falling water.

She couldn't answer. He took her breath away.

"Mary Beth?" he shouted.

"Yes," she managed to say. "I've got it. Right here."

"Toss it to me."

No way was she going to throw the bottle that far. It would fall in the river and they'd lose it.

She had to get in sometime. Now was as good a time as any. "Turn around!" she called.

She stripped off the wilted blouse and skirt. A last-minute suffusion of heat prompted her to keep her underwear on. She would pretend it was a bathing suit.

Taking a deep breath, she dived in and swam toward the falls. The water felt chilly and invigorating. She stopped a few feet from Nick in waist-high water and crouched down, careful to keep her chest beneath the surface of the swirling water.

"Here," she said, holding out the shampoo.

Stepping out from under the falls, Nick turned. Just above the rippling water, Mary Beth could see his navel. Water droplets glistened on his beautifully sculpted chest. With his hair plastered to his head, he looked sleek and imposing.

Tempting.

"Catch," she said, her voice a hoarse croak, and tossed the shampoo toward him.

Nick caught the bottle, his fingers curling around the plastic. Good thing he was in waist-deep water. He had thought the cold would render this particular response impossible.

And it was all because Mary Beth crouched ten feet away, water up to her chest, hiding her breasts. Across her shoulders he could see the straps of the white bra she'd kept on. He hated to think what his body's reaction would have been if she'd taken it off.

Below the churning water, the white lace of the cups had been rendered translucent by the water. Her nipples, dark and puckered, strained against the lace. His breath caught. His mouth watered. His pulse beat low in his body.

She stood, hugging her arms to her body, and licked water from her lips. He groaned. Helplessly, he stepped forward, his eyes locked to hers. He stopped a foot away and placed his hands on her shoulders. She didn't flinch, didn't protest, and moved closer.

He didn't want to misunderstand that simple move. "Your decision," he said, trying to keep a clear head.

"My decision," she repeated, her golden eyes dilated.

He toyed with one bra strap, wanting to be sure she understood, wanting her choice to be the one that led them to the inevitable. She touched his fingers and pulled down that strap, then the other. The bra fell around her waist. The sight of her beautiful, full breasts covered in shimmering drops of water made heat course through his body. He pulled her into his arms, feeling the hard little nipples against his chest. Then he tilted her head back and took her mouth.

Her body shivered against his; her mouth felt like a furnace. He ran his hands down her back and cupped her bottom. He felt the disappointment of cloth. She'd kept her panties on, too, but it wasn't enough to make him stop. Instead, he felt a greater urgency, the agony of the kiss beyond his control, a hunger beyond his comprehension. She reached up, looping her arms around his neck, straining for closeness. He crushed her to him, their mouths locked together.

Breaking the kiss, he looked down at her slumberous eyes. She looked wanton. And ready. God knows he was. Readier than he'd ever been. Her breasts beckoned him. He let her lean back, supported her back and took one nipple into his mouth, sucking hard, his tongue insistent against the sweet flesh, biting and sucking again. He repeated the movement with her other breast, until she grasped his hair, not to push him away but to pull him closer. She made delicious wanting sounds and wiggled against him, sending shards of flame through him.

He eased her down until she was no longer on tiptoes. Her nipples, wet now from his mouth, made him groan. Below the current he could see through the translucent white of her bikini panties. He put his hands on her hips and grasped the wet cloth, pulling down. She balanced herself, their eyes level, holding his arms, and stepped out. Then she fumbled with the bra, unhooked it, and let it float off with the panties. The sight of her, exposed to daylight, nearly brought him to his knees. He felt one of her hands trace the hair on his chest, touch a tight nipple and travel down to his waist. She paused, her eyes reflecting the green of the forest around them as they searched his for permission. He took her hand and moved it down.

Her hand skimmed him. He couldn't prevent the reflexive thrust of his hips, nor the need to pull her to him. He fitted their bodies together, his knees bent to bring him in contact with her feminine flesh.

She felt hot and slick. His mouth fastened to hers again as he thrust against her without entering her. Moments later she was gasping, her hands gripping his hips, her body moving in ecstasy against his, surprise pouring from her lips. Suddenly he felt her stiffen. And melt.

Then it hit him. He stopped, his body screaming, his mind tumbling down a deep tunnel of sudden clarity.

This couldn't happen. He would not repeat the mistakes of the past, would not break the vow he'd made when he'd learned the truth about himself.

He was doing what a man with no honor would do. What another man had done thirty-three years ago. He wanted Mary Beth Williams with every fiber of his being, but having her, a woman who needed commitment for this, no matter that she'd made the decision, would be wrong. He couldn't break the lifelong vow of silence he'd made. Couldn't abandon a family that had taken him in, given him everything. To have Mary Beth would mean doing just that. She would demand honesty. He couldn't give it.

In torment, he pulled away, struggling for control. When he opened his eyes, Mary Beth was staring at him, her eyes shadowed with passion.

"This can't happen," he managed to say through clenched teeth as desire ran rampant through his body. "We shouldn't do this."

She spun away, but not before he saw the pain he'd caused. He grabbed for her, his fingers sliding off her slick shoulder.

"Leave me alone!" The broken sound of her cry rose above the crashing falls.

"Mary Beth, please."

Without turning, she continued, her voice under control, hugging herself. "My choice, you said. We should have left it at yours."

He'd hurt her. And himself. It didn't matter whose choice it was. "It would be a mistake."

Mistake? How could something like that be a mistake? Mary Beth rubbed herself roughly with the towel she'd brought. She'd managed not to respond to Nick's appraisal of the situation, not that there was anything she could say.

She'd never felt anything like this. Never known anyone like Nick. Paul Martens had claimed he wanted her to be a virgin on their wedding night. She hadn't argued because she hadn't known what to want. Of course, Paul only cared about her as a source of information, not as a woman.

In the intervening years she had occasionally felt arousal at something she read or saw in a movie. She'd had what she'd called her obligatory romance, convincing herself that affection was enough to carry her through. It had, but all she'd succeeded in doing was hurting a perfectly nice man, knowing she hadn't been honest with him or with herself.

But she'd never felt this, this...heat. This wanting. And yet Nick had said it would be a mistake.

A mistake.

"Mary Beth?"

She wanted to ignore him, scream and cry. Make the whole incident disappear.

"Are you okay?"

No, she wasn't. She wanted to tell him so. She wanted to hide.

"Let's walk up to the house. We'll talk." His voice came from beyond the shroud of trees.

"I don't want to talk." She knew she sounded petulant. She couldn't help it.

"We have to."

"There's nothing to say."

"There's plenty to say."

She was not only embarrassed, she was devastated. Because she wanted him, really wanted him, while he could stop.

She took a deep breath and pulled herself together, taking control of the situation. "I'm going back to the house."

"Mary Beth." His tone was soft, cajoling.

She heard him move, heard him part the bushes she'd hidden behind. She didn't want to look at him, but she stiffened, held the towel tightly around herself and turned. He was already wearing his jeans.

"I've—"

"Please stop," she said, sure she would cry if he said anything.

"I've never wanted anyone as much as I want you."

She felt his words deep in her stomach.

"There's no way to protect you."

It took her a moment to understand. Pregnancy? He was thinking of pregnancy? Shocked at her own carelessness, she dared meet his gaze, searched the blue depths for the truth and saw it. And something else. Something deeper. More intense than any emotion he'd ever allowed her to see.

Regret.

And she knew that no matter the circumstances, no matter the availability of protection from pregnancy, he would never love her.

Nick stalked back to the bungalow. Frustration and anger battled with the knowledge that he'd nearly lost control.

His own affairs were for pleasure, not for commitment, and every woman he'd ever been with knew it. Mary Beth wouldn't know how to deal with such an arrangement. He'd never wanted anything else. Until now—when it would destroy the foundation of so many lives.

Because Mary Beth Williams was the sort of woman who would want honesty and a tomorrow. He could give her neither.

The reality of General Antonio Vargas made it all impossible.

But God, how he ached.

The vision of her, the remembered feel of her, the pleasure, all combined to make him hard again. With sudden clarity, he realized that even if he could have her once, really have her, it wouldn't be enough. She meant too much.

To save her pride, he'd used the concern for an unwanted pregnancy, but he'd never even thought of it. He hadn't thought about anything except getting inside her.

He pulled on clean clothes, jerking a shirt over his head. He would be gone by the time she got back. Gone so she wouldn't look into his heart and see the truth. She'd proved she had the ability to do just that. He had to get a grip on the situation. Had to focus on the reasons they were here.

Mary Beth wanted to find her brother, Nick wanted to protect his. Only one thing really mattered: Daniel's connection to Mark Williams had to be found or Nick would fail his brother.

Again.

He raised one thin shoulder. "*El rubio* was with my grandfather. They make him take his tools."

"Tools?"

"My grandfather is a printer."

"You've done nothing about this?"

"What am I to do? I cannot go to the Rangers and ask about my grandfather. I cannot go to the Guardia." Beto shook his head in defeat. "There is no one who can help."

"Where did the Rangers take your grandfather and Juan?"

"To the stockade."

Nick looked at the meager supply of magazines and comics. This boy would starve unless he had help.

"Where are your parents?"

"Dead," Beto replied, his eyes dark.

There, but for the grace of God and Elena Vargas, was what he could have become. "Go see Padre Franco. He will help you."

Mary Beth walked toward the sawmill. She didn't know what she'd do when she got there, but there was no way she was going back to the cabin. At least not now. She wouldn't risk running into Nick yet.

As she neared Padre Franco's house, she saw the priest come out and get into his battered pickup. He waved and she walked up to him.

"Where is Nick?" he asked.

"At the cabin."

"I'm surprised he let you come out by yourself."

"I, uh…thought I'd see what there is at the market." She wondered if the priest could sense lies.

"I am on my way to visit a nearby village. I will be back late tonight." Padre Franco seemed to assess her. "Are you sure everything is all right?"

"Yes, of course." But Mary Beth felt a flush along her cheeks.

"Nick is a good man, Mary Beth. He will not let you down. He will help you and your brother."

But at what price to her heart? Mary Beth wondered as the priest waved and drove off down the dirt track.

She'd walked most of the way to the market when she heard the rumble of an engine. As she made the final turn along the dusty path, a Jeep come to a screeching halt in front of an old woman's vegetable display. Inside were Elliot Smith and the three American soldiers who'd come by the day before. They stopped and asked questions. More than once, Mary Beth saw an old woman shake her head, or a young boy mouth the word *no*.

Afraid to draw attention to herself, she kept walking slowly. The men didn't seem to notice her. She managed to reach one of the low benches where a young woman displayed her weaving. Idly, she touched one of the ponchos and tried to listen to the nearest soldier as he asked his questions, but all she could pick up was the word *rubio*. Blond. That was enough for her to know they were still looking for Mark.

Somehow, she remained calm. As quickly and as efficiently as they'd arrived, Smith and the soldiers regrouped and drove away.

She put down the poncho she'd been holding and walked over to the woman who sold vegetables.

"Buenas tardes," she said.

"Buenas tardes, señorita."

"How much for the bananas?"

The woman made her an offer and Mary Beth countered. They haggled over the price of two apples, then Mary Beth asked about the men. "What did they want?"

"They look for your brother."

"Do you know where my brother is?"

"No, *señorita,* we do not. Two weeks ago the Rangers also look for him," the woman said. "Your brother is a good man."

The words echoed in Mary Beth's mind as she walked back

toward the cabin with her fruit. Mark was a good man. She'd always known that. But she hadn't known about his life here. A gift for carving wood into beautiful figures was one thing. Being involved in something that elicited accusations of criminal activity was another. What in the world had brought Mark to this place?

It was nearly dark by the time she reached the cabin and steeled herself for that first awkward encounter. She opened the front door to the cabin and stepped in, calling out, "Nick!"

He wasn't here. Looking around, she noticed a single sheet of paper on the small kitchen table. When she picked it up, Nick's writing, bold and strong, read: "I will be back late tonight. Maybe in the morning." A single scrawled N finished the note.

He wanted to see her even less than she wanted to see him.

The late-night breeze stirred the bushes surrounding the Rangers' stockade. Nick cupped his hands around his eyes and peered in the window, his boots sinking in the soft earth. He'd slipped past two guards and had managed to look inside two of the three buildings. One contained a holding cell, empty, the other, bunks, a bathroom and a kitchen. The entire thing looked abandoned, with no one in sight but the two guards.

This building seemed as unremarkable as the other two he'd seen. Just an office with some communications equipment. He made his way to the corner of the building, careful of where he stepped, holding his Glock down at his side. He waited patiently for any sign of a guard, then peeked around the corner. No one was there.

He checked the first window but couldn't see inside. All the lights were off. He moved down to the second window. Here, the lights were on. And Nick saw something he'd only seen once before—when he'd bargained with terrorists.

Assault rifles. Machine guns. Grenade launchers. Guns and

ammunition of every sort. None of them San Matean military issues. All spread out on a long table and across the floor.

A muffled sound drew Nick's attention. Turning quickly, he looked out into the darkness. Nothing.

He moved back to the corner of the building, waited twenty seconds and looked around.

The hot stab of pain in his back, on his lower right side, caught him unaware. Throwing his right elbow down, he turned, swinging his left arm toward his attacker's face.

A slashing pressure burst at his waist.

Mary Beth awoke with a jerk, her neck stiff from trying to sleep on the small couch. How she'd managed to even doze amazed her. She squinted at her wristwatch. Five minutes after five. The first light of day came through the window.

Curious to see if Nick had come back, she stood and tiptoed to the bedroom. The bed was empty.

She combed her fingers through her hair and stretched the kinks from her back. The couch was going to kill her.

Her first reaction to Nick's disappearing act had been anger. Then hurt. Now she simply felt tired. And edgy. She smoothed clammy hands down her thighs.

She'd give him a bit longer, then she'd go see if Padre Franco knew where he'd gone. Even if Nick was trying to avoid her, this was taking things a bit far.

A heavy thud from the side of the house made her jump. She ran for the duffel bag Nick kept in the bedroom. Her fingers shook as she pulled out a loaded gun.

She really was overreacting. It was probably an animal of some kind.

The second thud nearly made her drop the gun. She looked from one small window to the other. The light breeze billowed the cotton-print curtains. Outside, the sounds of predawn stopped.

Heart in her throat, Mary Beth moved to the front door. Why didn't this damn place have a back door?

Her fingers slipped as she turned the doorknob. The gun felt cold, the metal grip foreign.

She waited. Endless minutes.

And heard the heavy weight of something fall against the door, the groan of a wounded animal.

Torn between the need to see her terror and the need to flee, Mary Beth opened the door, her grip on the gun steady.

Nick lay sprawled on his back in the doorway, a bloodstain darkening his clothing from waist to thighs. Mary Beth's knees wobbled as she bent toward him. In the pale light, he opened his eyes, his face ashen.

"Have to get away." His voice was a rough whisper. His blue eyes, normally alight with life and intelligence, tried to focus on her.

"Oh, God, Nick!" She crouched down and touched his cheek. He felt cold and clammy beneath her fingers. That scared her more than the blood.

"No time," he muttered. "Got to get away." He struggled to sit, holding his left arm tightly around his middle. In his right hand he held his gun.

Maneuvering her shoulder under his right arm, she tried to support him as he stood. He weighed a ton.

"Tell Franco I'm hurt." He took the few steps necessary to reach the couch. "Bring his truck."

Mary Beth tried to ease him down, but he fell without a word. When she straightened, she felt the wet stickiness of his blood on her side and arm. She flicked on the light.

His head fell back against the couch. Perspiration glinted off his brow and his lips formed a straight line. His eyes were closed, his left arm glistened red.

She ran to the bathroom and grabbed all the towels she could carry. Kneeling before him, she pried the gun from his grip and tried to move his left arm from around his middle.

"Back," he protested weakly, fighting her hands.

"I've got a towel. Pressure should stop the bleeding."

His grip relaxed and he leaned forward, his head resting on

her shoulder. She pulled his T-shirt up, trying to support his weight. A two-inch cut on his back, below his right lower rib, welled blood.

Mary Beth folded a towel into a pad and pressed it to the wound. "Lean back."

He fell back, his arms lax at his sides.

Blood had to be coming from somewhere else for there to be this much. She raised the wet shirt from his abdomen, pulling to get it out of his jeans. The copper-sweet smell made her light-headed, but she tugged until she could raise it.

Shakily, she grabbed another towel and wiped. The second wound, also on his right side, above his hipbone, looked longer than the one on his back. She made a pad of the towel and pressed.

Desperation made her calm.

"Nick?" She waited for some sign that he was awake.

He rolled his head to one side.

"If you can lie down, your weight will put pressure on the back wound. You can hold the towel on the front while I go for Padre Franco." But she didn't know if he could hold the towel. She only prayed he could.

He grunted and opened his eyes. They were nearly black. She should cover him, keep him warm to stave off shock. If he wasn't already in shock. She didn't know. She knew nothing about emergency care.

"I'm sorry." His eyes were focused on her blouse.

She didn't understand.

"You're covered in blood...." His voice faded.

He was thinking of *her* when he was so weak? "Can you walk to the bed?"

Somehow, he stood again. Between them, they managed to get him to the bedroom. He fell on the bed. Mary Beth made sure both pads were in place and squeezed his blood-slick hand before leaving. Then she ran as fast as she could.

Praying he would still be alive when she came back.

Chapter 9

Padre Franco's truck hit another pothole. Nick flinched but didn't seem to wake. They'd been on the road to the Land Rover for endless minutes, Padre Franco driving as fast as he could. Nick's last words had been to insist that Franco take them to the Rover and that Mary Beth drive them back into the mountains, away from the mission. Then, exhausted, he'd drifted into either sleep or unconsciousness.

Now he lay with his head in her lap. They'd wrapped him in blankets, but even the jeans she'd changed into offered no protection from the cold metal of the truck bed. Icy shivers ran through her body. Her legs felt rubbery from the distance she'd run. She held a pad on Nick's stomach. The bleeding seemed to have slowed, but he had to have medical care.

The priest had told her where to go to find a doctor, one who could be trusted. She listened with every ounce of her being, afraid she'd get them lost.

Afraid Nick would die.

The sun rose over the horizon as the truck rolled to a stop, pulling in behind the hidden Rover.

"Remember," Padre Franco said as he helped her get Nick, stumbling, into the car. "Go east, around the lake. You will climb to around thirteen thousand feet. There will be an Incan ruin. Turn to the right there. It is a dirt road. Go to the second town and look for a low white wooden building. It will say *Clínica* in red letters. The doctor is a French-Canadian man named Jean Rousseau, a close friend of the family. Tell him no one must know it is Nick. I would go, but I must be here to cover for you."

"Thank you, Padre."

In the cool morning air, the priest put his hand on Mary Beth's shoulder. "He is strong of body. He is not a man to give up. Jean will make him well." He squeezed her shoulder gently. "You must save his life."

An hour later her hands ached from clutching the wheel. She'd driven relentlessly, careful only of the larger dips as she maneuvered the Rover over the rough terrain. Nick lay sprawled in the back seat, his legs bent to fit. She spared another glance at her watch. She should be able to see the ruins now. To her left, the lake reflected the rising sun. To her right, the low rolling hills of the Andean plateau were broken only by boulders and scrub plants.

Then she saw the looming outline of the ruins. Stark and square, the stones spoke of a culture long dead. She slowed to be sure she didn't miss the road, then stopped to make the turn.

Nick still hadn't moved. Mary Beth strained to see his chest. Her heart seemed to stop for a single instant, panic making her throw the car into neutral and pull up the emergency brake.

He wasn't breathing.

She nearly jerked the door off its hinges when she swung it open. Sunlight streamed in and hit Nick's face. His lids moved, then his eyes opened and connected with hers.

"Stop him. Have to stop him." His eyes closed again.

He was dreaming, having nightmares. Mary Beth touched

his face. He felt fevered now, but even wrapped in two blankets, he shivered. She pulled the blankets open just enough to reach in and feel the heavy towel she'd put on his abdominal wound. It felt sticky, but no wetter than earlier.

He flinched and grabbed at her hand. "I'm sorry, Laura," he said in a hoarse whisper. "He's dead."

She didn't try to understand. She had to get him to the doctor. Wrapping the blankets back around him, she closed the door and set off down the uneven road.

A few minutes later she came to the first small town the priest had mentioned. The early morning sun cast long angled shadows across the barren landscape. The few dusty adobe buildings of the town lay in somber stillness. Slowing a bit, Mary Beth drove straight through, her heart hammering in her chest when she could finally see the town in the rearview mirror.

Her attention focused on the road, she threw uneasy glances into the back seat. Nick mumbled a few words and went still again.

A half hour later, Mary Beth had found the place—and she wanted to scream. What the priest had called a clinic was nothing. She fought a sob of desperation. How could Nick get help in this isolated place?

She pounded on the rough wooden door, and began panicking when no one came. She banged louder, and heard movement from inside.

"*¿Qué pasa?*" came a man's voice.

"*¡Doctór!*" she shouted back. Beyond the door, she could hear the sound of shuffling feet.

The door swung open and a short, gray-haired man with a ruddy complexion stood before her. Hastily thrown-on clothes drooped on his body.

"I need the doctor," she said.

"I am the doctor. What is wrong?"

"Padre Franco sent us. It's Nick Romero. He's hurt."

Without another word, the middle-aged man stepped outside, opened the back door of the Rover and bent down. "Good God, Nick! What happened?"

"He's bleeding. Stabbed, I think."

Even as she answered, the doctor was opening the blankets, hastily lifting the bloody towel. "How long ago?"

"Sometime last night. I don't know exactly when."

"Let's get him inside."

With some help from Nick, who seemed to understand what they were doing, they managed. Halfway through the struggle, she realized she and the doctor were speaking English, but there was no time to wonder about it.

The inside of the clinic made Mary Beth feel better. It wasn't as well-equipped as a city hospital, but it was clean and there seemed to be all sorts of supplies stored in the cabinets around the room. They put Nick on an examining table.

"Jean," he said once, then closed his eyes.

The doctor cut Nick's shirt off, peeling it away from his body. He worked the jeans down low on his hips, then turned the light from an examining lamp onto his abdomen.

The sight made Mary Beth sick with dread. The floor moved beneath her.

The doctor turned on her. "Get out of here. You'll do him no good if you faint." His words brooked no argument. "There's a bathroom beyond that door," he said, signaling with his eyes. "Sit down and put your head between your knees. Then splash cold water on your face. Don't come in here until you can be of help."

Mary Beth stumbled through the door. She found the bathroom and, taking big steady breaths, did as she was told. After the woozy feeling passed, she stood and looked at herself in the small mirror. Blood smeared her cheeks. With jerky movements, she turned on the cold water and scrubbed her face.

Finally, with her head clear, she stepped through the examining room door and stood watching the doctor work on Nick, his movements sure and practical.

Nick looked like a mannequin. Angular features, dark hair, ashen skin. Perfect body but for the dark stitches marring the beauty of his abdomen.

"Don't come in here if you're going to faint."

"I won't faint."

"Good." He put aside something he held in his hand and turned toward her. "I'm Jean Rousseau. You're…"

"Mary Beth Williams."

"Mary Beth, we have to turn him over. Help me."

Somehow she did. Maybe it was the knowledge that Dr. Rousseau was in charge, that she was no longer solely responsible for Nick's life. She even watched as the doctor cleaned and stitched the straight cut on his lower back.

"How did this happen?" Jean Rousseau asked when he'd finished.

"I don't know." Mary Beth helped turn Nick back over again. He was so still. She gently brushed his hair away from his forehead, wishing she could do more.

"Through some miracle, nothing vital was cut. I had to clean the wounds, which caused him a lot of pain. I gave him something for it, so he's going to sleep." The doctor lifted the bandage on the abdominal wound, looked closely, then pressed it down again. "I wish I'd had more local anesthetic, but the injection I gave him seemed to help. I don't have any way of giving him a transfusion, but infection is the biggest threat now."

"Will he be all right?"

"He'll wake up a little groggy from the narcotic. The antibiotic injection I've given him should keep any infection away. Like I said, he should sleep for a good while. Rest is what he needs."

"No one must know he's here."

The doctor's gaze shot to hers.

It took only a second for Mary Beth to decide whether to tell Jean Rousseau all of it. If Padre Franco and Nick trusted the man, she would, too. "San Matean Rangers and an

American army contingent are after us. It has to do with my brother.''

The whole story bubbled out of Mary Beth as the doctor finished with Nick. They moved him into the doctor's living quarters. Nick was of no help, but Dr. Rousseau shifted him over onto a cot.

"So you believe Daniel knew your brother?"

"That's what it looks like."

"Nick will help you save your brother."

Mary Beth knelt down next to Nick, who'd slept through the entire transfer, and took his hand. "He was dreaming about his cousin's death earlier."

"You mean Daniel."

"Yes."

"Then it was a nightmare," the doctor said.

"I've heard bits and pieces of what happened. Can you fill in the blanks?" Mary Beth asked.

Jean Rousseau looked up and seemed to assess her before pointing to a nearby cot. "Sit."

He stood next to Nick and checked his pupils, then moved away, leaning against the doorjamb. "Nick was in New York when the news broke that Daniel had been taken hostage. He rushed back, determined to negotiate as he had so often, not just here, but all over the world. The generals, unbeknownst to Nick, pushed for a military option—a raid to rescue the men. They didn't want a two-month standoff like the one at the Italian embassy. Nick met with the terrorists and came out. While he was preparing for a second meeting, the generals went ahead with the raid. It was a horrible mistake.''

Mary Beth shivered and hugged herself. The doctor took a blanket from a nearby shelf and handed it to her.

"Nick couldn't stop General Vargas, Daniel's father, from ordering the assault. He personally led the raid. It was a purely political move. There were others much more capable."

"That's why Nick blames him."

"He's right. Daniel and those men should be alive." Jean

Rousseau shook his head. "As it was, Nick and Franco found Daniel's body inside the compound after the failed raid. He'd been executed, as had the other captives. The general let the terrorists get away. He didn't save the men. The whole thing was a disaster. But as in everything that man does, he salvaged something. Politically, he sold many people on the idea that he was tough on terrorists."

"Daniel?" Nick's voice sounded strained.

Mary Beth knelt down next him, her hand reaching for his. "You're safe, Nick."

"I'm sorry." He sighed and slipped into unconsciousness.

Mary Beth's eyes flew open.

Nick!

He was shifting, mumbling, his voice rough. She jumped from the cot next to him and bent over him, holding his shoulder down to keep him from sitting up. He'd uncovered himself, so she pulled the sheet up over his bare bandaged abdomen.

Strong fingers grabbed her hand. "No," he whispered, his blue eyes glazed. "No."

"It's okay, Nick. You're safe. At Dr. Rousseau's."

"No." He held her hand with increased pressure. "It's in the blood." He took a deep breath. "Angela!"

"It's me, Nick. Mary Beth."

"It's in the blood…" His words trailed off, his hold on her loosened, and he slept again.

She heard the door open, and turned.

Jean stepped into the room. "Is he awake?"

"He was, I think. But he's restless and he's not making sense."

"What did he say?"

"Something about blood."

Jean nodded and checked the bandages.

"Who's Angela?"

He straightened and looked at her. "His real mother. She

was an American. Died shortly after childbirth. He mentioned her?''

''Yes.''

Once again, he bent over Nick, this time to check his pupils. ''Let me know if he says anything else odd or if he becomes restless. I'm making a list of supplies. Wish I'd had more local anesthetic. He's not reacting well to what I gave him for pain.''

Three women looked at him. All casualties of a Vargas.

Angela Crosby. Beautiful, forever young. Forever lost. She'd had no life after giving birth to him.

Elena, a survivor who deserved a life after giving up hers for the child he had been, the man he'd become.

Laura, alone. A woman who needed a man. A woman without a man.

He owed each of them.

''Nick?'' Mary Beth's voice intruded on his vision. ''I'm here.''

But she wouldn't be when she found out who he was.

A noise from the front of the clinic pierced the fog of Mary Beth's dreams. She was glad for it. Her dreams had been nightmares awash in Nick's bright red blood.

''You're awake.'' Jean Rousseau's friendly face smiled down at her.

''Yes.'' She sat up, instantly looking toward Nick. ''He's been very restless. Sometimes reaching for things that aren't there.''

''I saw. He's reacting to the narcotic. If only I'd had— Well, doesn't make any difference now. It'll wear off. He's sleeping now, so I'm not going to disturb him. I'll have to change the bandages later, but first, you need to eat.''

The thought nearly made Mary Beth gag. ''I don't think I can.''

''You'll have to if you want to be of any help to him.''

A few minutes later, while she washed in the small bathroom, she understood what the doctor had done. He would make her take care of herself for Nick. Somehow he'd seen her infatuation.

The small kitchen smelled of coffee and hot bread. Despite her earlier reaction to the thought of food, Mary Beth's stomach rumbled. Jean heard and smiled.

"I guess I am hungry." She glanced at the time. Nearly 6:00 p.m., about twelve hours since they'd left the mission.

"Eat and we'll try to get Nick to take something."

Nick didn't protest when Jean woke him changing the bandages. He said a single word before letting himself be propped up enough to take a few swallows of orange juice. *"Gracias."* Then he fell asleep again.

Jean took his pulse, then looked at Mary Beth. "The drug is wearing off. I have to go check on some patients. Try to give him some juice every hour or so. Sweet tea would be good, too."

Patiently, Mary Beth spent hours feeding Nick spoonfuls of liquid. He didn't protest. He didn't open his eyes. He said nothing.

The slamming of the door woke Mary Beth. She'd fallen asleep again slumped in a chair next to Nick's cot, even though she'd dozed all day long and most of the evening. The tea had gotten cold.

"I brought steaks and bananas." Jean smiled. "We have to build his strength back up, so I asked for my payment to be beef. The bananas will restore his potassium levels."

Mary Beth stood, stretching. "I'll cook if you'll tell me where things are."

"Be my guest." He led Mary Beth into the kitchen. "Has he been awake at all?"

"No, not really. He's still talking nonsense, but he hasn't tried to get up again."

"Good, good," he said. "That's a good sign. I'll give him

another injection of antibiotics and look at the wounds." He walked to the door. "Oh, Mary Beth, I hid the Rover."

Mary Beth half listened to Jean's explanation of where the Rover was hidden, until she realized that in her concern over Nick she'd pushed Mark aside. She couldn't afford to do that.

Four more days and the terrorists would kill him. Nick was in no shape to go anywhere.

She would have to go on alone.

"Well, my fine young friend," Jean said, smiling from the foot of Nick's cot. "You're going to live."

He swallowed, his mouth dry. "I feel like hell."

"You look it, too."

"Have I thanked you?"

"Yes. But it's Mary Beth you should thank. She got you here before you lost too much blood."

He didn't want to owe her. "I'm sure I thanked her." But the words came out too harshly and he knew Jean would pick up on his discomfort.

"I certainly hope you don't use that tone with her."

Nick didn't have the energy to argue.

"Unfortunately, I didn't help you very much. I ran out of local anesthetic as I cleaned your wounds. Do you remember?"

"There was a lot of pain, that much I remember."

"I had to give you a narcotic painkiller. You didn't react well. You'll have to remember in the future. You don't want to hallucinate again."

"I hallucinated?"

"Had your pretty nurse very worried about you."

Nick didn't like the thought of being out of control. What had he said?

"About her brother?" Jean said. "Are you helping her for her sake or for Daniel?"

Jean Rousseau knew him too well. "I just hope we find him alive," Nick replied.

"What happened to you?"

"I got a tip that the Rangers had him." He tried to breathe slowly, to avoid moving, afraid the pain would intensify. "So I went to the Ranger stockade. Williams wasn't there, but there were weapons. Grenade launchers. Guns. Ammunition." He shut his eyes against the burning at his stomach. "Lots of them." He took a another careful breath. "And a guard with a knife."

"And you think they've got Mary Beth's brother?"

"They had him, but I don't know what they did with him." He tried to shift but thought better of it. "Took him and an old man named Demetrio Vazquez."

"Oh, you mean the counterfeiter."

Surprised, Nick rolled to one side, ignoring the discomfort, and looked at Jean. "Counterfeiter?"

"Got out of jail a few months ago. He was one of the best counterfeiters of American dollars around. Daniel was involved with that arrest, I think. So was the American Secret Service."

He had to think, but the heaviness of exhaustion made it impossible.

"Rest a while," Jean said.

Nick closed his eyes, unaware of the line between wakefulness and sleep.

Mary Beth stood over Nick. The aroma of steak drifted up from the plate she held in her hand. She hated to wake him.

"Nick?"

He shifted a little but didn't open his eyes.

"Nick?" She put the plate down on the small table next to the cot and leaned over him. "Jean says you have to drink and try to eat."

He opened his eyes and looked straight at her.

"It's counterfeiting."

"What?"

"Whatever is going on," he mumbled. "It's counterfeiting."

She brushed her hand across his forehead. He was still reacting to the drug. "I'll get Jean."

He took her hand, pulled it to his chest and spoke firmly. "The numbers on the scrap of paper. The hundred-dollar bill. It has to do with counterfeiting," he insisted.

"What are you talking about?"

"Is that steak?" He tried to lift his head.

"Yes, it is."

He shifted, attempted to sit up, and winced.

She bent down, putting her left arm under his shoulder as he clutched the bandage on his stomach. Finally, leaning his weight back against the wall, he took a deep breath and closed his eyes.

"What happened? Where did you go?"

He opened his eyes briefly, then shut them. "I found a boy at the market who told me his grandfather and Mark were taken by the Rangers."

"If the Rangers took Mark, how did the terrorists get him?"

He ignored her question and told her what had happened.

As she listened, Mary Beth's thoughts raced. "Currency serial numbers."

"American dollars." His words were more of a breath than a sound.

"Don't talk. You need to eat."

She helped him eat as much of the steak as he wanted, in the end feeding him herself when he rolled onto his good side. Then he slept.

Mary Beth sat back in the chair and stared at him. And worried. The one-hundred-dollar bill in Mark's safety deposit box. It was a counterfeit. It had to be.

Surely Mark hadn't done this.

What about Daniel Vargas? What did he have to do with all of it?

"No!" Nick jerked awake, his eyes wild.

Mary Beth bent and tried to soothe him, her hand on his cheek. "It's okay. Just a dream."

"No." He shook his head. "Not a dream."

"It's okay," she repeated.

She didn't expect him to say anything else since he'd closed his eyes again. When he did speak, his words were lucid, but they were the words of his delirium.

"It's in the blood."

Chapter 10

Nick slept the night through, waking only once to reach for juice on the small table. Mary Beth lay on the narrow cot next to his and stared at the ceiling, bright morning light gleaming across the room.

The more she thought about what he'd been repeating, the more curious she became. *It's in the blood.* What was in the blood? Were the words a reaction to the drug in his system? Or was it more?

Like those old sayings. *Blood will tell. Blood ties.*

She and Mark were tied by blood, by kinship. By love. And it was beginning to look like Mark was involved with some pretty bad things. Had he been duped, as she had been years ago, and gotten in over his head?

Nick shared a blood tie with Daniel Vargas. Was he thinking that his cousin had gotten involved in gunrunning and counterfeiting?

Not likely. From everything she'd heard and read, Daniel Vargas was considered a San Matean national hero. The man responsible for the rescue of foreign hostages from the same group that had eventually killed him. He'd been buried with full honors.

She sat up and looked at the man she'd nearly made love with, the man she had to remind herself she didn't know. She was sure of only one thing—if Nick was willing to go so far as to take responsibility for Daniel Vargas's son, then it only stood to reason that if Daniel had broken the law, Nick would do everything in his power to keep it from coming to light.

No matter the consequences to Mark.

Nick opened heavy eyelids. The disembodied feeling he'd experienced seemed to have passed. Pain, not particularly intense, centered on the two wounds and pulled at him as he tried to reach for the juice on the table by the cot.

He grimaced. He was going to have to get up.

Raising his left arm to shade his eyes against the morning light pouring through the small window, he saw that Mary Beth's cot was empty, her blanket folded neatly at the foot. He moved his arm enough to focus on his wristwatch—midmorning. He'd wasted too much time. Even if he wasn't completely well, he had to think, plan.

And believe in Daniel, who'd given him so much. Who'd counted on him. Whom he'd let down.

Daniel couldn't have been involved in counterfeiting or gunrunning. His relationship with Mark Williams simply indicated an investigation cut short by his death.

But that didn't explain the numbers in both their writing. And if that wasn't enough, the two men had been seen together and Daniel's dog tag had been in Williams's safety deposit box. That spoke of friendship. Or collusion.

"You're awake." Mary Beth's voice pierced his thoughts.

She stood at the door, looking fresh. Beautiful. Memories of how she'd looked at the river raced across his mind, but he pushed them away ruthlessly. He couldn't afford to think like that. He had nothing beyond a fabricated life to offer her.

Then there was that other problem. What would he have to do once he found Mark Williams?

She gazed at him long and hard, as if she were thinking about what to say. Afraid she might see the questions he was still asking himself, he cleared his throat.

"I have to get up."

"You really shouldn't. You might tear something."

He smiled at her abrupt shift in emotions. Ever practical Mary Beth. "But I have to."

She stared at him a moment before her expression reflected her understanding. "Oh."

"Yes, oh." He rolled to his left side, holding his stomach. "Jean's gone."

He paused in mid-roll. "I still have to get up." He used his arms to push himself up, trying to avoid any use of his stomach muscles. "Just help me get there. I can take care of the rest."

She steadied him as he swung his legs off the cot.

They'd stripped him. He had borrowed boxers on, but his pants were gone. When he stood, the room swayed. Mary Beth stood next to him, balancing him as best she could. He couldn't help but turn his face and inhale the scent of her. Holding on to her and leaning against the wall, he managed to get to the bathroom.

The return trip was much worse. By the time he fell back into the bed, he was cold and sweaty. The room seemed to be spinning in ever faster circles.

"I've made breakfast," she said, wiping his brow with a cool, damp cloth.

God, he felt horrible. The thought of food made him queasy. "Can I have it later?"

"Sure."

Her voice soothed him. He managed to straighten out and relax, aware that the pain was not bad at all. It was the dizziness that wouldn't go away.

Until she wiped the cloth across his neck and chest.

She was trying to comfort him, while he was the son of a bitch who hadn't yet decided what he'd do about her brother's involvement with his.

He wouldn't be beholden to her. Knowing he was being a jerk, knowing she was only trying to help, he said, "Stop," and grabbed her hand, yanking the cloth from it.

She jumped up and fled.

He swore in English.

Mary Beth squeezed the orange with vengeance. All she wanted to do was make Nick comfortable. Well, she'd forget about his comfort. She'd feed him, make sure he drank enough liquid and let it go at that. It was obvious he didn't want her to touch him, so she wouldn't.

She was a fool.

No, she was an idiot for reacting to a wounded man. She had to quit reacting and start acting, taking charge. Nick wasn't well. She had to go on. As soon as the road opened, she'd have to take her chances alone. Jean would tell her how to get to Los Desamparados.

With renewed purpose, she washed her hands and put the orange juice on a tray along with fried bananas, eggs and hot rolls. He'd damn well better eat.

Prepared to treat him like a stranger, she found him on his left side, his face pale. She wanted to cry.

"Jean left some pain pills," she offered.

He shook his head, his dark hair ruffled against the pillow. "I don't want to even think about drugs," he said with a humorless laugh. "Besides, I'm not in pain." He turned toward her. "The Rangers know someone was at the stockade. They'll know to search for a wounded man. Once they look around the mission, they'll come straight to Jean's."

He was right. She hadn't thought of that. Everyone was searching for her. What would they do to him if she left?

"Where's the Rover?"

"You can't move yet. Jean said—"

"Mary Beth." His tone sounded a warning.

"He hid it in some trees. But you need—"

"To get better. I have today, at least."

"You can't be serious. You're not well enough—"

"Time is running out. There's no choice." He struggled to sit up.

With Mary Beth's help he did, and he ate all the food she'd fixed. She hadn't left the room before he fell asleep again.

The long day wore on. Nick woke to drink and go to the bathroom. Every time he got up, she was sure he was going to collapse. But he treated his weakness like he would a recalcitrant politician who refused to agree to a compromise by ruthlessly pushing ahead.

By late afternoon, when Jean got back from checking on patients, Nick had convinced himself that he could take a shower. She was only convinced he'd kill himself, and told him so.

"I am perfectly capable of showering."

"You're perfectly capable of falling down and ripping your stitches out."

"You're not my mother, damn it!"

She bit back a sharp retort, knowing she'd argued with him when he'd needed someone to cajole him.

"Of course she's not your mother." Jean stood in the doorway smiling at them. "You have a wonderful mother. Mary Beth is simply trying to follow my instructions."

Nick turned on him, holding on to the table for balance. "Which were to keep me in this damn bed until I rot?"

"No. Which were to keep you still so you don't destroy my stitches."

"Funny," Nick replied. "They feel like *my* stitches."

Jean shook his head and gave Mary Beth a look that begged patience. He directed his words toward Nick. "You want a shower?"

"Of course I do. I stink."

Mary Beth saw the militant glint in Nick's eyes. He was

going to get a shower one way or the other. She hoped Jean didn't insist on refusing him.

"For the sake of your pretty nurse, I'm going to help you." Jean winked at Mary Beth. "She shouldn't have to put up with your bad temper and your smell."

Nick released the table and eased back onto the cot. "Thank you." He gasped as he relaxed. "I think."

Jean laughed, winked at her again and spoke to Nick. "Don't let the water hit the stitches directly and don't use soap on them. You're healing quickly, no point in pushing your luck."

Mary Beth left them, and a few moments later, as she busied herself in the kitchen, she heard the shower running. Jean had brought back a *matahambre* from one of his patients. The steak roll contained spinach, eggs and carrots and smelled wonderful. She hoped Nick wasn't too tired from his bath to eat.

She had just put the *matahambre* into a pot to warm, when she heard the knock on the door.

"*¡Doctór!*" a woman shouted.

Afraid that it might be the Rangers or Elliot Smith, Mary Beth peeked out the window and saw a woman and child. Jean couldn't possibly hear anything in the bathroom. The knocking continued as she went to get him. She stepped into the steamy bathroom and told him.

"Don't leave him in there more than another minute or two," Jean said to her. To Nick, he said, "I'm going to answer the door, Nick. Mary Beth is here."

Mary Beth heard the door close behind her and turned toward the shower. Behind the yellow vinyl curtain, she could make out the shadow of Nick's body. He leaned against the wall, his head bent forward, letting water run down his neck and back.

Moments later, Jean opened the door and said, "I've got to go. There's been an accident. There are clean bandages in the examining room." He left, then Mary Beth heard the front door slam.

She looked back at the shower stall. How in the world was she going to deal with this forced intimacy?

"Nick?" She hated the awkward sound of her own voice. "Jean had to leave. You have to get out."

"Hmm?"

"Jean's left. You have to get out of the shower."

A thud resonated through the small bathroom. Muffled mumbling followed. Nick's silhouette tilted precariously. He tried to push himself upright, away from the wall. She forgot about anything but the possibility that he might fall, and threw open the curtain.

He listed slightly, both hands on the tiled wall, his back to her. In a single instant, she took in the beautifully sculpted muscles, the soft hair under his arms, the dark hair plastered to his head. And the horrible stitches at his waist.

Reaching out, she placed a hand on his shoulder. He flinched, his muscles tense.

"Turn—off—the water." His words came in pants. "Hand me—a towel."

She released his shoulder and did as he'd asked. Holding the towel toward him, she waited.

"Turn around," he ordered, wrapping the towel around his waist.

This was ridiculous.

He turned his head—to see if she had, she presumed.

His blue eyes fastened to hers. "Turn around," he repeated.

His words brooked no argument, so she made to turn.

But at that moment, he tilted forward and began to fall.

He didn't, because she steadied him as he caught hold of the towel rack. Balancing his wet, slippery body, she braced herself as he struggled to push against the wet tiles.

With awkward effort, he stepped out of the shower and stumbled down the hall with her, soaking her clothes. Finally in the bedroom, he lurched onto the fresh sheets, pulled up the top one, and closed his eyes.

"Nick?" she asked, afraid he'd passed out. She reached out tentatively to touch his shoulder.

"I'm okay," he mumbled. Rubbing a hand down his face, he added, "I'm getting everything wet."

Relieved to hear his voice, Mary Beth looked down at him. The white sheet clung damply to his chest and legs, molding to them. He was the most beautiful man.

"I need another towel," he said.

She met his gaze, a flush spreading across her face as she realized he'd caught her staring. "I'll, uh—" she muttered "—get one."

"Wait," he said, grabbing her hand. "I'm sorry for behaving like a wounded bear. Worse. I would have fallen if you hadn't been there. I would have bled to death if it hadn't been for you."

His eyes seemed so intense, so open. She pulled away, afraid of what he might say.

"No, Mary Beth. Wait. Give me a minute." He took a deep breath. "Don't think I stopped before, at the river, because I don't want you. God knows I do."

He smiled, but it was such a sad smile, Mary Beth didn't understand it.

"Sex involves a lot more than bodies." He released a pent-up breath. "It involves..." He paused, as if searching for words. "What matters is innocence of spirit."

"Nick—"

"Let me finish." He placed his hand over the sheet against his stomach. "I don't have innocence to give you. Neither of body nor of spirit. You need that."

"Please don't—"

"No way to protect you." He closed his eyes for a single moment, then opened them, searching her face. "Neither your body nor your spirit."

"I'm responsible for myself," she replied, wanting to stop him.

"I can't give you the life you should have." His words came out as a harsh whisper.

"You can't know what I should have."

His voice gentled. "What's the most important thing to you?"

The answer that came to mind surprised her. Love. She'd wanted love from her parents, but had only gotten it from Mark. The yearning for it was something she could no longer deny, but something she would not voice, certainly not to him. She couldn't bear for him to know. Instead, she focused on the mistakes she'd made. She'd wanted love and had been given a pretense. What she should have been given was something else.

"Honesty," she said, knowing it would have saved her so much.

"I can't give that to you."

She turned, unwilling to let him see what she so desperately wanted to hide from herself.

She'd fallen in love with him.

"I'm sorry." His words rumbled in the quiet of the room.

Her parents had never spoken of love. She'd been guilty of fearing the emotion, too. She remembered the man in college, the hurt on his face when she told him she was leaving town. She'd lied to him, telling him she'd keep in touch. She hadn't known how to soften the blow.

Nick had tried to be kind, to give her some dignity to hold on to. Whether he admitted it or not, he was an honest man.

"I'll bring dry sheets."

"How'd Nick make out?" Jean asked when he came back four hours later.

"Okay. He's asleep." Mary Beth closed the days-old newspaper she was reading at the kitchen table. She didn't want to think about anything he'd said. "Is the road to Los Desamparados open yet?"

"No. I'm told it will open tomorrow." Jean put his black medical bag down on the table. "I'll pack bandages and antibiotic capsules. Put them in the bag where Nick keeps his guns."

"Is there anything I should know to watch for?"

"He knows how to take the stitches out. You may have to help with his back, but that's—" Jean looked at her for a long silent moment, then sat down and tented his hands together. "You can trust him. There are few men who deserve trust more."

"He warned me not to."

Jean shook his head. "You have to understand Nick's sense of responsibility. He doesn't let anyone down. I haven't figured out how he does it without allowing anyone to get too close—with the exception of Daniel."

She wanted to understand this man who had been so important to Nick, who still was. "I know Daniel was stationed in the Río Hermoso Valley, but why did he have a house there? Why not live in Ciudad San Mateo?"

"Daniel bought the property years ago. Long before that famous hostage rescue that made him a household name in this country. He and Nick used to go fishing there." Jean stood and poured himself a cup of coffee. "That land was one of the first signs that Daniel wasn't going to do as his father wanted. The general opposed the purchase and certainly didn't want Daniel to build the house. But Daniel was his own man. He did it, smiling at his father the entire time."

"The general seems to be a difficult man."

"The general is a son of a bitch." Jean's green eyes seethed with emotion. Anger and something else. Something the doctor wouldn't allow her to see. Regret, maybe?

"Sorry. I didn't mean for that to come out like that."

"You know him?"

"Well enough to wonder why in the world Elena allowed her father to tie her to him," Jean replied.

Jean didn't call her Doña, Mary Beth noted. "It was an arranged marriage?"

"Oh, yes. The money and influence of the Romeros, the up-and-coming military officer."

"So the general wanted the marriage for the good it would do him politically?"

"There is nothing the general does that isn't geared toward that end. He tried to groom Daniel to follow in his footsteps." He grinned. "But Daniel wouldn't play his game. The general handpicked a girl from a powerful family for Daniel's wife. Daniel simply refused."

Mary Beth wondered if that was why Daniel hadn't married Laura. It didn't seem like much of a reason. "He must have been very angry."

"He was, and he blamed Nick because Nick had always been Daniel's confidant. But behind that anger is envy, I think. It makes the general furious that Nick was so close to Daniel. It galls him that Nick is so successful, that he's succeeded at everything he's ever tried. Have you met Carlos Montoya?"

Mary Beth shook her head.

"He's Elena's oldest sister's son. He influenced Nick more than anyone, other than Elena. When Nick left the Rangers, Carlos introduced him to diplomacy. Nick is very, very good."

"I've read some of the stories."

"There's a lot that doesn't get into the newspapers. Nick's been sent all over the world. He's had more success in more areas than anyone, always able to find a compromise. He's a master at it."

"What am I the master of?"

Mary Beth turned. Nick stood in the doorway, leaning against the frame. He'd put on his jeans, but he wore no shirt or shoes. The bandage at his waist was the only reminder of why they'd come here. His dark beard seemed to fit now. He looked lean and dangerous, as far from a diplomat as anyone she'd ever met.

"Compromise," Jean repeated.

Nick walked into the kitchen and pulled out a chair. "Sometimes compromise is failure."

Did he blame himself for his cousin's death?

Jean spoke quickly. "It wasn't your fault—"

"There is always fault, Jean. You know that."

"I've seen too much suffering to believe that."

"I've seen too much not to."

Both men fell silent. In the charged stillness, her own voice sounded tight, "I'll, uh, go—"

"I have to finish a new supply list," Jean said as he left the room.

Nick lowered himself to a chair, holding his stomach. "Jean has few complications in his life."

Mary Beth could think of one complication—whatever Jean felt for Elena Vargas. But this was not the time or the place to mention it. Instead, she leaned back against the sink, trying to relax the knot of tension in her stomach.

"I don't want it on my conscience that I hurt you," he said, his eyes steady on her.

"You won't."

"I already have."

"You're giving yourself too much credit."

"Ah." Nick smiled his urbane smile. Behind the beard it didn't look the same as it had at his formal party. "Mary Beth Williams is back." He placed his hands on the table. "Cool and in control."

"It's who I am."

"Yes," he said, his voice dropping. "It is."

She stood without looking at Nick again.

As she walked out of the room, she thought she heard him say, "And I'm who *I* am."

*   *   *

Nick woke suddenly. He'd dreamed of Daniel again.

Across the room, he could hear the even sound of Mary Beth's breathing. The nearby clock said it was just past 4:00 a.m. He'd spent the day aware of the distance Mary Beth had placed between them. A distance that had to be maintained.

He wanted to curse at the heavens.

Jean had said he was the master of compromise. But he could find no compromise that would overcome what made Mary Beth unreachable. Just as he hadn't been able to find a compromise to save Daniel. It was the general's fault, but he was at fault, too. He could have saved Daniel if he'd admitted sooner that compromise was out of the question. That only violence would free Daniel.

If he'd allowed himself to be what he was, instead of denying it, he could have picked off the terrorists and freed his brother.

And he could have Mary Beth if he was willing to ignore her need for honesty.

He rolled to one side, surprised that the wounds barely hurt. Pulling on his jeans, socks and a shirt, he made his way quietly across the room.

Bright moonlight lit the kitchen. The single window, its curtains slightly parted, served as a conduit for the intense beam. Nick didn't bother to turn on the light as he made his way to the refrigerator.

He should send Mary Beth back to the city. Back to the States. She didn't belong here.

But she wanted to help her brother, just as he wanted to help his. And he hadn't solved the dilemma of what he'd do if helping one precluded helping the other.

The sound of a car's engine came through the window. It intensified until it was obvious that the driver was coming toward the clinic. One quick look outside at the vehicle confirmed the identity of the occupants. Careful to avoid the window, Nick hurried back to the room he shared with Mary Beth. He picked up the bag that held his guns and spare clothes and moved toward her.

She woke with a start, struggling against his hand as he held it over her mouth.

"Shh!" When she nodded he removed his hand. "Get dressed. Rangers are coming."

He barely registered that she'd slept clothed. He pulled his Glock and holster from the bag, pocketed a box of ammunition and tied his boots as quickly as possible. In the shadows, he saw her bend to tie her shoes just as someone began knocking on the front door.

From the next room, Jean yelled a reply as he stumbled out of bed to answer what had now turned into pounding.

Nick signaled to Mary Beth to follow him. He pushed aside the curtains and opened the window. From the front of the clinic he heard Jean's mumbled words.

Then suddenly there was shouting and the sounds of the front door crashing open.

Chapter 11

Mary Beth had barely had time to gather her wits when she heard the crash. Nick grabbed her arm and propelled her toward the window.

"Go!" he whispered against her ear. "Head for the Rover."

Stumbling, she rushed to do as he ordered. At the last moment, she remembered the bag with her clothes, the ransom money and Mark's papers.

"I'm right behind you," he said, turning away briefly.

She ducked to fit through the small opening. The bag hung on the windowsill, but she jerked it free. She turned to see Nick maneuvering his much bigger body through the window, gun in his right hand, his bag in his left.

Bright moonlight glowed off the yellow dirt-filled yard. To her left stood a chicken house, to her right a dilapidated barn.

The Ranger search party would look in both places first. They had to get to the cantina, which stood past the dirt track behind the barn. She only hoped she could outrun them. That Nick could in his condition.

"Which way?" he whispered, his breath frosty in the cold, Andean night air.

Pointing, she answered, "The cantina, past the barn."

He grabbed her hand and started running. Her bag bumped against her legs. She was too scared to look back, too scared to look forward.

They made it to the barn in time to hear a man yell from the clinic. *"¡Encuéntrenlos!"*

Find them! he'd said. They would. There was no way out of this.

Nick swung her against the outside of the rough-hewn barn. Dust and particles of hay drifted up as they walked along the side of it. She tried not to breathe hard, not to make noise.

He led her around to the back of the barn, careful to stay in shadows. Sounds of running feet broke the silence of the night.

A loud *bang* reverberated through the old building. She held her breath. Nick froze in place. Two men spoke quietly to each other as they passed through the center of the barn, only yards away from them. More men approached. Her heart pounded in her ears. She wanted to close her eyes and make this nightmare go away.

Nick pressed her against the coarse wooden boards. Beams of light from several flashlights streaked past, missing them by inches. He pushed harder, his heart beating against her, and winced slightly as their bodies pressed together.

She felt the ridiculous urge to jump out, to tell the men she was here, to tell them to quit looking. Flashlight beams skirted around them again, never penetrating the deep shadows.

By the time they moved on, her knees were so weak, only the force and heat of Nick's body kept her upright. She dared a look over his shoulder and saw the backs of the search party as they spread out. Two of the men headed for the cantina.

With icy fingers, she tugged at Nick's shirtsleeve and pointed toward the men.

"I see," he breathed into her ear.

His warm breath pierced the cold dread and she relaxed a bit.

"Wait," he said.

The minutes dragged; he stepped away slightly. "Where's the car?" he whispered.

"In the copse of trees across from the cantina."

"Let them move on."

Mary Beth discovered she wasn't patient. The moments lasted an eternity. In the shadows of the barn, she couldn't make out Nick's face. Only his scent and the knowledge of his presence kept her sane.

"Let's go." His softly spoken words startled Mary Beth.

Taking her hand, he led her, ducking and running, out of the shadows and across the open ground toward the cantina. Mary Beth felt like a moving target. Despite the awkwardness of the bag, she tried to match his long strides, but she had to skip a little to keep up. By the time they reached the bushes surrounding the cantina, altitude and exertion had robbed her of breath.

Nick stopped and looked around. The Rangers had taken the small dirt track back toward the central road in town, the one directly in front of the clinic. From inside the cantina, sounds of music and laughter poured into the night.

Moonlight glinted off Nick's hair as he pulled her across the road into the trees.

Jean had taken the time to cover the Rover with hay. Mary Beth supposed he thought that would keep light from reflecting off it and make it less noticeable. Nick began brushing off the car, leaning in and stretching. She saw a small hesitation as if something hurt him, but he kept at it. She knew it would be useless to tell him to stop, so she hurried to help.

But when she started to open the passenger side door, he stopped her by grabbing her hand.

"Wait," he whispered. "Let them move toward the other side of town."

On wobbly legs, she rubbed her nose, still itching from the

particles of hay she'd inhaled. Nick sat gingerly on the front bumper.

"Are you bleeding?" she asked, also whispering.

"No."

"You need to be—"

"We have bigger problems than my stitches right now."

"I thought Padre Franco said the Rangers had gone on to the Río Hermoso Valley and that the road was blocked."

"Maybe the road is open, or this is another contingent of Rangers."

A door slammed in the distance and a dog began barking.

They waited. Mary Beth hugged herself against the cold and wondered how they would get away. The search party continued through the tiny town, their movement made obvious by the sounds of the dogs and more slammed doors.

Finally Nick whispered, "Let's go." He opened the driver's side door, climbed in, then put his bag next to hers at her feet before placing one of his guns on the seat between them. In the dim morning light, the glow from the dash seemed bright and intrusive.

The rumble of the Rover's engine filled the early morning. He threw the car in gear and inched forward between the trees toward the back of the cantina. Before pulling out of the cover of woods, he looked back over his shoulder, then his gaze rested on her.

"Hang on," he said.

She did, her hands gripping the armrest on the door.

While the cantina was alive with sound, no one else seemed to be awake at this early hour. The wooden building loomed between them and the main road in front of the clinic. The wide-open plain would provide little cover for their escape. They could only hope that surprise and early dawn would let them outrun the Ranger search party.

The Rover broke from the trees.

Minutes later, Mary Beth could see the poor excuse for a

town falling behind them, but her relief was short-lived. A
Jeep lunged from behind a mass of boulders.

"They've seen us!"

"Get down," Nick said, checking first the rearview mirror,
then the side view.

She felt the Rover accelerate at the same moment she heard
shots.

One shattered the rear windshield, spraying bits of glass on
them.

"Get down!" Nick shouted.

The shooting continued as he pushed the car across the
dusty, bumpy road. One shot pinged on metal and almost
immediately the Rover lurched to a sudden stop.

Nick reached down onto the floorboard and grabbed the
other gun from his bag. Mary Beth looked around them in
panic. They were on the open plain. No place to hide. The
only cover, an enormous boulder, lay more than a hundred
yards away.

Behind them, the soldiers quit shooting.

"Stay down," Nick ordered, carefully tucking one pistol
into the back waistband of his jeans. He grabbed the other,
holding it down on the seat next to him. "Don't move until
I tell you to."

The rapidly approaching Jeep held his attention. Finally, it
pulled to a stop behind them. Numb, Mary Beth waited, half
turned in the seat, her attention on Nick's tense body. He
seemed to be moving easily, his wounds causing no problems.

Elliot Smith and three heavily armed soldiers materialized
from the blinding headlight beams. They surrounded the
Rover, rifles aimed and ready.

"Mr. Romero, Ms. Williams," Smith said, his voice so
pleasantly menacing that Mary Beth's heartbeat accelerated.
"Please get out and throw down your weapons."

"You're in San Mateo, Smith. You have no authority
here," Nick replied, still holding his gun out of sight.

"Be realistic, Romero, we have you surrounded. The Ranger search party in town could be here at any minute."

"You wouldn't want that, would you?"

"Don't waste my time. We simply want to talk to Ms. Williams."

"What about?"

"Her brother."

"What about Mark?" Mary Beth asked.

"Throw out your weapons and move away from the car," Smith replied.

Nick tossed out the gun in his hand. It skidded across the dirt road. Then he took her hand and pulled her across the seat toward him. "Watch my face. When I tell you to fall, do it."

He opened his door and stepped out, hands in the air. "Tell them to lower the rifles."

Smith nodded at the soldiers. They lowered the rifles, but the biggest of the three kept his attention on Mary Beth.

Nick nodded and Mary Beth stepped out. "What about Mark?" she asked again.

"We have to find him, Ms. Williams. He's in danger. I'm afraid he's gotten involved in a gunrunning operation."

"It's not true—"

"If we don't find him soon, San Matean Rangers will capture him. I don't think I have to tell you what conditions are like in the jails here, if he lives long enough to see the inside of one."

"Mark wouldn't do anything like that."

"Ms. Williams," Smith said with exaggerated patience, "I know this must be difficult for you, but you have to trust that the embassy is doing all it can to find your brother before anything happens to him."

"Why did you ask me to leave the country?"

"I was trying to keep you out of this," Smith replied. "Your persistence in staying, in trying to find your brother, has made it necessary for me to come after you."

"What about the—"

"We didn't know this involved gunrunning," Nick interjected, his arms lowered. "If we had—"

"Romero, I wasn't born yesterday. You know exactly what's going on." He smiled. "The question is, how much does Ms. Williams know?"

"I know you're wrong about Mark," she retorted.

"Your loyalty is commendable, Ms. Williams, but your friend here has an interest in seeing your brother dead."

Mary Beth kept her gaze on Smith, but in her peripheral vision she could see Nick, unmoved by Smith's accusation.

"Romero is only interested in preventing the public humiliation of his family. All he has to do is find Mark and kill him in order to eliminate any question about his cousin's involvement in this gunrunning operation."

"Mark isn't a gunrunner," Mary Beth insisted. But she had her doubts and knew Nick wanted to prevent anything about his cousin from coming out. She'd thought of it herself. His family would always come first.

"No arguments, Romero? No defense of your cousin or your own sterling character?"

"Why aren't you working with the Rangers?" Nick asked, ignoring Smith's question.

"The State Department has decided to work it this way."

"They assigned these men to you?"

Mary Beth noticed a pause before Smith spoke again.

"I'm not here to explain the actions of the United States government."

Turning to his men, he ordered, "Check them for weapons."

One of the soldiers started toward Nick just as the heavy one approached her.

"And mind your manners, Wyatt," Smith warned as the soldier reached out to her.

Mary Beth's skin crawled at the look in the man's eyes. If he was an American soldier, he'd escaped from prison to enlist. Despite Smith's warning, Wyatt rubbed his thumbs down her breasts as he frisked her. Repulsed, she jerked away.

"Get your filthy hands off her," Nick said, stepping toward the soldier ready to search him.

"Unless you want a bullet in your head, I suggest you stand still, Romero." Smith's voice brooked no argument. "Wyatt, don't provoke a situation. Get away from her."

The man obeyed, but not before running one hand across her bottom.

Nick responded immediately. "Stay away—"

The soldier standing beside Nick used the butt of his gun to strike Nick across the left cheek. He fell and didn't move.

"What are you doing?" Mary Beth asked, rushing toward Nick.

"Don't do anything foolish, Ms. Williams." Smith grabbed her. "You're in no position to help him."

"You could have killed him!"

"He's not dead. I wouldn't waste any sympathy on him."

"Have you lost your mind?" she asked, trying to wrench her arm from his grasp.

"Ms. Williams," Smith replied. "Stop, or I'll have you bound and gagged."

"We have to help him!" She looked at Nick, still on the ground, immobile.

"He'll be fine. We don't need him."

"You don't understand. Mark—"

"Your brother is why I'm here. We have to find him. He's in danger."

"Of course he is. The Primero de Mayo is holding him for ransom. If I don't get the money to them in two days, they'll kill him."

Smith laughed. "You believed Vargas?"

"Vargas? What do you mean?"

"General Vargas, the man in charge of the operation to catch Mark. He had you called, lured you here."

"I don't understand."

"It's really very simple. Vargas can't catch Mark, so he gets you to come to San Mateo in the hopes that if he has you, Mark will come out of hiding. Those are his men going through the town back there."

It was too much to take in—Nick on the ground, Smith claiming the kidnapping was a hoax.

"Now, get in the Jeep," Smith said. "Wyatt, check out the Rover, see if they have anything in there. A bag, anything like that." He directed Mary Beth to the Jeep and nodded at two of the soldiers, who moved toward Nick, still on the ground, illuminated by the Jeep's headlights.

Then she saw him move. He mouthed a single word: *fall.*

Her decision on whether to trust him was instinctive.

As she dived for the dirt, shots rang out. The two soldiers who were approaching Nick fell to the ground and didn't move. The soldier named Wyatt froze, his rifle still down at his side.

"Drop it," Nick ordered from the ground, his pistol aimed at Smith.

Smith did.

"Tell your man to drop his rifle," Nick said.

"Shoot him!" Smith shouted at Wyatt, who stood unmoving. "Shoot him!"

"The hell I will," Wyatt replied. "He dropped Jonah and Ed too fast. They need a doctor. You're not paying us enough to get killed." He threw his rifle down.

"Both of you turn around and start walking," Nick ordered. "Go get the doctor."

Smith seemed to waver for a moment. "Do it," he said to Wyatt. To Nick, he said, "I'll find you, Romero. I'll find you." Then he smiled. "She'll pay for this."

He should have killed him. Instead he'd used his fist to bloody Smith's nose and knock him out, forcing the animal named Wyatt to carry him.

"I thought you were unconscious," Mary Beth said as Nick

cranked the engine of Smith's Jeep. They'd transferred their bags from the Rover to the Jeep. Jean would take care of the wounded.

"He didn't connect as well as he thought he had." He'd managed to duck just in time; otherwise that animal—

"How did you do it?" Mary Beth asked.

"Do what?"

"Pull out your gun so fast. Shoot them, but not kill them."

"Lucky, I guess."

"That wasn't luck," she replied. "That was fast. And accurate."

Nick thought about how much to tell her. Maybe it was time to divulge a bit more. It might make her feel safer. "I was a sharpshooter when I was with the Rangers. I have a good eye." And an ability he'd tried his damnedest never to use again. It bore proof of his heritage from Antonio Vargas.

She said nothing. It made him uncomfortable. Made him want to explain. And that was the worst thing of all. What was he going to explain? That he wasn't who he pretended to be? That he'd inherited some of Antonio Vargas's worst traits?

He'd wanted to shoot Smith and his men, had wanted to do something that would show them they couldn't touch what was his.

But she wasn't.

Nick turned the headlights off and pulled out, guiding the Jeep down the road a few hundred yards, then off, over the rough highlands terrain. Instinct would have to be his guide. They couldn't afford to have the Rangers find them. Smith was out of the picture, at least temporarily. They had to reach the Río Hermoso Valley to get their answers. To keep his promise.

"They're mercenaries, aren't they, Smith's men?" Mary Beth said.

"Yes."

"And General Vargas is behind all of this, trying to use me to get Mark to turn himself in."

It was time she knew what he'd suspected for some time. "It never made sense that Primero de Mayo would kidnap and ransom their source of guns. If they thought Mark had double-crossed them, they'd..."

"Kill him," she filled in while he struggled to find words that wouldn't hurt her. "And you're using me."

He glanced at her quickly. "Not to hurt your brother."

"For what, then?"

He turned down a steep hill, carefully avoiding huge boulders. "I want to stop Vargas from regaining power."

"And you think chasing after Mark will do that?"

"Vargas is hiding something in this investigation. That something could be his downfall." It all involved him somehow. Otherwise there was no reason for Vargas to ask him to burn the house, no reason to even approach him. Was there really something he thought Nick should cover up for Daniel?

"Revenge," she said. The word sounded obscene when she said it. "It's revenge for what happened to your cousin."

"It's necessity," he argued, unwilling to admit the truth to her. He knew himself, understood the emotions he kept hidden. He didn't want her to see them.

"It doesn't matter what you call it. Mark is all that matters to me. You want revenge, I want my brother. If Vargas wants Mark, then one way for you to bring Vargas down is for us to find Mark."

"You're not afraid that I'll give Mark to Vargas in order to get my supposed revenge?"

She looked at him with an unwavering gaze that made him wonder what she saw.

"No. You won't do that."

She turned in her seat and faced forward, her chin high. He understood. She was challenging him to meet her expectations.

If only he could meet his own.

* * *

Nick rolled down the Jeep's window. Two hours out it became obvious they were on the eastern slopes of the Andes. It was warmer and muggy. Rain clouds hovered on the horizon. By the time they reached the four-thousand-foot level, it would probably be raining. The narrow pass that had closed the road earlier in the week was still ahead of them. That was the last chance anyone had of catching them before they could vanish into the high jungle of the Río Hermoso.

Their luck held out. The pass was clear. No one paid them any attention.

They stopped on the outskirts of the old colonial town of Trujillo and bought bread, cheese and bottled water. Mary Beth insisted they also buy bananas, oranges and beef jerky, which they found at an open-air market.

When they got back into the Jeep, Nick winced as his stomach wound protested the movement.

"How do you feel?"

"Like somebody stuck a knife in me."

"Funny." She opened a bottle of water and handed it to him as he started the vehicle. "I find it hard to believe that the American embassy has given Smith the authority to use mercenaries."

"Smith has his own agenda," Nick replied before taking a long drink. "There's no point in guessing what it is. Your brother is the only one who can straighten out the whole mess."

"You think he's guilty of everything they've accused him of." Defeat had crept into her words.

"I don't know what to think." Except that Daniel was involved with Mark. If only he could figure out why. "I wish we had the papers we found in Mark's safety deposit box."

"They're in my bag," Mary Beth replied. "I've looked at the numbers and compared them to some bills I have with me. The total numbers and letters match." She reached down to the bag she'd moved from the Rover to the Jeep and pulled the papers from the folder they'd found them in. She'd put them in a plastic bag. "You look," she said, passing the bag to him.

He stopped the car and removed the papers from the plastic, careful not to drop anything. The first thing he saw was the stiff, folded copy of Mark Williams's will. Opening the folder, he scanned the single page. Whatever Mark had, he left to his sister. It surprised Nick that such a young man would even think of making a will, much less have one. Did Williams have some reason to think he might die? Nick noted the date of the document. Three years ago.

He put the will aside, and looked at the carbon and its scrawled dates. What were Mark and Daniel doing? Were they trying to make use of the counterfeit money? But Daniel didn't need the money.

"The money you took from the bank. Is that all the money your brother has?"

"As far as I know. He inherited some beach property. It's worth a lot." She looked at him. "If you're implying that Mark's into counterfeiting because he needs the money, you're wrong."

He understood how she felt. Loyalty to a brother.

"Did your cousin need it?" she asked.

"No. There's plenty of money. Daniel is—was—a Romero, too. Besides that, the old man has done well for himself. Daniel's salary wasn't much, but—" He stopped. He knew he was trying to convince himself. "Daniel didn't need the money."

"If neither of them needed the money, then it's something else. Maybe gunrunning, as Smith said."

"We're back to money if it is. Daniel didn't need the money to be made in the gun trade. If Mark didn't, it still makes no sense."

He handed the bag and its contents back to Mary Beth. Rain splattered the windshield.

"Mark will explain it all."

Nick didn't answer or look at her. By now, the chances of finding Mark Williams alive, with so many people after him, were fading. He'd have to rely on the few clues they had to get to the truth, and protect Daniel and the family from whatever had brought these two men together.

"Will we be able to get into the valley without being seen?"

"There's only one road. It'll be watched, but there are other ways down." Ways that might keep her safely away from whatever her brother had gotten himself into. Ways she wouldn't like, not if the rain kept coming down.

"Then we'll have to use one of those other ways," she said.

Nick tensed. He knew what those other ways meant.

The rain kept its relentless grip on them as they continued the descent out of the mountains. Finally, at midafternoon, Nick pulled the Jeep under the cover of deep, undisturbed tropical forest. He fell asleep in the front passenger's seat while Mary Beth did the same in the back.

An hour later, he woke and sat up. The rain had stopped. Turning, he could make out only her shape under the darkened canopy of the forest. He wished he could see her. Touch her.

But he didn't trust himself, didn't trust what faith she had placed in him. She might have come with him this far, trusting him to protect her, but if she felt that a challenge was necessary to make him do the right thing, she'd never completely trust him without the unvarnished truth. Which he couldn't provide.

There was no solution, nothing he could do to make everything work out the way it would in a fairy tale. There had never been any happily-ever-afters in his life.

But God knows he wanted nothing more than to kiss this sleeping beauty. That made him smile to himself. She'd laugh if she knew he'd thought of her that way.

Whatever Daniel and Mark Williams had been doing together stood at the center of the entire mess. Dragging Daniel's name through the mud was not acceptable. Not to him. Not to Doña Elena. Not to the Romero family. He couldn't let it happen. He didn't owe Mark Williams a thing.

What he felt for the man's sister was going to haunt him forever. With one last look, he carefully opened the Jeep door and got out.

And walked into the shaded darkness of the misty forest.

Chapter 12

Mary Beth couldn't wake up, even though she knew it was a dream. A really bad one. An ominous darkness settled over her, chilling her.

In the distance, at the edges of the forest, Mark ran, as if dodging some invisible menace. Huge trees blocked her view of him until he finally disappeared into the dark mouth of the jungle. She had never seen him like this. Dirty, an unkempt beard, his clothes ripped and bloodied.

Oh, God, Mark. What is going on?

She came awake with a start, alone, in the Jeep. Daylight barely penetrated the forest canopy, giving everything an otherworldly glow. Animals moved, birds chirped high overhead.

Nick was nowhere around. What if she'd been wrong to trust even half of what he'd said? She had to decide what to do in case he didn't come back. She was alone at the back of beyond in a foreign country. Maybe she could get back to Trujillo and find a telephone. She could call for help. She just didn't know who to call. The ambassador to San Mateo was one choice, but if he'd approved Smith's methods, she'd only be giving herself up to him.

Her father was the better choice. Asking him to again pull her out of a mess of her own making was galling. But there was no one else if she expected to help Mark. She should have called him immediately, instead of trying to deal with this on her own.

Or with Nick's help.

She had to start thinking instead of depending on anyone. She knew better, yet she'd come to rely on Nick. She rummaged in the bag and pulled out Mark's papers again. The numbers. Mark had to have put the numbers in the safety deposit box because he didn't want anyone to get to them. He'd trusted her to see them. She had to protect them. Not sure she was doing the right thing, she carefully tore the numbers out of the will. After folding them and the carbon, she ripped the plastic bag to make a small piece, wrapped the paper and carbon in the plastic, and put them in her pocket.

Climbing out of the Jeep, she scanned her surroundings. Watery sunlight filtered through the trees casting unusual shadows. She couldn't shake the sense of doom her dream had given her. And despite every cautionary warning she'd offered herself, she couldn't believe Nick had really left her here.

Hunger, exhaustion and plain fright gave way to tears. She never cried. Never. Yet she wanted nothing more than to let the sobs engulf her.

Then she heard it.

A twig breaking. Followed by deathly silence. No birds sang, no animals moved.

Then another rustling of vegetation.

Desperate, Mary Beth sought a hiding place in the dim forest. The high canopy prevented much undergrowth. Trying not to panic, she rushed toward the biggest tree she could see, away from the Jeep. The sob she'd been fighting froze in her throat. Leaning against the rough bark, she angled her body and peeked into the clearing, toward the sound.

Nick, leather holster across his shoulders, walked toward her.

Relief made her sag against the tree.

"Mary Beth?" he said softly.

She swiped furiously at the tears she'd shed. Because of a man. Because of him. Because she'd thought he had left her alone to cope with finding Mark.

Then anger took over. Anger at herself for trusting him, for so easily depending on him. That anger pushed away the tears and brought her back under control. She grasped it as if it were a life raft.

She could do this. She could deal with him, with the way he made her feel, until they found Mark. The only thing that mattered was helping Mark.

"Mary Beth?"

Did the sound of his question reflect fear? She didn't want to let that thought sway her from her resolution.

"Here I am," she said, stepping into the open.

She saw it then in an instant, in the light-speckled forest. The steel-nerved diplomat momentarily let down his guard and she saw what could only be described as relief. Just as quickly as it was revealed, it was hidden again.

"I woke up and went to look around. Did you get any sleep?" he asked.

She couldn't let this get to her. Wouldn't let emotions she was reading into his actions affect her. "Yes," she said.

He turned away, saying, "Let's eat, then."

They ate cold bread, cheese and jerky, washing it all down with bottled water. Nick cut up oranges. With Nick's pocket-knife as their only utensil, they were forced to eat with their fingers. Mary Beth tried to keep the juice from dripping onto her clothes.

He smiled at her efforts. "Don't mind your manners because of me."

"I suppose you could do better?" There was an annoyed bite to her reply.

"I'm not trying to eat this as if we were at a White House reception."

She licked her lips. "And I am?"

"You try too hard."

"This is all too easy for you." She reached out for another slice of orange.

"That bothers you?"

"Shouldn't it? We've been chased and shot at—you've been stabbed. You act like it's just another day at the office."

Nick wanted nothing more than to tell her it would all be okay. Fear for her had pushed aside both anger and possessiveness when Smith had caught up to them, and again when he thought she'd left the Jeep and gotten lost...or worse. He'd forced his chaotic emotions aside in order to do what had to be done. Now he chose the most innocuous of the many things rolling around in his mind, trying to avoid the feelings she engendered.

"It will end soon."

But she got to him once more. Those light, whiskey-colored eyes focused on him with deep intensity. "I won't be left behind," she said.

So that was it. She thought he'd left her. This woman who had seen the truth of his relationship to Alex and Laura thought he'd abandoned her.

"I won't leave you." His words were intended for the moment. They begged a more permanent sentiment.

The sound of birds again filled the silence as they sat crosslegged, facing each other.

She was the one to break eye contact. She raised an orange slice to her lips. He saw her fingers tremble, saw her lips part.

"Look out," he warned, reaching toward her.

Nick grabbed the slice just as it fell, catching it in her lap.

Juice oozed through his fingers onto her jeans despite his efforts. She grabbed at the drops, instinctively taking her slim fingers to her mouth. Nick's breath caught, his gaze frozen on her mouth. He raised the fruit to her lips.

She watched him with wary, alert eyes. He wanted to tell her to move away, not to let him make another mistake, but the words were caught somewhere between his heart and the overwhelming pull of desire. She parted her lips, accepting his offering, her breath warm, her teeth white against his fingertips.

She would taste of oranges and passion. Of everything he'd ever wanted. Everything he'd ever dreamed of. Bravery, honor and loyalty.

"I'll clean all of this up," she said, her voice rasping over his senses.

Nick saw her pull away, both physically and emotionally. She'd done the right thing. He knew she had. Because if he had kissed her, he wouldn't have stopped.

Mary Beth, nerves stretched beyond endurance, sat in the Jeep as Nick drove through the pouring rain with what appeared to be concentrated desperation. He'd been unfailingly polite. She'd been unfailingly silent. She could think of nothing to say.

She felt she knew him, understood him, yet there was this barrier, a barrier he'd established. Not just a physical one, but one that kept everything about him at a distance. One that would forever make her wary of him, wondering what other secrets he kept.

The rain came down in sheets, slowing them to a near crawl. The wipers proved ineffective against the deluge, but Nick kept driving, his attention fixed on the miserable excuse of a road.

Mary Beth glanced down at her watch. Nearly seven-thirty. "How much farther?"

"We won't make the valley today, but we'll have a place to stay the night."

The rain tapered, then quit, clouds racing east. Far ahead, lights twinkled through the mist.

"What's that?" she asked.

"San Vicente. The end of the road for us." Minutes later, he pulled the Jeep into the sheltering cover of a metal-roofed, dilapidated barn. They got out and walked into the town square. It was illuminated by towering light posts that reminded Mary Beth of a ballpark. Rolling mist replaced the rain, but from the looks of the carefully tended square, San Vicente had had its share. Puddles covered the grass in the center of the square, and mud lay thick on the unpaved road.

"They have power way out here?" They were hours away from civilization.

"These small towns go into cooperative efforts, like the Incas used to do. They get an engineer to come in and plan it all, lay the power posts, then connect to the next small town."

"I can't believe there's another town out here. We're in the middle of nowhere."

"You'd be surprised at how close we are to Trujillo."

"Where we stopped for food?"

Nick nodded.

"That was hours ago."

"A straight line from Trujillo to San Vicente would take less than half an hour."

"But I thought Trujillo was on the edge of the mountain."

"It is. San Vicente is on the next eastward mountain." Nick shifted the bag he carried to his right shoulder. "Let's go."

Cool and humid, the night air revived them after the long trip. Mary Beth followed Nick as he walked toward a white-washed two-story frame house at one corner of the square. He knocked on the heavy wooden door and waited, the streetlights casting them in tall shadows. She hoped it was only the light that made him look so tired.

Finally, they heard footsteps and the door opened. A short, heavy woman stood framed in the doorway. She blinked at them, then laughed in pleasure.

"Nicholas!" She opened her arms and he stepped forward. *"Qué bien,"* she said, hugging him. *"Ven, ven. Pasa."*

Nick pulled away, still holding the woman's hand. "Doña Inez, this is Mary Beth. Mary Beth, Doña Inez Alvarez, a good friend of the family."

Inez stretched out her hand toward Mary Beth. "It is a pleasure, no?" She cast a quick curious glance at Nick as she said the words.

"My pleasure, Doña Inez," Mary Beth replied.

"Ah, Nicholas," she said, looking Mary Beth up and down. "Your mother, she is well?"

"She is. Very well."

"Muy bien." She nodded, then looked back at Mary Beth. "I have two rooms and food."

"Gracias," Nick replied.

Doña Inez led them through a darkened living room decorated with heavy Spanish furniture and into an immaculate kitchen.

"Siéntate, Nicholas," she said, tying an apron around her ample middle. "Please, you too, Mary Beth."

Nick sat down on a wooden chair beside a small table as their hostess kept up a constant chatter that told Mary Beth she was a close friend of Doña Elena's. Finally, she set plates before them and wiped her hands on her apron.

Mary Beth hadn't known how hungry she was. She and Nick ate huge ham sandwiches and drank the sweet national cola, following it all with strong black coffee.

Finally, Nick gave Doña Inez an edited version of the purpose of their trip. Without lying, he let her believe they were simply touring, giving Mary Beth a chance to experience the wild untamed areas of San Mateo, showing her those places he'd loved when he was a boy. Somehow he managed to tell her that if anyone looked for him she was to say he was not here. He was sneaking away from work, he explained, and wanted to have the time off without interruption. It amazed Mary Beth that anyone who knew Nick would think he would shirk any duty.

And she wondered if Nick knew his old family friend had her own version of the trip, a more romantic one. The gray-haired woman kept giving her speculative looks.

Then she led them up a finely carved wooden staircase to the second floor. "Nicholas, this is your room," she said, opening the first door. Nick stepped in, and Doña Inez continued down the hall. "Mary Beth, this is your room." She opened a second door and walked inside. She flicked on a lamp on a tiny ornate table in the entrance and continued inside. "You will share a bathroom, *bien?*"

"Of course. *Gracias.*"

In the intimate light of the bedroom, Mary Beth saw a look of concern cross the woman's face. She seemed to struggle with something she wanted to say.

"Is something wrong?"

The woman stared at her for a few seconds, then took a deep breath. "It is not my concern, no? But Nicholas, he is a good boy. He has a kind heart. You will be good to him, no?"

Mary Beth drifted awake. The quiet rain she'd heard all night had stopped. Outside, weak sunlight washed the morning in a golden glow. The house stood still and quiet.

Stretching, she rolled over and plumped the pillow. She felt new. After a hot bath, which included a shampoo that washed out more of the fading hair dye, she'd fallen into a sound sleep in the clean comfortable bed.

She'd pondered Inez Alvarez's last words to her as she'd fallen asleep in a borrowed floral knit gown. Why would this family friend ask her to be good to Nick? Mary Beth had no power over him. He held the power to devastate her if she let the feelings she had for him blind her to who and what he was. She'd seen him work his charm on Doña Inez. He didn't lie, but he avoided the truth.

Then it hit her. Did Doña Inez believe her to be like Laura Morales? A lover who might come back to haunt Nick with claims of a pregnancy? How little people knew him. How did he and Laura put up with their families' and friends' erroneous beliefs about them?

There was only one answer. Their love for Daniel Vargas and his son took precedence over all else.

Mary Beth would do well to remember this fact.

With deliberate effort, she pushed aside the troublesome thoughts. Stretching again, she got out of bed. Donning her jeans and a navy-blue T-shirt—her last clean one—she carefully opened the bathroom door. It was dark. Nick had closed the door to his bedroom. Did he think she would come in search of him? That she wanted him so badly she would embarrass herself again?

Won't happen, she told herself, flipping on the light.

The mirror revealed that she looked…well, bad. Really bad. The black dye streaked her hair. Maybe another half-dozen or so washings would get her back to normal. Right now she looked like a beautician's nightmare. Grimacing at her reflection, she turned on the cold water, grateful that at least water was plentiful here, that the sink didn't gurgle as had the one at the bungalow at the sawmill. Moments later, eyes closed, face dripping, she reached to her left, where she'd seen a towel rack with a fresh towel.

"Looking for this?"

Her eyes flew open. Nick, hair ruffled, stood next to her, holding the towel.

"You scared me to death!"

His only response was a half grin.

Jerking the towel from him, she scrubbed her face dry.

"Leave some skin, *niña*," he said as she finished.

"Bathroom's yours," she said with as much dignity as she could muster.

"You wet your hair," he said. He was too close. Too close and barely dressed, barefoot, wearing only black jeans.

"It'll dry," she replied, but before she could turn around, he reached out and pushed the wet strand of hair behind her ear. Why she stood still and let him, she would never know. Worse yet, she closed her eyes. She was a fool.

A distant, mechanical *bang* resonated around them. Jerking her eyes open, she could see nothing. It was pitch dark.

"Turn on the lights," she said, trying to catch her breath.

"Power's out. Something just blew." Did his voice sound scratchy?

Reaching toward her right, she sought the wall of the small bathroom, but instead, backed into the sink. Realizing her mistake, she turned and stepped in the direction of her room. Only to run into Nick.

"Watch out," he said, grasping her arms.

She could hear him breathing, the rhythm altered and quick. Then, with velvety blackness all around them, he ran his hands up her arms to her shoulders and stepped even closer.

She knew what would happen next, knew but did nothing to move away. She was a *total* fool.

He was a solid presence—a warm, hard, solid presence in an otherwise unearthly void. She didn't protest when she felt his hand on her cheek. Didn't question when the touch of his fingers on her lips blotted out all doubts. The heat of him, her passion for him, was something she couldn't deny. The fact that *he* had come to her obliterated all other thoughts. When his mouth touched hers, tentatively at first, she was lost.

Then he was holding her to him, holding her when it wasn't necessary because she wasn't going anywhere. In the dark, the kiss was her only reality.

"Nicholas!" Doña Inez called, pounding on Nick's bedroom door.

Opening her eyes and pushing away from him, Mary Beth realized the lights had come back on. Nick stared down at her, seemingly as confused by what had happened between them as she was.

"*¿Sí?*" he replied.

"*Desayuno,*" Doña Inez said. "Breakfast."

Mary Beth took the cup of coffee Doña Inez handed her and sat down at the kitchen table. She'd practically run down the stairs.

"I hope you slept well, Mary Beth. The power, it is erratic in the rainy season. I am sorry if it frightened you."

"I slept very well, and no, the outage did not worry me."

"Did Nick sleep well?"

"I wouldn't know," Mary Beth replied, sure she was blushing. But she was saved from further embarrassment because her hostess had her back turned, putting something up in a cabinet. She seemed to presume she and Nick had spent a passionate night together. If she only knew.

He still hadn't come downstairs. She'd heard the shower running when she'd left the room.

Doña Inez turned and said, "Nick, he is—"

He picked that moment to bound down the stairs. Had he been listening? She was sure everything could be heard in this small house.

"*Buenos días,*" he said, and bent to kiss Doña Inez.

Moving easily this morning, he poured himself a cup of coffee as the older woman placed hot rolls and sliced ham and cheese on the table. "How is Arturo?" he asked.

"Good. Very good." Doña Inez turned toward Mary Beth. "He likes your United States," she added.

"Arturo is Doña Inez's son," Nick explained. "He's a pilot, training in the States."

"I see," Mary Beth replied.

"When he returns, he will live in the city." Doña Inez opened the curtains before joining them at the table. "San Vicente is a town of old people. All the young ones leave."

Outside, the fog began drifting upward from the square. A

middle-aged couple picked their way carefully around the mud and puddles. An old man sat on the single bench in the middle of the square, a dog at his feet.

"When Nicholas and Daniel came here as boys, we had no electricity. They would play hard all day, then fall asleep as soon as the sun went down.

"Your mother, Nicholas, she loved it here. Years before, when Doctor Jean lived here, she helped him in the clinic."

Mary Beth remembered what Jean Rousseau had said about Nick's mother. Maybe there had been something between them, something brought to an end by her family and the general.

Doña Inez continued. "Elena said that was what life was meant to be." She sighed and sat down heavily. "But that was before she lost Daniel, and I my Pepe...."

Nick reached across the table and took Doña Inez's hand.

"I am fine, *hijo*. I like to remember Pepe alive." She used the corner of her apron to wipe away a tear, then looked at Mary Beth. "Pepe is my oldest son. He died with Daniel."

Mary Beth saw the grim line of Nick's mouth. This was another death he blamed on General Vargas.

"Pepe, Arturo, Daniel and Nicholas. Ah, that was a wonderful time." Doña Inez looked beyond her small kitchen into the town square. The church bell began tolling. "Nicholas, do you know that Manuel is here? He is the priest. You must go see him before you leave."

"How did he get an assignment to his hometown?"

"He tells the bishop he knows the people, so he comes. He is a good priest."

Relieved to no longer be the center of Doña Inez's scrutiny, Mary Beth gazed out the window, enjoying the last few sips of her coffee. Nick and Doña Inez continued their conversation, but she tuned out, fascinated by the way the mists rose and tumbled outside the window....

"No, Nicholas," Inez was saying firmly.

What had Mary Beth missed?

"It is insanity. You were wild boys. I told your mother we should not let you do these crazy things, but she wanted—"

"It will be fine."

"Estás loco, hijo."

Nick started to reply.

"What will your mother say?" she asked, cutting him off.

"I'm not a boy anymore. My mother knows this."

"With her head, perhaps. Not with her heart."

"This is something I must do."

"For whom?" she challenged. "For you?" She gave him a look of disapproval. "You do nothing for yourself." She shook her head.

Turning toward Mary Beth, she demanded, "If he does this for you, can you stop him?"

Confused, Mary Beth looked from Doña Inez to Nick.

"Why do you want to go on this foolhardy...*aventura?*"

Mute, Mary Beth stared.

"Bah, you are both fools. You will break your necks." She turned toward Nick again. "And I will have to tell your mother she has lost another son." Doña Inez pushed back her chair. "Eat your breakfast," she said, shaking her head. "We should have stopped you then. Now that you are a man, you do not listen."

With an angry challenge in her eyes, she turned to Mary Beth. "You are a woman. You will see reason. Ask him what he plans. You will see. It is foolish."

"Doña Inez—" Nick began.

"I must go to my sister today. She is sick. I will not be back for a week or more. You know where I keep the key." She pinned her gaze on him. "You will go see Manuel. He must hear your confession before you do this." Then she stalked out of the kitchen. The door slammed behind her.

Mary Beth spoke into the ringing silence. "What was all that about?"

"She doesn't want me to go into the valley."

"She's worried, like your mother, about the place?"

Nick pushed back his chair. "It's a little different."

Suspicious now, Mary Beth stood. "In what way?"

"She knows how I intend to get there."

Mary Beth carefully examined his choice of words. "What do you mean *you?* What about me?"

"I don't think it's a good idea that you go with me."

Mary Beth crossed her arms. "We've been through this before. You told me you wouldn't leave me."

Outside, the bell had stopped tolling. People were coming out of the church. A young priest, still dressed in his robes, stood outside, bidding goodbye to the parishioners.

"Why does she think you should go to confession?"

His lips turned up, but the smile didn't reach his eyes.

Mary Beth didn't like it. "What's going on?"

"Come on," he said and led her out into the square. They walked around the church and, with a quick wave at the priest who waved back, Nick continued until the only thing they could see was the thick fog drifting up, at times revealing a magnificent panoramic view of the emerald-green *ceja de montaña* at the edge of town.

Then he took her hand and led her toward a crude wooden railing two feet high, in front of wild vegetation. Beyond lay an abyss misted in tropical wetness. Small breaks in the fog bank revealed a sheer drop of hundreds of feet. He brought her to stand before the railing and pointed down.

"This is the other way into the Río Hermoso Valley."

Chapter 13

"You must be kidding." Mary Beth squinted into the valley, against the still rising sun. She had never seen anything like it. During the moments when the mists parted, she could see the overgrown precipice, the boulders, the trees, the vines. The mud slides. "We can't go down here. We'll break our necks!"

"I won't. But you will," Nick said with a certainty that made Mary Beth clench her fists.

"What makes you the expert?"

"Daniel, the Alvarez brothers and I used to go down to the valley this way."

"When you had less brains than a peanut." The tactless words poured out, prompted by fear.

"Thank you, Miss Ambassador's daughter." Nick smiled as if he'd just learned some secret of hers.

Mary Beth watched the mists float away, revealing more of the treacherous drop. "How far down is it?"

"Three thousand feet."

"What?" She choked on the word.

"Give or take a few hundred." He sounded so reasonable. "It'll take at least a half a day to get there."

"What about a road?"

"The only one into the valley will be watched by Vargas and his Rangers. They control this whole area. There's no choice."

"It's suicide." They'd die. Both of them. In an endless fall. She felt her knees tremble. "Is there no other way?"

"Not if the goal is to get there." He took her frozen hand in his warm one. "You're not going. You'll be safe here."

How she wanted to stay! But there was no choice. "I have to go."

Nick cursed. She hadn't heard some of the words he used, since some were in Spanish. But the majority were in English.

"Mark is down there." She looked into his eyes, the color muted by the gray tropical mists. "It doesn't make any difference what's happening with him. He won't trust you if I'm not along."

Nick shook his head and cursed again.

She faced him more fully, intent on making him see she was serious. "I have to go." As much as the thought of descending into the cloud-shrouded nothingness of the tumbling cliff frightened her. Because no matter how badly she wanted to believe Nick would help her find Mark, that kernel of doubt lingered.

Nick would do anything to protect his family.

The unspoken hung between them as they began the trip down. Nick knew why she'd insisted on coming. He would have if he'd been in her position. It didn't make him feel particularly proud of himself to admit that she was right. He didn't know what he'd do once they learned what had gone on between Daniel and Mark Williams.

But that wasn't the only reason he didn't want to bring her. The physical demands of the effort were too much. But Mary Beth didn't make it harder for him, at least not physically.

This daughter of privilege had guts and strength reinforced by determination. Nick admired her tenacity. She didn't like the height, so she didn't look beyond her own feet. They'd been on the downward descent for a little more than half an hour, slipping and sliding down the treacherous cliffside.

He didn't know when he'd learn to handle his fear that she would slip and fall and tumble to her death. Every time she grabbed a vine that broke, his heart stopped.

"Let's rest here," he said, standing on the first piece of flat ground they'd encountered. It was a ledge of sorts, firm because of the vegetation and rocks that anchored the rich earth.

She came down the steep grade and joined him, covered in mud. He'd insisted she wear work gloves they'd gotten from Doña Inez to protect her hands from the bite of the vines. She hadn't argued with anything he'd asked of her from the moment he'd agreed to let her come. Now her cheeks were smeared with drying mud and her hair had come loose of the pins she'd used to hold it away from her face. With shaking fingers, she removed the gloves and lay them aside carefully. Pulling the pins out, she held them between her teeth as she readjusted her hair before again using them.

"Water?" he asked, holding out the canteen.

"Please," she replied with her pristine manners.

Nick smiled. Mary Beth Williams had crept into his heart, and his heart was having a hell of a time dealing with her. She was all polished manners and perseverance and loyalty.

"It's not as steep as I thought it would be," she said after taking a sip. "There's actually a path."

"Years ago, people took mules down this way. There have been too many landslides for that."

"How long do you think it'll take us from here?"

"Another couple of hours, at least." But he knew it would take longer. She was trying, but he wasn't going as fast as he would by himself. "How are you doing?"

"I'm tired," she admitted.

"Me, too." The stitches on his stomach pulled and burned.

He should have removed them before attempting the descent, but that was hindsight.

She stretched her arms high, then moved her neck around, loosening overworked muscles.

God, she was beautiful. And he wanted her for himself, as that one something that was his and only his. Not something that came to him by way of the name he used, not something that had been touched by the truth of his paternity.

They rested, then continued. The midday sun broke through the mists, warming the air. Perspiration plastered Nick's shirt to his back and mud caked his jeans. Mary Beth fared no better, but she never complained. They stopped again and ate the bread and cheese he had in a backpack.

"Which way?" she asked when they'd finished.

Nick looked down, then from side to side. He'd followed the route he had taken years before, but from this point on, a landslide had taken away everything he recognized. He'd have to scout ahead to see which way to go.

"I'm going this way to see if we can get down. You stay here."

"If you don't know which way to go, why don't we split up? It'll save time."

She was right, of course, but the thought of her alone frightened him. He didn't like the feeling at all. To prove to himself he wasn't as vulnerable as he feared, he agreed.

A half hour later, with Mary Beth hidden by thick vegetation and boulders, Nick knew he'd made a huge mistake.

He'd lost sight of her.

It wasn't that steep, Mary Beth repeated to herself for the umpteenth time. Not steep at all. But it was still too frightening, the wet earth barely anchored in places by overgrown greenery. She followed along a barely perceptible path, leaning to her left, her weight against the mountainside, both hands grabbing bushes and vines, wishing desperately that she'd stayed with Nick.

She saw it then. A better way. Slightly up and to the right. Taking one step back, she turned, reached up and grasped a sturdy vine. Pulling on it gently before committing her weight to it, she stepped up, pleased when she realized how much more level this path was. Confident now that this was it, she moved forward, needing no handhold, intent on seeing if this did indeed promise a route down.

It gave way to nothingness in a heartbeat.

She struggled for a toehold on the muddy incline, her gloved hands tearing down the length of a sturdy vine as she slid down fifty feet or more before stopping.

Praying the vine held, she scrambled to her right, intent on reaching a more level area that would see her clear. Then she'd go back and find Nick. She wished she hadn't been in such a rush that she'd failed to watch where she stepped.

Then she heard it—someone breathing hard, a rustling in the vegetation below. "Nick," she called tentatively.

Frightening moments later, the vine began to break free. Mary Beth felt the ripping and dug her toes deeper into the mud. Reaching out with her right hand, she grabbed a bush and pulled, testing its ability to hold her. It fell away. She dropped another foot as the vine continued to give way.

Surprisingly clearheaded, she clung to the cliffside, her eyes scanning for anything she might use for support.

She identified sounds. Breathing. Clumps of mud tripping down the incline.

The vine ripped from its mooring and she slid, her hands clutching for a firm hold, her legs churning for support. Panic lurched in her heart.

Suddenly she stopped. Something had caught her right arm, stopping her downward descent. Looking up to where her arm was trapped, she saw a large male hand grasping her.

Mary Beth peered up and froze at the sight of the coarse features of the man who held her, a salacious grin on his face. The one soldier Nick hadn't shot. The one named Wyatt.

"Gotcha!" he said.

Mary Beth struggled to pull free of his grasp, but he dragged her up toward him and held her down on somewhat even ground, pinning her arms to the muddy earth.

"Let go!"

"There's no need to shout," he replied, his fingers biting into her arms.

"Where's Smith?"

Wyatt smiled. "Looking for you." He raised one leg over her prone body, anchoring her thighs with his own. "He's gonna have to wait."

Mary Beth saw something mean and ugly settle into Wyatt's eyes. She fought the hold of his hands and tried to scoot out from under him.

He jerked her arms back down into the mud. "No reason to fight," he said softly.

But there was a reason. There was no doubt in her mind as to what he planned. "Smith won't like this."

Wyatt laughed. "I don't think he'll care."

She was on her own. If she was going to survive this, she had to do something. She twisted beneath him, turning to one side and thrashing her legs—until he settled against her, crushing her into the mud.

But the mud proved her friend. Wyatt couldn't hold her, as slippery as she was. She twisted, flipped onto her stomach and scrambled away, crawling frantically to escape his clutching hands as he laughed, one hand around her ankle. Her hands grasped handfuls of mud and grass, but she could find nothing to help her. He began inching up one of her legs, pulling her down as she kicked with her other leg. Her hand found a rock about the size of a brick. She hurled it at him. It hit his shoulder and bounced off. Desperate now, she kicked at the hand that held her, kicking herself in the process. He grabbed her free leg, again pinning her to the muddy earth.

Never before a quitter, Mary Beth feared this time she'd been defeated. She had no more fight in her. The cliff had exhausted her. This man might do as he wanted. But she'd make him pay a heavy price first.

With one last effort she jerked her leg, attempting to unbalance him so he'd release her.

"Let her go." The words, so calm, rose over the sound of her desperate breathing. She barely had time to register Nick's presence before she felt herself freed.

Choking back sobs, she scrambled away from the detestable man.

"Take it easy," Wyatt said, sitting back, his arms wide.

"Where's Smith?" Nick demanded, the gun he carried pointed at the man.

"In the valley, looking for you. I told him you'd find another way down," Wyatt replied with a smile. The smile faded as Nick's expression hardened.

"Stand up," Nick ordered.

"Sure, just take it—"

"Now."

Reluctantly, his eyes frozen to Nick's gun, Wyatt did as he was told. "There's no need to play the hero here. I was just having a little fun. It's got nothing to do with you."

"Pull the pistol from your holster," Nick ordered.

Mary Beth had missed that. He'd been armed all along. He could just as easily have shot her. But that hadn't been his intention. At least, not until he was through with her.

She watched the drama unfold, trying to control the trembling she felt spreading through her limbs. She clutched her knees to her chest.

In the blink of an eye Wyatt pulled the pistol from his hip and swung his arm up toward Nick, just as Nick fired. The man collapsed to the muddy ground.

Before she could suck in a breath, the slope where Wyatt lay gave way, sending him sliding, tumbling down.

Mary Beth closed her eyes and heard the sounds of the mud slide, then long moments later, the muffled moment of impact.

Nick had said he'd been a Ranger, a sharpshooter. But the memory only briefly connected after she realized the shot Nick had taken had landed squarely between Wyatt's eyes.

She didn't know how long she sat there, the echoes of fear and death screaming around her, when she felt a gentle hand on her shoulder.

"Are you all right?" Nick asked.

All she could manage was a nod. Despite the heat, she felt cold. Strong arms gathered her close. She turned into the solidity of Nick's body. The sobs she had felt bubbling to the surface burst from her. She buried her face in the welcoming space between his neck and shoulder. His flesh, warm and damp, felt comforting.

He rubbed his hands up and down her back and rumbled his reassurances. Finally, her nerves soothed by his presence, by his attention, she pulled away marginally and met the intense blue of his gaze.

"*Dios mío*," he said, his voice hoarse and raspy.

She caught a glimpse of something deeper in the emotions he allowed her to see for an instant—in that single instant before he lowered his mouth to hers.

It wasn't a kiss of passion. It was a kiss of relief. Of overwhelming thankfulness.

With shaking hands, he held her face, then as if reluctant, he pulled away and took a deep breath. "We're going back up. Smith thinks we're in the valley. He won't look for us in San Vicente." He pushed aside strands of her hair that had come loose.

She didn't argue. She couldn't.

How she ever made it back up, she never understood. Nick's strong hands, his own determination and unwavering strength got her back up. She'd turned into a spineless robot, one hand before the other, one foot after the other.

Late-afternoon mists had drifted back to cover the deep abyss by the time they reached the top.

The people of San Vicente were taking their afternoon tea,

Nick explained, so the square was empty as they made their way across. He led her to Doña Inez's house and pulled a key from one colorful pot full of blooming flowers.

Once inside, they pulled off their muddy shoes, and Mary Beth fell into one of the kitchen chairs as Nick opened the refrigerator and pulled out two bottles of cola. Removing the caps, he handed one to her and sat down on the floor next to her. Neither said a word as they drank. The clock ticked over the stove.

Long minutes passed. Nick removed his holster and put it on the floor beside him. Mary Beth could think of nothing to say. She couldn't formulate logical thought. Finally, the sugar and caffeine from the soda kicked in. She wanted to get up. To move. To feel something besides terror.

Reaching out her hand, she brushed her fingers against Nick's wet hair. He turned toward her, the bottle halfway to his lips. She tried to look away, tried to turn from the intensity she saw there, but couldn't. He held her with his eyes as he finished the drink. She watched his throat as he swallowed, but couldn't move her hand away. He put the bottle down without breaking eye contact, then reached up and took her hand from his hair and held it pressed to his lips.

He was filthy, muddy, just as she was. She'd thought before that his beard made him look dangerous. It did. He was, he'd proved that today. Very dangerous, she acknowledged, aware of the male intensity rolling off him. Not the sort of man she had ever thought she'd find herself drawn to, not the sort of man she'd thought he was. Yet he fascinated her. She could deny her feelings until hell froze over but nothing would change them.

"Mary Beth—"

"I'm sorry you had to shoot—"

"Don't talk about that miserable excuse—" He cut himself off, shifting on the floor so that he sat on his heels in front of her, his hands on her knees, over her muddy jeans. "I should not have let you go off alone."

She couldn't bear not to feel his warm flesh beneath her fingers. Reaching out, she touched his cheek.

His nostrils flared. "Nothing has changed."

"Don't. Please don't." She took a jagged breath, her heart pounding out a rhythm that threatened to make her light-headed. "I don't want to analyze. I just want you."

He tensed, his gaze pinning her in place. His hands moved from her knees to the arms of the chair. "Are you sure?"

"I've never been more sure of anything in all my life."

Nick felt his control slip. She represented something fine and wonderful—hope for himself—and he'd almost lost her. If he'd had the chance he would have shot the bastard on the cliff twenty times. For hurting her. For even looking at something that was *his*. Clutching the arms of her chair, he tried to tame the savagery he felt trying to surface. He let a moment pass, hoping he wouldn't scare her with his feelings.

But she took things out of his hands with a simple touch, the pad of her thumb across his lower lip. A soft caress, sliding under his control.

Sure he was shaking, sure he'd topple them both over, he shifted onto his knees, his hands gripping the chair. "I don't want to hurt you."

Her eyes darkened to the color of mellow whiskey and she whispered, "You can only hurt me if you stop."

Blood pounding through him, he leaned toward her, toward her mouth. She watched him, only closing her eyes when his lips touched hers. The heat of her mouth pulled him in. He couldn't get enough. He'd wanted her for so long. Wanted her with more than his body. But it was his body that took over, leaning into the chair, pulling her roughly against him as he plunged his tongue into her mouth.

She welcomed him, drew him to her, her fingers clutching his head. It felt like coming home, like finding something precious there, something he'd missed with all his being. The scraping of the chair across the tile brought him back to what he was doing. He pulled away, only inches, and watched her.

Her eyes opened, blinked as if surprised. He'd pushed her chair against the wall. He wanted to slow down, to bring some sort of control to what raged through him, but she did it again.

She pressed her mouth, open and hot, against his. And he lost it. Lost whatever modicum of sanity he'd been able to maintain from the moment he realized what she was to him. Tearing his mouth from hers, he buried his face in her neck, ravenous for the feel of her flesh against his tongue. He could feel her hands tearing at his back, trying to pull his muddy shirt out of his jeans. He had to feel her against him, couldn't wait.

Pushing himself away, he pulled at her shirt, ripping it over her head, then tore his own off, tossing them both to the floor. He felt like he was sliding down a slope, unable to put on the brakes, unable to stop.

The chair tumbled over and she sprawled onto him, her mouth clinging to his, her teeth bumping against his. He tangled his fingers in her hair, needing more. She moaned, her hands stroking down his chest.

The feel of her fingers against his nipples made him shake. He pulled the straps of her bra off her shoulders with clumsy haste. She grappled with the single snap of his jeans, her hands trembling against him.

Their breathing filled the kitchen, ragged gasps that covered the sound of Nick's zipper. But he didn't need air, he needed her. Rolling, he pulled her under himself, his elbows supporting his weight, his hands holding her face for the onslaught of his mouth on hers. Her hands, trapped between them, against his belly, pressed against him. He raised up on one knee, and the feel of the tile brought him back to reality.

He was tearing at her, prepared to take her on a cold floor with no consideration for her exhaustion. For anything. He almost lost it again when her hands clutched his back as she raised her hips against him. He felt the give of desire but fought it, holding her still, trying to soothe her with quick kisses to her face, gentle touches along her shoulders.

She stopped moving and stared up at him. Looking down at her, he saw that one breast was exposed. She followed his gaze. "Don't stop," she whispered.

He touched her, feeling the swell of her breast against his hand. "Not like this. Not on the floor." He pulled her bra up and kissed her, pushing himself up and pulling her with him.

"Nick," she said, grabbing his hand.

"Not like this, Mary Beth." He wanted perfection for her, knowing he couldn't give it to her. "A bath, a bed."

She seemed to relax, seemed to understand.

He knew he'd never get his zipper up again, not in the condition he was in, so he didn't try. She pulled him out of the kitchen into the living room and up the stairs. At the top, she stopped, turned and kissed him, as if challenging him.

He accepted the challenge, letting her place his hands on the front fastener of her bra. He released the clip and she let the white cotton slide off. When he stood one step below her, their faces were almost level. He broke the kiss and looked down at her.

Gorgeous. She was perfect.

Her hands, which had rested on his shoulders, traced the line of his collarbone, then lower to his chest. She leaned forward and placed her mouth gently at the juncture of his neck and shoulder. Her hot breath tickled, tantalized.

Somehow he managed not to trip as he stepped up and, one hand tangled in her hair, the other around her waist, backed his way to the first bedroom. Later he wouldn't remember how they got to the bathroom.

But he'd never forget the feel of her. The taste. The explosive need came back to him so quickly he couldn't slow down for finesse. She didn't seem to mind, and seemed to encourage the madness with her mouth and her hands.

They managed to tear off the rest of their muddy clothes and toss them aside. Nick was surprised he had enough clarity of mind to turn on the hot water. Then they were in the shower, the spray washing the mud and grime off. Soap and shampoo added to the slickness of their bodies.

He'd never realized how finely muscled she was. She looked so trim, so feminine, but there was strength in the lithe lines of her body. Strength that she used to hold him to her, to push him and entice him until he thought he'd go roaring mad if he didn't get inside her.

Unable to breathe from the intoxication of desire, he opened his mouth over hers and, cupping her bottom, raised her off the shower floor. She moaned and wrapped those perfect legs around his waist, her ankles crossed at his flanks. Nearly slipping down, catching himself and her against the tiled wall, brought back his sanity. He jerked the shower curtain open and carried her into the bedroom, her legs still wrapped around him. He fell back onto the bed, clutching at her wet body.

She straddled his hips, her hair wet and wild, the way he loved it. He tunneled his hands through the still dark mass and pulled her to his mouth. She melted onto him, hot and damp from the bath. Then she pulled away and rose slightly, aligning them. He couldn't wait, couldn't contain what had burned in him for so long. Flipping them over, he thrust into her.

Surprise, and pleasure, etched her features. The feel of her beneath him, around him, nearly pushed him over the edge. She moved with him, met his urgency, until her pleasure made her call his name and he allowed himself the release he sought.

Mary Beth could hear the water still running in the bathroom.

"Can you," Nick said, "breathe?"

She wasn't alive, she thought. This hadn't happened.

"Mary Beth?" he asked.

"Mmm," she replied. He weighed a ton. A beautiful, heavenly ton. Still slightly damp from the shower. Still buried inside her. She ran a hand down his back. It was the feel of the stiff stitches at his waist that made her shift. "Your back," she said, pulling her hand away. "Your stomach."

She felt the effort he made to push himself up. "I can't feel anything." His eyes focused on her. There was laughter in his voice.

"I can feel a lot," she said, and immediately felt the hot rush of embarrassment as they both realized what she'd said.

He chuckled, sending the most amazing sensations spiraling through her body. Her sexual experience was limited. There had never been anything as intense as what had just happened to her. She'd never wanted the…intimacy of what had happened. She supposed she'd never thought anything could be so spontaneous. And so carnal.

"The water," she hurried to say before his mouth settled on hers again.

"Water?"

"In the shower. It's on."

He stared down at her and shifted. "It bothers you?"

"Hmm," she sighed as she felt his growing fullness.

He levered his upper body away. "I'll go turn it—"

"No! Don't you dare leave now."

"Why, Miss Williams—" Nick breathed against her mouth "—where have your excellent manners gone?"

Chapter 14

Nick put the cloth he'd used to clean his Glock into his bag. After reloading the semiautomatic, he put it into the holster under his left arm and stretched. He'd cleaned the floor and washed the few dishes they'd left last night when he and Mary Beth came down to get something to eat. Just being in the kitchen reminded him again of all that had transpired. The exhaustion, the fear, the terror of losing Mary Beth. Survival had brought on an incredible hunger that had started as a physical craving and had turned into much more. The too-proper Mary Beth had delighted in him, had let herself go, had relinquished control.

She was his now, more truly his than anything or anyone in his life. And as his, she was his responsibility. He would protect her with his last breath. That meant leaving her here while he went into the valley and confronted whatever had brought her brother into contact with his own. Whatever had placed San Matean Rangers and an American who claimed to act in the name of the American embassy into a collision course with a mysterious American who pretended to be anyone but who he was. And who had pushed Antonio Vargas into admitting what he'd denied for thirty-three years.

He poured himself a cup of coffee, his gaze drawn to the chair Mary Beth had sat on before they'd gone upstairs. The memory of her fingers in his hair tempted him.

Maybe there was a chance. A chance she'd want the pleasure enough to accept the outward Nicholas Romero, accept the hot passion and not demand his soul, not demand the secrets that bound him to who and what he was.

If he didn't have to make a choice that would affect Mark Williams. If Daniel hadn't become a Vargas in the end, compromising everything they'd sworn to believe in. If he himself didn't fall into the same trap to protect his brother.

Grimly, he realized he'd be better off, as far as Mary Beth was concerned, if Williams was dead. That pragmatism was too close to a Vargas trait for comfort.

He put aside the troublesome idea. He'd already done too much he didn't like, pushing the envelope of what was reasonable in the man he wanted to be. He'd killed one man and hurt two others. Those actions had kept Mary Beth safe. For the moment. He had to ensure that safety by keeping her out of it from here on.

Carlos had to know more about what was going on by now.

He stood, his thoughts upstairs where Mary Beth lay sleeping. The temptation to go up, to sink into her and forget his duty, his responsibilities, was strong. But he had no choice. No other option.

He picked up the telephone.

The inside of a shower would forevermore bring back some pretty fantastic images, Mary Beth decided as she turned on the hot water. Stretching, her body aching from the climb down and then up the cliff, she adjusted the spray and stepped in. The rush of water brought back memories of the night—the hot passion, the joy that had blotted out the events of a frightening day.

Her lips felt swollen, her body felt…different. Stronger. She blushed at the memory of what she'd said, what she'd done, the things she'd felt. But Nick had reveled in her, his body hers for the asking. And she had asked. She'd abandoned all caution, all the barriers she'd put up years ago against any invasion of her emotions. It was entirely too late for barriers. Nicholas Romero owned her heart.

What would she say to him? What would he say to her?

The question of what they would do brought her out of her brief shower and made her hurry to dry off.

Dressed in bra and panties, the last clean ones she had, she rummaged through a dresser and a closet until she found a man's white shirt and some khaki shorts that fit a little loosely. Drumming up her courage, she made her way down the quiet stairs and into the kitchen. No sign of Nick. Gingerly, she touched the side of the percolator on the stove and found it warm. She took the grounds out and turned on the burner.

In a paper bag, she found rolls and took one. She felt ravenous, shaky from the long night.

Then she heard Nick talking. She walked through the dining room, following the sound of his voice, drawn to him.

Nick paced as he talked, pulling the phone cord with him. "There's nothing on Elliot Smith?"

"Nothing at all. No one at the embassy will talk about him," Carlos replied. "But something is happening. Many new faces coming and going. One of my contacts tells me there are three Secret Service agents working out of the embassy."

That clearly indicated counterfeiting, Nick thought. "Are they new?"

"These men are, but there have been men from that department here for a few years. Since before Daniel died. I think one group worked with him."

There was the connection again. He had to know what Mark Williams had to with it all. Why Elliot Smith and his men were so desperate to find him. The answers were to be found in the valley.

"Any word on the general?"

"It is rumored in some circles that Francisco Arenales has been given command of the Río Hermoso troops. Many within the Army are saying that means that the general's power has ended. Arenales, they say, will play by no one else's rules." Carlos paused as the line crackled. "Be careful, Nick. It is common knowledge that you have taken the American's sister with you. Neither the Americans nor the Rangers mention the man's name. You know what that means...."

Yes, he knew. He completed Carlos's thought. "Mark Williams is expendable."

Mary Beth sucked in a quick breath at Nick's words. She didn't need to hear anything else.

She'd been duped. Again.

Somehow, she managed to get back up the stairs, undress and get into bed. She didn't know what she would do if he touched her, but she knew she couldn't face him. She had to push the betrayal and anger aside if she was going to help Mark.

Nick came upstairs. Mary Beth heard him open the bedroom door and quietly walk to the side of the bed. It took everything she had not to roll over and scream at him. She was sure she was trembling with rage when she felt the soft touch of his hand on her cheek.

Then he walked out and down the stairs. She moved only when she heard the front door close.

Running to the window, she watched as he walked toward the mist-enshrouded descent into the Río Hermoso Valley.

Nick slid the final few yards to the valley floor and landed on his feet. Though exhausted and covered in mud, he knew he had to be alert. Rangers would be everywhere. They'd either found Wyatt's body, or it lay buried beneath rock and

mud. He wondered if Elliot Smith would even bother looking
for the man. There appeared to be no one around. Five
minutes later, after walking through an untended coffee patch,
he came to the bank of the Río Hermoso.

What a misnomer. There was nothing beautiful about the
river now. The rainy season had turned the sparkling waters
of the placid river into a muddy torrent. Initial surprise at
finding no Rangers guarding the swinging bridge built of
tightly wound vines gave way to frustrated reality. The bridge
wouldn't be guarded because it couldn't be called that anymore. The only things that remained were the two vine-ropes
that held the bridge up. The sides and the floor had fallen.
What was there barely cleared the chocolate-colored water
that sprayed up from the larger boulders. The only other
bridge was the stone one that was part of the main road in
the valley. That one would be guarded.

Nick wiped sweat from his face and reached up to test what
was left of the bridge. He pulled and the rope swayed but
didn't give. It felt sturdy enough. And he had no choice. With
the river so high, there would be no place to ford it. It was
either this or swim. Or both, if the vine broke.

The long morning crawled by, each minute longer than the
one before. Mary Beth concentrated on Mark.

She'd spent a frantic hour trying to make the overseas connection to contact her father. To no avail. Spencer Williams
was not to be found, neither at home, nor at his office. Mary
Beth left messages everywhere; she even broke down and
called her mother, the senator's wife. Of course her mother
hadn't heard from her father, but someone from Mark's company had called repeatedly about his whereabouts.

She remembered the Jeep, but Nick had taken the key. So
she went to the church, hoping the priest could find someone
to start it for her, but he was away.

Finally, she admitted that her hands were tied. She could

do nothing but wait until her father called. *If* he called. And then what? What could he do from so far away?

She broke down and called once again. And again did not contact him.

Now, desperate for something to do, she cleaned the bathroom and washed her muddy clothes, hanging them on the clothesline beside the house, all the while banishing thoughts of Nick. She studied the papers with the numbers again and again, trying to see what she was missing. Giving up, she decided to wrap them in the plastic again and tuck them into her bra. She was just finishing when she heard a car engine. A quick look out the living room window confirmed her fear. San Matean Rangers.

She ran up the stairs to the bedroom they'd used and, with her back against the wall, peeked out the window in time to see two Rangers step out of a Jeep.

They walked to the door and pounded. Mary Beth held her breath, her gaze darting around the room in search of a possible hiding place. The bang of the door being opened and hitting the wall downstairs propelled her into motion. She ran into the bathroom, then into the next room, desperately seeking a place they wouldn't check.

The men climbed the stairs.

The only place to hide was under the bed, but it was too low to the floor to allow her underneath. With nowhere left to go, she urgently sought some sort of weapon. Nick's bag was in the other room. She bit back a moan of despair when the only thing she could find was a single brass candleholder. She curled her fingers around the cold metal just as the soldiers opened her door.

"*Señorita,*" the Ranger with lieutenant's stripes said. "Please come with us."

Mary Beth felt a bubble of nervous laughter threaten to escape. Such perfect manners from such a fierce-looking man.

She held the candleholder in front of her. A silly move. "What do you want with me?"

"You are to come. Quietly."

"No," she said in a shaky voice.

"Please, *señorita*, we mean you no harm."

"And pigs fly."

"Pardon me?"

"The American embassy won't stand for this."

"The American embassy is not here, *señorita*," the lieutenant replied.

There was no way out. She'd never get away.

She placed the candleholder on the dresser and followed him.

Outside, the reflection of the sun off the Jeep blinded her momentarily. The lieutenant held her arm and pushed her into the back seat.

They drove down the muddy, washed-out switchback road that kept Mary Beth clutching at the seat as they wound their way into the Río Hermoso Valley. Parts of the side of the mountain had crumbled, taking pieces of the road with it, causing the Jeep's driver to hug the mountainside in several places. No one said anything to her. Both men were unfailingly polite—in their own menacing way.

The road in the valley was in much better condition than the one on the mountainside. They drove for a few minutes, first across a single-lane stone bridge over a raging, muddy river that had to be the Río Hermoso, then through rows and rows of coffee trees. Finally, a few, small wood-frame houses with tin roofs came into view. The Jeep pulled up in front of the one closest to the riverbank.

Without a word, she was hauled out of the Jeep. The lieutenant held her arm and led her inside.

Mary Beth looked around. The inside of the house was surprisingly modern for this rural part of San Mateo. Air-conditioned—a real surprise—it also had two computers with large industrial printers attached. The furniture was utilitarian. An open door led to a small kitchen. Another door was closed, a Ranger standing in front. From beyond the door, she heard the sound of a chair scraping across the wooden floor. Moments later, the door opened from the inside.

Nick's uncle, Antonio Vargas, opened it wider. She could see inside.

Mark.

In a chair, his hair long and tangled, one side of his face bruised, one eye swollen shut, his lower lip split open. A bloody bandage rode high on his left arm. Handcuffs dangled from his right wrist, as if he'd just been released from the left one. He looked glassy-eyed and disoriented.

She tore free of the lieutenant's grasp, but he grabbed her before she took a single step.

"Let her go, Lieutenant," General Vargas said.

Mary Beth ran the few steps necessary to reach Mark, and knelt to embrace him. He jerked, as if she'd woken him, shaking the chair, then pushing her away with his right hand.

"Damn and hell."

Ignoring his exclamation, Mary Beth hugged him. He winced when she touched his back. "What have they done to you?"

He focused on her. "What the hell are you doing here?"

"Mr. Williams," the general said.

Mary Beth turned.

"Perhaps now you will cooperate with us."

"Let her go, Vargas," Mark said in a hoarse whisper.

The general laughed and shook his head. "I admire bravery, not stupidity. She will go when you tell me what I need to know."

Mary Beth clutched Mark's hand. It was icy cold. "My brother needs medical treatment," she said. "We demand access to the American embassy."

Vargas laughed again. Mary Beth noticed that the lieutenant who had brought her here wasn't smiling. He stood outside the room. The general walked around behind Mark's chair.

"Your sister is fierce, no? That is good." Turning to the

lieutenant, he said in Spanish, "I will deal with them from here. Leave us."

As the door closed behind the lieutenant, Vargas moved around so he faced them both. "Now, Mr. Williams, we will continue our discussion."

"I have nothing to discuss with you," Mark said, his voice only slightly clearer.

"Then I must persuade you." The general's hand rested on the pistol he had strapped to his hip.

"Mark," Mary Beth said in what she hoped was a fearless tone. "What's going on?"

"A misunderstanding, Miss Williams. Nothing more," the general replied. "Your brother has refused to take my demands seriously."

"What demands?"

"He knows." With that, General Vargas pulled the pistol from its holster and aimed the gun at her head.

For a breathless instant, no sounds interrupted the fear screaming through Mary Beth.

"Let her go," Mark said.

"We will talk." The general glanced at Mark, then brought his attention back to her. He kept the gun steady.

"What guarantee do I have that she will be unharmed?"

"My word."

Even beaten, his features distorted, Mary Beth could read the expression in Mark's eyes; he didn't trust this man.

"What you want is not in one place," Mark said.

"Do not lie to me."

Mark stared at the general through his good eye. "It's in the city. You can't get it without me."

"There is a simple solution, no?"

"You will never get it if I'm dead or she's harmed. It'll be waiting for you, like a ticking bomb." He straightened in the chair. "Waiting to blow up in your face."

"Ah, Mr. Williams. You are in no position to make threats."

"Just as you're in no position to threaten my sister."

Vargas laughed again. "I am holding the gun."

"You won't get what you want from me until my sister is safe and unhurt."

Vargas moved the gun off of her and aimed it at Mark. Mary Beth saw his steady hold on the weapon. No emotion whatsoever showed on the man's face. Or on Mark's. She was so frightened she couldn't move.

The general lowered the gun and smiled. "This is what your Western movies call a Mexican standoff, no?"

Nick came up behind Daniel's house. It appeared deserted, but he'd have to circle around to the front to make sure no men were posted there.

Careful to stay behind the shelter of trees and bushes, he moved to the east of the house as quietly as possible. He saw no one standing outside and decided to go in through the back door.

The doorknob had been broken off, so the door swung open easily. The house was empty, anything of value taken, probably long ago. Drawing his gun, he made his way to the back, to Daniel's room.

He checked the closet. There was nothing there. He closed the closet door and knelt beside it, his hands searching the baseboard for imperfections.

There! The notch he and Daniel had fashioned. Carefully, he pulled the wooden baseboard aside to reveal the crawl space and the dirt below. Momentarily confused, he sat back. If Daniel had something to hide, he would have put it here. The general wouldn't have gone to the trouble of confronting Nick about the house if he weren't convinced Daniel had hidden something there. Lying down on the dirty wooden floor, he felt inside. Finally, his fingers felt metal.

Stretching, he pulled out a small safe and twisted the lock. Snatching a packet of papers from atop something heavier in a rough cloth sack, he sat back on his heels and read the words written by his dead brother.

Days of wondering were over.

Now he knew the connection between Daniel, Mark Williams, Elliot Smith and Antonio Vargas.

Mary Beth bent over Mark and examined his face as soon as the general left the room.

"I'm fine."

"Yeah, you look great," she replied, gently wiping dried blood from his brow with her T-shirt.

"Ouch!" He pushed her hands away. "What are you doing?"

"Trying to see if you need stitches."

"Like the general is going to get me a doctor, Mary Beth. He's the reason I look like this."

"He's crazy, Mark."

"He's a criminal and a cold-blooded son of a bitch," Mark said.

In the silence of the little room, the words sounded harsh, deadly. Mary Beth hugged herself. "What does he want?"

"You don't need to know what he wants."

"It's a little late to be hiding things from me. He just pointed a gun at us! Of course I need to know!"

"What I want to know is how the hell you got here. Why?"

"I got a call saying that the Primero de Mayo terrorists were holding you for ransom."

"So you jumped on the next plane? Are you insane? Did you think you could travel to the far edge of nowhere without help?"

"I had help."

That stopped him. "Who?"

"Nick Romero."

"Damn, Mary Beth! Of all people!" He ran a hand through his filthy hair and winced. "How the hell did you get him tangled up in this?"

"I, um…asked, and he agreed."

She thought he said, "I bet."

"What?"

"So where the hell—"

"Your mouth sounds no better than it—"

"Where is Romero?" he asked through clenched teeth.

"I don't know. He came down to the valley this morning."

"We'd better pray Vargas doesn't get his hands on him."

"What does that mean?"

Mark ignored her, pushing himself out of the chair and onto his feet before Mary Beth could help him. "Do you see anyone outside the window?"

"You can't be serious. We can't outrun these men."

"Look!"

Mary Beth went to the window and looked out. The river was about fifty yards back. Pressing her face against the glass, she tried to see down both sides of the house. A Ranger sat on the ground beneath a short tree, his rifle across his lap.

"There's one man with a rifle, to the right."

"Okay," Mark said, slowly making his way to the open bathroom. "We wait."

"For what?" Mary Beth had to struggle to keep from yelling at him.

"For me to feel a little better and for something to give."

She didn't have the courage to ask what it was he expected to give.

Nick bent over a stream that fed into the Río Hermoso. Splashing water on his face, he considered his options. He could go back up to San Vicente and get help. But Mary Beth would insist on coming back down. That was not acceptable. Or he could try to make everything work out. Find some compromise. For Daniel, for the Romeros. For Mark Williams, and for the woman he cared too much about.

Maybe even for himself.

He glanced at the towering cliff on the other side of the

flimsy vine bridge across the Río Hermoso and remembered Franco's question: *Has your life been your choice?*

His heart ached to choose Mary Beth. But before he could even consider the possibility, he had to remember duty, honor and the promises of two thirteen-year-old boys.

"What's going on?" Mary Beth asked.

"Someone has driven up," Mark replied.

"Can you hear anything?"

"No. You're talking too much," he whispered, limping to the door.

Mark hadn't told her a thing. He hadn't let her see about his wounds. He'd gone into the bathroom and washed, coming back out looking surprisingly better. He was in pain, she could tell, but now she wondered if he'd been faking in front of the general. She'd asked all her questions and gotten not one single answer.

The sounds of various voices came from the front of the house. Mary Beth could not pick out any words—just the mumbling that filtered through to the room.

Mark leaned against the door, listening. "Damn!"

"What?" she asked.

"Look out the window. Is the guard still there?"

She pressed her face against the glass, straining to see.

"No, he's gone."

"Anyone else?"

"No."

"Bring the chair over here."

He took the chair from her and jammed the back under the doorknob. "Won't hold 'em for long, but it might help." He hurried, still limping, to the window and tried to open it, but his left arm was next to useless.

Mary Beth pushed his hands away and struggled to raise the wooden frame that had been painted shut.

"Cough, really loud," Mark ordered.

Mary Beth coughed until her throat hurt as he used his right hand to pound against the window frame in an effort to un-stick the paint.

"Now try it," he said.

It slid up, with only a single *squeak* at the end. He leaned out the window, looked both ways, then ducked back inside.

"Okay. Go for the river. Straight back. Don't look to either side. Don't look back. If I don't make it, cooperate with them. Tell them you can take them to what they want. Tell them it's all in Ciudad San Mateo. Once you're there, tell them I sent it all to Dad."

Frightened, she asked, "What do they want?"

"Stuff I put in my safety deposit box."

She touched Mark's arm. "If it's those numbers, I have them with me."

He stared at her for an instant, then glanced toward the door. "Where?"

"In the lining of my bra," she answered.

"You've got both sets of numbers?"

"Yes."

He moved away, toward the window.

"Mark, what have you been doing?"

"The numbers have to get out of the country. Give them to Dad," he said, his one good eye focused on her.

"Tell me you've done nothing wrong."

He stared at her. "The only thing I've done wrong is trust someone I shouldn't have trusted."

Mary Beth nodded. "Do you really think we can outrun them?"

"There's a church, a little thing, if you follow the river down about two or three miles from here. Ask for Sister Ana. Use her phone to call Dad. Tell him not to work through the embassy." Mark paused, took a nervous step toward the window. "He needs to find someone he trusts...."

"I could call Rachel, my college roommate. She's married to Enrique Norton."

"The OAS chairman?"

"Yes."

"Do that, then, but call Dad anyway. Tell them both you need help out here. Tell them where you are." He took a deep breath. "And tell them not to trust either General Vargas or Elliot Smith. Whatever happens, don't give up the papers to the general or to anyone from the American embassy. Only to Enrique Norton or to Dad."

He wasn't talking as if he'd make it, Mary Beth realized. When she searched his face for reassurance, he smiled, his battered face distorting his features.

"You've got guts, Mary B."

She didn't. She wanted to cry.

Nick approached the Ranger compound from the banks of the Río Hermoso. Only a few feet below, the river roared east, down to the Amazon basin. The rush of muddy water hid branches, even trees, as it swept eastward on its inevitable path to the sea, thousands of miles beyond. He found an outcropping of vegetation and drier earth that had not succumbed to the raging waters. Using this as a perch, he peered over the bank at the back of the three closely clustered buildings.

A San Matean flag flew from the first building, only fifty yards from where he stood. Beyond it stood two more buildings with two Jeeps parked between them. As he watched, the Ranger positioned to the side of the first building stood and ran toward the front. Looking to the right, Nick saw another Jeep approaching.

The roaring of the river made it impossible to hear the vehicles. Knowing he had to get closer, he pulled himself up the slippery bank and prepared to make the dash to the back of the first building.

Movement caught his eye. A man pulled himself out of the window and jumped down. Crouching low, he looked around, then turned and held his right arm up.

To Mary Beth.

* * *

She leaped to the ground, unwilling to take Mark's out-stretched hand for fear of hurting him. As soon as she straightened, he pushed her back against the outside of the building as he looked both ways.

"Go," he said softly. "Run straight for the bank. Careful when you go over not to slide into the water. I'm right behind you."

Mary Beth nodded, automatically felt for the papers lodged in her bra, then sprinted for the river. Mark was, indeed, right behind her. She could hear his uneven breathing. As they got closer to the river, the damp earth gave way to mud. She tried to widen her strides, but couldn't without sliding.

Ten yards from the river, Mark stumbled, bumping into her. That's when Mary Beth heard the gun. She grabbed at his arm and felt the second shot slam into him before she heard it. Her fingers clutching his shirt, she tried to help him regain his balance, but he was already falling, pulling her down with him.

Chapter 15

Someone was shooting. Nick levered himself up the slippery riverbank, staying behind some thick bushes, and positioned himself to see what he could do without making the situation worse.

Mary Beth and Mark lay only a few yards away, sprawled on the ground. Nick's mind screamed, fighting the urge to run to her, but he couldn't give himself away and still hope to help her.

She sat up, instantly turning toward her brother, who lay immobile on the ground. As she reached out to him, another shot echoed around them, making her flinch.

Elliot Smith ran toward them, rifle at the ready. Nick pulled the Glock out of its holster and judged the distance between himself and Smith.

Then Nick saw the general and three Rangers coming from the compound. If he took the shot, Mary Beth and her brother would be caught in a deadly cross fire.

"Move away from him!" Smith yelled, standing only a few feet from her, aiming at Mark.

"He's bleeding," she said, her attention fixed on her brother.

"Stand up. Move away."

But she stayed down. Smith fired again, the bullet kicking up grass and mud a few feet away from Mark's prone body. The shot echoed across the river.

"Move!" Smith yelled.

"But he's—"

"Stand up!"

Taking steady aim, Nick concentrated on Smith, his finger on the trigger. Mary Beth stood and blocked his view.

Turning, Smith spoke, "Vargas, have one of your men check him."

Down the barrel of his gun, Nick saw the old man walking toward them.

"We need him alive," the general said.

"It doesn't matter. With both of them dead, there's nothing to find," Smith replied.

Mary Beth moved, slowly leaving Nick's line of fire. He aimed carefully, praying Mary Beth would give him a chance to get a shot at Smith.

"Mark said whatever you want will blow up in your face without him." Her voice rang out. "Get him a doctor."

"She's bluffing. When we couldn't find Williams, his sister was important. It doesn't matter now. It ends with them," Smith replied.

Nick picked his targets. He had only seconds to take out Smith and the other four men.

Elliot Smith aimed his rifle at Mark.

Blood roaring through his body, Nick willed Mary Beth to move just enough.

A shot rang out and Smith fell.

The general turned toward the compound in search of the shooter, and Nick trained his gun on his back.

"General." The voice came from the side of one of the buildings. Francisco Arenales, the Ranger colonel Carlos had said was now in charge, held a rifle, smoke coming from the barrel, aimed at Smith's body. Behind him stood a contingent of seven Rangers.

"*Gracias,* Francisco," the general said. "Have your men move Smith. Check Mr. Williams."

Arenales nodded at his men and they moved forward.

"General," Arenales said as one of his men examined Mark. "My men will take over here. Your men should join the rest of mine at the bridge. There is word that Primero de Mayo will destroy it."

Nick lowered his gun. The game had just changed.

Drastically.

"Miss Williams," the man who'd introduced himself as Colonel Francisco Arenales said. "My man is a medic. He will see to your brother."

Mark lay on a narrow bed inside the second of the buildings in the compound. A soldier was, indeed, working on him.

"He needs a hospital."

"I will see that he gets to one," General Vargas said from behind her. "But first, we will talk, no?"

Mary Beth had to force herself to look away from Mark. "There's nothing to talk about. My brother needs help."

"Calm yourself, Miss Williams. Now that you have a reason to work with me, I am sure we will reach a compromise."

She glanced at Mark again, but couldn't see him because the medic blocked her view.

"What do you want?"

"First, I want to know where Nicholas is."

"I have no idea."

"Miss Williams," the general said. "Do not expect me to believe this."

"Believe what you want."

"Nicholas brought you here."

She stared into the general's cold eyes. It made no difference where Nick was. He'd betrayed her and Mark. "He left. I don't know where he is."

"He came into the valley?"

"That was his plan."

"What else did he plan?"

"I don't know."

"Miss Williams," the general said with exaggerated patience.

"His plan was to protect his cousin—your son."

"Ah, so he did come because of Daniel."

Nick had used her to protect his cousin. Used her…and she'd fallen in love with him. How rich was that? Now she and Mark were alone, at the mercy of this man.

"What have you done with Elliot Smith?"

The general smiled. "Your dependency on the American embassy was ill-informed. As you saw, Mr. Smith was not here to help you."

"And you are?"

"I can see to it that your brother gets medical attention."

"In exchange for what you want."

"Of course."

"Mark's unconscious. He can't tell you anything."

"Perhaps you know more than you think you know, Miss Williams. Perhaps if we discuss this further—"

"*Coronel!*" a voice from the front called.

"*¿Qué pasa?*" Arenales shouted back.

When no answer came, the general turned his attention away from Mary Beth. "Francisco, go see what is wrong," he said to the Ranger colonel.

Arenales left the room and made his way to the front door.

"How is he?" the general asked the medic in Spanish.

"He needs to go to a hospital. His wound is too much for field treatment."

The general addressed her. "I will get him to a hospital, Miss Williams. Tell me where your brother hid what I need."

Mary Beth wanted to give him anything that would get

Mark the help he needed. Her fingers itched to pull out the scraps of paper she had hidden in her bra. But she couldn't trust the general. She remembered what Mark had said. *"It's in the city."*

"General!" came the call from outside.

"Leave him," the general ordered the medic. "Go see what *Coronel* Arenales wants."

After the medic left, he continued. "Miss Williams, you have no option. Do not waste my time. Your brother will die without medical treatment. I will not give it to him until I get what I want."

She couldn't trust this man, but time was running out. Mark needed help. "I can take you to what Mark hid."

"Where?"

"Mark gets a doctor," Mary Beth said, knowing she was gambling with Mark's life, "then I'll show you."

"Or I could kill him now," the general said, aiming his revolver at Mark.

Nick took the M-16 Arenales handed him. The colonel had not been surprised to hear what Nick had found in Daniel's house. It quickly became apparent that this man was here to clean up the mess of the so-called investigation the general was conducting. He'd sent Vargas's men to the bridge where other Rangers had taken them into custody. Arenales was in charge. Antonio Vargas would be the last to know.

If he ever did.

"Williams is on the bed," Arenales said. "The woman and the general were standing when the medic left. It should be an easy shot."

The rifle fit comfortably in Nick's grip. It felt familiar. He walked around one of several parked Jeeps, braced his left elbow on the hood and aimed through the window.

The general was talking, his back to the window. So easy. But Mary Beth stood a few feet away, in front of him. The shot would go straight through Vargas and kill her.

If she would move…

"I will leave you to your job," Arenales said.

His job. He'd been good. Excellent. Better than the man he could see down the barrel of the M-16. They'd been compared often. He knew exactly what he could still do, despite not having used the skills in years. It was second nature.

The general moved slightly. Mary Beth kept glancing down—to her brother, Nick figured—but the general didn't move.

It would be an easy shot, if only…

"If you kill Mark, you'll never know if I've turned everything over to you." Mary Beth was sure her voice trembled. She only hoped she could bluff the general well enough that Mark would get the help he needed.

"I can make you talk, Miss Williams."

The door opened. Vargas's attention shifted instantly.

"I'm sure you can." Nick's voice surprised her.

Nick stood there, arms spread wide at his sides.

"Ah," the general said, lowering the revolver. "You have come as I knew you would."

"As you planned."

The general smiled. "What terms do you have to offer?"

She'd believed that Nick and the general were enemies. Had Nick come to *help* him?

"Your life," Nick said.

The cold detachment of his words shocked her. Confused and scared, she didn't understand. Did he intend to kill General Vargas? Mary Beth had seen his abilities. His gun was still in its shoulder holster, but she'd seen him. He could do it.

Vargas laughed. "You would not do this."

"Believe it," Nick replied.

Vargas's expression changed from one of confidence to grudging admiration. "I can kill you and take her with me."

He raised the gun and aimed at Nick, his finger squeezing the trigger.

"No!" Mary Beth yelled, lunging toward the gun. She managed to hit the general's wrist, but didn't knock the gun from his hand.

He recovered instantly, grabbing her arm and twisting it behind her as Nick went for his holstered gun.

"Do not be so foolish, Nicholas. You know you cannot draw before I can shoot."

"Let her go," Nick said, holding his hands wide again.

"She is brave," Vargas said, holding her arm back. "She cares for you. And you care for her. She is what I have to negotiate with. What do you have?"

"The proof."

Mark's uneven breathing filled the silence in the room. Then, from outside came the sound of several vehicles driving up.

"It's over. You cannot get away."

"My men?" the general asked.

"Arenales has them. He knows you sold arms to Primero de Mayo. He knows about the counterfeiting. Don't expect help from him. From anyone."

The general threw a quick glance around the room, as if searching for an exit.

"There's no escape this time. You have to make a choice."

"I always said you were good, Nicholas. Always." He sounded remarkably friendly.

"Don't flatter me."

"Ah, it is not flattery. It is the truth."

"You wouldn't know the truth."

"I know who you are, what you are, Nicholas. I know you."

"You don't know anything about me."

"You are the other side of me," the general declared.

Tension crackled in the room. The conversation was beyond Mary Beth's understanding, but she fully expected one of them to begin shooting.

"Walk out now. Arenales will arrest you."

"The charges?"

"Treason." The single word resonated around them.

"I am no traitor."

"You are worse," Nick said with conviction.

The general did not reply.

"Show some sense of honor. Let her help her brother. Let them go. You and I. We can settle this."

"Ah, this woman. She is the one, no, Nicholas? The one you will kill for."

He already had. The thought struck Mary Beth as insane, unbelievable. Beyond uncivilized in this uncivilized place.

"Let them go."

The two men looked at each other. The silence around them grew.

"No, Nicholas, I will not."

It happened so quickly, she didn't have time to react. The general pulled her close and held something hard and cold against her neck. His gun.

Over her own harsh breathing, Mary Beth heard the general say, "Now *you* have to make a choice."

Nick's blood ran cold. There had been an instant when he could have taken a shot, pulled out his Glock and killed Vargas. He knew he was that good. But he'd paused, afraid that in the confusion Mary Beth would be hurt. That single second of fear for her would cost her life.

"You make few mistakes, Nicholas. Why did you not shoot through the window? For you, it would have been very easy."

"Let her go."

"I hope it was not sentimentality that stopped you," Vargas added. "Or perhaps you doubted your skills? Does your Miss Williams know we are often compared, you and I?"

A single second, and he'd failed. Again.

"Shame, jail—they are not acceptable to me," Vargas continued. "You should know this."

"And death is?"

"I need a Jeep."

"Arenales will not negotiate."

"I am not negotiating with him. I will go or this woman will die."

"Then you will die."

"So be it." Vargas pulled Mary Beth tighter against him, the barrel of the gun pressed into her jugular.

Nick needed an opening, a break. Something that would allow him to save her. He could draw on the general, hope that his reaction would be to turn the gun away from Mary Beth in an automatic defensive move. But he couldn't gamble. Vargas couldn't be counted on to react the way any other man would. She could die. She would, unless he did something.

"I'll talk to Arenales."

"Talk quickly, Nicholas. Two minutes. No more," Vargas said. "Put your hands on the top of your head before you turn around."

Nick walked out, hands clasped on the top of his head. He wanted to turn and take the shot, but knew he couldn't. His best chance lay with Arenales.

As he stepped outside, bright sunlight reflected off one of several Jeeps surrounding the compound. Shading his eyes he said, "Have them move back."

"I cannot make such an order," the colonel replied.

"The woman's life is at stake. Her brother's, too."

Arenales seemed to consider what Nick had said. He looked around at the Rangers surrounding the compound, then back at Nick. "What does he want?"

"A Jeep."

"Impossible. I cannot allow that."

It was happening again. The offer, the counteroffer, the refusal. Only this time it wasn't Daniel who would die because of the general's need for glory. Mary Beth would pay the price of his mistake—a second's pause.

He couldn't let it happen. Wouldn't. Vargas had to die.

And he would. When he came out, the Rangers would kill him. And kill Mary Beth because Vargas would not let her go.

That left him with only one option. To do what he should have done minutes earlier, what his fear of hitting Mary Beth, or his conscience, or both had prevented. Antonio Vargas had stopped him from going back in for Daniel nearly three years ago by launching a disastrous assault. This time Nick would go back and do what had to be done. This time he would not fail, no matter the cost.

Mary Beth had to live. Nothing else mattered.

Surprised at how calm he felt, he made sure the safety was off the Glock and turned to walk back inside.

"Nicholas," Arenales said.

Nick turned back.

Arenales tossed a 9mm Beretta toward him. "It is always better to have two weapons."

Moving the Glock to the back waistband of his jeans, he pulled his shirt out enough to cover it. The weight of the Beretta in the holster reassured him.

But the Glock was his weapon.

All he needed was an opportunity.

Perspiration rolled down Mary Beth's back. The room was hot and stuffy. Someone had turned off the power. Fear choked her.

The general had nerves of steel. His body heat made her hotter, but she could almost swear he wasn't sweating. He simply waited.

Mark's now labored breathing was the only sound in the room. He was getting worse. If he didn't get the help he needed soon, it would be too late.

"I'm coming in," Nick shouted from the front. The door

opened and he came in, calm and businesslike. He'd probably done this sort of thing a hundred times.

"He refused?" the general asked.

"Yes."

"He does not compromise. I trained him well."

"Leave her here."

"The Rangers will have a difficult time shooting at a woman," the general said. "You underestimate chivalry, Nicky." The use of his nickname caught Mary Beth by surprise.

Nick's eyes flickered in reaction before he replied. "You don't stand a chance."

"This is where you are wrong. There is always a chance." He pulled back, dragging Mary Beth with him, always facing Nick. "With your left hand, throw aside your weapon and put your hands on your head," he ordered.

Nick complied, and the general continued dragging her backward, toward a door just past the cot where Mark lay. A door that faced the river.

"Come here," he told Nick.

Nick didn't hesitate. With his hands on his head, he passed the general and came to stand beside the door, always facing Vargas.

"You will open it with your left hand. Keep the right one on your head. The moment you open the door, put your hand back on your head and walk out. You may ask the Rangers to hold their fire."

"Let her tend to her brother. Take me instead," Nick said from the doorway.

"No, my best chance is with her."

"You use yet another woman. You hide behind women."

The general flinched at the insult. Mary Beth felt it and knew he'd shoot one or both of them. Moments dragged by.

"*Eres un caballero,* a gentleman," the general finally said. "Elena did well with you."

The admiration in his tone surprised Mary Beth.

"She did well with your son. If you had not armed his enemies, he would be alive. Alive and shamed by what you have done."

"Ah. Daniel did have evidence. I thought perhaps it was only Arenales who thought he could benefit."

"Arenales is honorable. You hoped I would doubt Daniel. That in order to protect him, I would protect you."

"He hid the proof. He did not give it to Williams."

"That's where you're wrong. He and Williams worked together. But you killed him before they could use what they gathered. Arenales has everything. There is no escape."

The general's arm tightened around Mary Beth. "You will not allow him to use what he has. It would hurt Elena."

"You will be dead. You won't gain a thing."

"My name will not be shamed."

"Your legacy, your name—both are dead."

"The boy, Nicholas," the general said. "He is my grandson. His mother is useless, but Elena will see to it that he is the Romero heir. He will have it all. He is my future."

"He will live a life without the knowledge of you."

A dark, heavy silence fell over the airless room.

"But there is you, Nicholas," the general said finally. "Because of you, I still win."

The last statement made no sense to Mary Beth. Her brain wasn't working, and fear dominated every breath she took.

"You will never get anything from me. Arenales won't cover up for you. He owes you nothing."

"Let us see, then, shall we? Open the door."

Nick lowered his right hand to the doorknob. "Francisco, we're coming out!"

Mary Beth's heart nearly stopped. A dozen Rangers stood on either side of the door, all aiming rifles at Nick. To the left stood Arenales. More Rangers had to be positioned around the front. About fifty yards away lay the heavy growth along the embankment of the Río Hermoso.

"Step outside, Nicholas."

"Last chance," Nick said. "Let her go."

"Ever the diplomat," the general said. "Step out."

Nick walked forward. Mary Beth held her breath, expecting shots that did not come.

"Stop," the general said once Nick stood well away from the house. "Turn around."

Nick stopped, turned and waited. The Rangers and the colonel were behind and to the left and right of him. The gun at Mary Beth's neck slipped a little, on her sweat.

"We have a dilemma," the general said. "I must get to the river. Nick wants to protect you, Miss Williams. He knows I will pull the trigger if I am shot." He kept walking, pulling her along, gun at her neck. "What do you suppose he will do?"

Nick had another gun. He had to. He would shoot Vargas. She knew he would. She tried to think clearly enough to decide which way to jump when it happened.

"Francisco?" Nick called, his gaze steady on the general, his hands on his head.

"Let them pass," Arenales said to his men.

All lowered their rifles slightly but kept them on their shoulders.

She and the general reached Nick. "As I said, Nicky, chivalry," the general said in a conversational tone. He pulled Mary Beth along and, as they passed Nick and the Rangers, began backing toward the river, keeping her as a shield.

"Do not turn around," he ordered Nick. "Walk to the river."

Their shoes squished as they reached the soggy ground. Nick's back became Mary Beth's focal point. Finally, the river roared behind them.

"You may turn around now."

Nick turned toward the general and Mary Beth, remembering the exact position of each Ranger, of Arenales. Vargas had reached the overgrown bushes at the edge of the river and now stood about fifteen feet away from him, back to the river, facing him and the Rangers. The rushing river would make it impossible for Arenales and the Rangers to hear and react quickly to anything that was said. The general's hold on Mary Beth had relaxed, but only slightly. The gun was still aimed at her neck but was not pressed to it.

"We reach the end," Vargas said.

"Let her go. She will only slow you down. This is a mistake."

"I do not make mistakes, Nicholas. I never make mistakes."

"Your greed was a mistake."

"Perhaps a flaw, not a mistake." The general shrugged. "Your character, Daniel's character, these are things I did not anticipate. Perhaps they were my errors in judgment."

"Your whole life has been an error, a mistake," Nick said.

"You, of all people, cannot mean that." He stepped slightly away from Mary Beth, as if daring him to try a shot. "Nicholas has another gun, Miss Williams. Did he tell you that our marksman's abilities are equal? He is looking for an opportunity. We are much alike, Nicholas and I."

"Move away from her."

"Will you kill me? You are a diplomat. A man of peace, yet you show no compassion. No mercy."

"Just as you showed none for your own son."

"You know nothing, Nicholas. Nothing."

"You armed Primero de Mayo. Did you expect them to let him go when you betrayed them?"

"You failed him with your *negotiations,*" Vargas sneered the last word.

"I would have gotten him out."

"No one could get him out."

"I could have. I *would* have."

The general's grasp on Mary Beth loosened slightly. He looked at Nick as if seeing him for the first time. "You were going back in," he said, surprise in his voice.

Mary Beth shifted away ever so slightly. All Nick needed

was a moment. A small movement in the right direction. He waited.

"You were going to kill them all and save him," the general said, his right arm slightly lower, the gun aimed now at Mary Beth's shoulder.

Nick said nothing. The silence grew.

"Your failure, then, Nicholas," he said finally. "You should have done what I would have done with your talent, your first opportunity. You could have killed them all the first time. Instead you negotiated your failure. Did you doubt your skills?" he asked. "It was not fear for yourself. That is not something that is in you. You feared for him. Your fear for him stopped you."

Nick heard the words but refused to allow them to affect him. He needed an opening.

"You are not a man who doubts himself. In that, you are like me. You let your love for Daniel weaken you," Antonio Vargas continued. "You can never allow any emotion to weaken you."

He suddenly seemed smaller, weary against the backdrop of the muddy river. But he straightened and raised the gun to Mary Beth's neck again. "You will see. It is all in the blood. You cannot avoid it."

No, he couldn't, Nick realized. He would have to kill this man. "You gain nothing by killing her. Throw down your gun. Move away from her."

"In exchange for what?"

"Your life, old man."

"You cannot heap such sin on your soul, Nicholas."

"My soul is not your concern. Move away or die."

The roar of the river filled the air.

"You should have taken the shot when I was inside. It would have been easier for me."

"But not for me," Nick admitted.

"Then Elena did raise you well," the general said, backing

to the edge of the crumbling riverbank. He pushed Mary Beth forward, toward Nick.

Seeing his chance, Nick reached back for the Glock as she stumbled to the muddy ground.

The general, gaze steady on Nick, no expression on his face, jumped into the raging river.

And vanished.

Mary Beth scrambled to her feet and ran to the edge of the river. Brown spray flew around her. Nick, his unfired gun dangling from his right hand, stood silently staring down into the boiling waters that had swallowed Antonio Vargas.

Confusion overwhelmed her. She couldn't describe her jumble of emotions. Relief was the only obvious one. Questions she couldn't sort out tumbled around in her mind.

"Miss Williams?" the colonel, said jogging up to her. The Rangers were already on the bank searching the river. "Are you hurt?"

"No. No, I'm not," she replied, shivering with a sudden chill. "My brother?"

"A helicopter will arrive within minutes to take him to the hospital in Trujillo. My medic has stabilized him."

"May I ride with him?"

"Of course. I will tell my men that they are to help you aboard the helicopter." With a brief, stiff nod, he walked away, leaving her alone with Nick.

He was still standing on the riverbank, as if all his strength had been used up. It probably had been. He'd spent the better part of an hour trying to find a way to save her.

He hadn't abandoned her.

She had to understand, had to make sense of things. "You said Mark was expendable."

He turned sharply toward her. "I never said that. I would never—" He nodded, as if remembering. "You heard me talking to Carlos on the phone."

She wouldn't help him, refused to help him come up with an excuse.

"He was filling me in on what he'd learned. It was so bad, he didn't want to say it, so I did. According to everyone, Mark was expendable."

He'd saved her life, but did she dare believe him? Trust him? He'd told her all along he couldn't give her honesty.

There was something different about him now, a stillness. A quietness. Not sorrow, not defeat. Not anything she could name.

"Do you know what their involvement in the counterfeiting was?"

He turned back toward her again. "Mark didn't tell you?"

She shook her head.

"He is Secret Service. Daniel was his San Matean contact. They had a good deal of evidence. Enough to bring General Vargas and Elliot Smith down. Daniel's death left Mark out in the cold since Smith was his contact. I don't know exactly what happened, but Mark and Daniel were investigating, not participating, in the counterfeiting."

"So they are innocent?"

"Yes."

"Then they've been vindicated."

"Yes."

From downriver came the clap of helicopter blades. Nick shielded his eyes and looked up.

Mary Beth had one last question. "He knew about Alex, but what did he mean when he said he still wins, that there is you?"

Nick looked back at her, his face drawn, the expression in his eyes tearing at her heart.

"That monster was my father."

Chapter 16

He'd told her the truth and she'd left. Intellectually, Nick knew Mary Beth had run back to the compound because the helicopter had arrived. She'd had to go to her brother. He'd even told her to, unable to stand her scrutiny any longer.

But as he stared into the Río Hermoso, as he watched more of the muddy bank tumble into the brown waters, taking with it bushes and trees, he found he couldn't be pragmatic.

He couldn't be like the man who was surely dead.

He wanted something besides the shock on her face.

All along, he'd told himself that he couldn't tell her the truth because it would hurt his family. He'd been lying to himself. She would have kept his secret, just as he knew she would keep the one about Alex. No, he had not been able to tell her because he couldn't stand to see that look on her face, couldn't stand to have her know such a horrible thing about him.

And it was much worse than he'd imagined. Antonio Vargas had sold weapons to Primero de Mayo and, when he double-crossed them with his attempt to capture them, they had taken his son. Simple greed had motivated the counterfeiting operation. Demetrio Vazquez, the expert counterfeiter, had proved a temptation the general and Elliot Smith could not resist. They'd organized a huge counterfeiting operation that continued even after Vazquez went to jail and the American authorities became involved. Vazquez had told Arenales about the general's scheme after Mark had helped him escape from Vargas.

Now Nick had to see if it was really over. Had to find the general.

Arenales quickly organized a search party. A few Rangers walked; others drove on either side of the river, searching for Vargas's body. But they might never find it. The Río Hermoso flowed into another larger river, a tributary of the Amazon, when it reached the town of Los Desamparados.

The Forsaken, as he'd told Mary Beth only days earlier. Funny, he'd tried to frighten her with the word, had tried to make her go back to the safety of her life. Yet he was the one who felt lost.

The blast of air from the helicopter as it left for the hospital pushed him into action. Arenales loaned him a Jeep. He got in and drove along the riverbank, ahead of the search party on this side of the river. Once, he thought he saw something, but it turned out to be a wooden fence post bobbing in the churning waters. The river turned about three miles ahead, just before it passed by a tiny mission church. The bank there wasn't eroded, but slopped to the shallows along a rocky shore. Eyes scanning the bank, he slowed the Jeep to a crawl when he saw something wash up. He drove to the shore.

It was Antonio Vargas.

Nick stopped the Jeep and got out. If the general was still alive, he'd go to trial. As his wife, Doña Elena would suffer. Better that he were dead.

He walked slowly, deliberately, over the big rocks that kept this part of the bank from eroding. The general lay half in, half out of the river, facing skyward.

He was battered, bruised, cut up.

Dead.

Nick didn't touch him. He didn't want to.

Instead, he studied him, trying to see the man who was no longer there. He'd told Carlos he wouldn't stop until the general burned in hell. He was surely there. Yet Nick felt no elation—only relief that no one else had died.

That Mary Beth had not died.

There had been no physical resemblance between them. No one would ever have guessed they were related. Nick's eyes came from Angela Crosby, who had been a blue-eyed blonde. The only physical attribute he'd inherited from the general was his black hair and his hand-eye coordination. Those reflexes that had given him a deadly ability.

And there it stopped. Because everything else he was had been given to him by Elena Romero. And it was that side of him that wanted a future.

"You found him," a young lieutenant said.

"Yes," Nick replied. "It's over."

Mark hadn't regained consciousness even as he was loaded into the helicopter. For Mary Beth, the entire day in the military hospital became a nightmare of dread and waiting. A bullet and several fragments were taken from his shoulder in a two-hour operation. The doctors said he would need a great deal of rehabilitation to regain full mobility—rehabilitation better completed in the States.

From his bedside, she called her parents and informed them of Mark's condition. Both immediately made plans to come to San Mateo, expecting to arrive within a day. An orderly brought a message saying that a Señora Vargas had made arrangements for her parents to get to the hospital quickly and that they would all have a place to stay.

But Mary Beth didn't hear one word from Nick.

He'd pushed her away. He'd finally told her the truth, and he'd pushed her away.

Eight hours after leaving the Río Hermoso, Mark woke and managed to speak a few words, telling Mary Beth not to worry, he'd be okay. Typical Mark. Then he drifted into a drug-induced sleep.

She spent the night in a chair beside his bed. Nurses came and went, checking on Mark every few hours. They urged her to leave, but she couldn't bring herself to go until one of her parents could watch over him.

As the first streaks of dawn brightened the eastern sky, she sipped hot coffee brought to her by a nurse's assistant. Mark stirred, twisted slightly in the bed, and reached up to touch his heavily bandaged shoulder. Mary Beth stood quickly and bent to hold his hand. He opened his eyes.

"It's okay," she said. "You're in a hospital."

He nodded and through dry lips said, "Water."

She gave him small sips as he tried to rouse himself. After that, he slept intermittently. Once she was sure that he would be okay, Mary Beth sat back and dozed.

She woke to the sound of his voice. "Mary B., you okay?"

Rushing to her feet, she bent over and kissed his forehead. "I'm great. How do you feel?"

"Groggy," he replied in a raspy voice.

"You're on so many drugs, I can't begin to name them."

"What happened?"

She told him, answering all his questions, leaving out only what she'd learned about Nick's relationship to the general.

"Elliot Smith is dead. They weren't able to save him."

Eyes closed, Mark shook his head. "He had the agency thinking I'd gone rogue."

"They know what happened now. There are a couple of agents waiting to talk to you when you feel better."

He nodded and fell asleep again.

An hour later he woke, asking for more water. After taking a sip, he asked, "Those agents still out there?"

"They left to get something to eat," she replied.

He stared out the window.

"I want to know something, Mark. Why were Daniel Vargas's dog tags in your safety deposit box?"

With a sigh, he said, "I couldn't get anything out past Smith. When things started going to hell, we didn't know what else to do, how else to make sure we were believed, should something happen to one of us." He paused, shifted slightly in the bed. "I gave him my ID and he gave me his. Then Daniel was killed." He paused, seemingly for a breath.

"You tried to help him, didn't you."

He closed his eyes. Moments passed and she thought he'd gone to sleep, but then he said, "Vargas had already ordered an assault on the terrorist compound. I was too late."

As Nick had been. Two men would forever carry a sense of failure because of what one selfish and evil person had done.

"You did all you could, Mark."

"Daniel's death stopped the investigation. Vargas found out about it after Daniel died. At first he thought it would end, but I kept at it. I needed the evidence Daniel had hidden and someone I could trust."

"I understand there was a counterfeiting plate."

"Vargas kept them. I don't know how Daniel got one, but he did. That and a counterfeit hundred dollar bill, single-sided, that General Vargas had written on. Daniel told me he had them, but he died before I could add them to our collection of evidence."

That was what Nick had found, what he'd given to Arenales.

"Why didn't you tell me you'd joined the Secret Service?"

"I started to, but I didn't want Dad or Mother to find out. Either of them could have made it impossible. I was afraid you might slip up and tell them."

"But you sent me the safety deposit box information."

"Insurance." He smiled and his eyes closed again. "I figured if something happened to me, you'd see the things and contact Dad."

"When the call came from who I thought were the terrorists, they told me they'd kill you if I told anyone," Mary Beth explained. "I was afraid Dad would launch some grand plan to rescue you."

Mark opened his eyes. "Vargas set it all up hoping to use you to get to me."

"And I walked right into it."

"But you did good, Mary B."

A nurse came in, quietly checked the monitors and left.

Mark appeared to have gone to sleep again, so he surprised her when he said, "Tell me about Nick Romero."

Doña Elena had booked them all rooms in a *pensión,* a beautiful Spanish ranch house with huge bedrooms and private baths. By noon, Mary Beth stood under the pounding spray of a steamy shower until she was sure the boarding-house staff would knock on her door and order her to stop. When she got out, she found someone had brought the suitcase she'd left at Doña Elena's. It felt wonderful to slip on her comfortable nightshirt and eat the light lunch left on the sitting-area table. Finally, exhausted, she crawled between the sheets of the big bed, and slept.

The next thing she knew, she heard knocking on her door. The bedside table clock said it was four o'clock. She rolled onto her stomach and scooted her arms beneath the pillow. But the knocking persisted.

Finally, she sat up and asked loudly, *"¿Quién es?"*

"Nick."

She had quit expecting him. During the hours she'd spent by Mark's bedside, she'd replayed everything that had happened, the secret he had kept, and had come to one conclusion. Had she been in Nick's position, she would have done the very same thing. She would never have disclosed the truth about such tangled relationships. Honesty, as she'd told him she must have, could not come at the cost of damage to so many lives. At least, not without the utmost faith of love.

And he did not love her.

As her mind raced through these thoughts, he knocked again.

"Mary Beth!"

He wasn't going to stop. He would keep knocking until everyone on this wing of the *pensión* heard him.

She'd forgotten to pack a robe, so she grabbed clean jeans from her suitcase and pulled them on, leaving her nightshirt hanging out. Standing in front of the closed door, she took one deep breath, ran her fingers hastily through her tangled hair and reached for the knob.

When she swung the door open, Nick was leaning his forehead on his hand, his upper arm braced against the doorjamb. He was clean, he'd shaved. He looked exhausted. She made that assessment quickly as she stood, one bare foot over the other, staring up at him.

"Can I come in?" he asked.

She was too tired to do anything but open the door wider. He stepped inside and waited for her to close it.

"I went by the hospital and spoke with your brother. Your mother told me you were here."

She'd left her father with Mark. Her parents had somehow managed to arrive separately. Neither spent more than a few minutes in the company of the other. Her father had no doubt found a reason to leave her mother alone with Mark. Her family was being true to itself.

Nick looked at her as if he expected her to say something. She couldn't think of a thing. They stared at each other for what seemed like an eternity before he spoke. "You said you needed honesty, *niña*. You finally heard it."

She couldn't answer, didn't know what to say, except "I understand now."

He studied her as if trying to see beyond her words.

"I'm sorry," he said finally. His words hung suspended between them.

"For what?"

"For nearly allowing you to be killed, for not telling you the truth…" He seemed to struggle for words. "For everything."

He was the type of man who was never at a loss for words. A man who had probably never apologized for anything, yet he had to her. Twice. Or was it three times?

Maybe there was some hope. Maybe he'd come to see her because she mattered. He'd told her secrets she was sure he'd told only those closest to him. Maybe he'd given her the honesty she craved not because it was expedient or necessary, but because he wanted to. Because she was important to him.

Afraid to hope, she asked, "Are you okay?"

He avoided her gaze. "We found him three miles downriver. He was dead. Arenales has agreed to let the blame fall publicly on Elliot Smith. The official reports will have it all. There will be rumors, but they won't hurt my mother. She can go on with her life without the stigma of being the widow of a man who did so much wrong."

"I'm glad you're able to protect Doña Elena, but I still want to know if you're okay."

He looked up then, his gaze steady on her. "I'm as okay as I'll ever be."

"Are you sorry he's dead?"

"No." There was no doubt in his voice. "I'm sorry you were caught in the middle. I'm sorry you had to save my life while I couldn't guarantee yours."

"I was there through my own choices."

"But I knew better. I should have left you in the city, sent you home."

"I would not have gone. You know that."

He smiled. "No, you would not have gone. You are very brave."

She remembered that the general had said the same thing. She didn't think of herself as brave. She'd been terrified most of the time. Only when she'd been with Nick, knowing she could count on him, had she felt safe. Yet she'd been afraid to trust him.

"I wanted to destroy him," he said quietly. "For all that he'd done. But I didn't know how bad it was. Arenales told me about the sale of arms to Primero de Mayo. Vargas wanted the instant political glory of a victory against the terrorists. He double-crossed them and, in doing so, he set up Daniel's death. But he was right. I should have gone into that compound the first time and killed all those men in order to take my brother out. Instead, I tried to talk to them." He laughed, a quick bitter laugh.

"Do you think you could have negotiated with them if the general hadn't—"

"No. They knew the general was going to kill them. They had nothing to lose. But Daniel would have lived longer." He paused. "There would have been another chance to save him."

"Mark tried to help, but he said he was too late."

"He told me."

"You both did all you could do."

He didn't reply. He walked to the window and opened the curtains, letting afternoon light in, then turned back toward her. "When Vargas was in the compound with you and Mark, alone, I wanted to kill him. I could have. Arenales had given me a rifle."

"What stopped you?"

He looked at her. "I couldn't risk your life. Then, when I went in, there was one instant, a single moment when I could have done it, but you were there. If I had missed..."

She reached out and took his hand. "Then I'm glad you made the choice you made."

He shook his head. "You don't understand. He had you. He would kill you, given that he had a better reason for doing that than keeping you alive. And he was right, you know. Fear stopped me. I was afraid you would die."

She wouldn't read more into those words, wouldn't interpret them to mean he cared for her that much. He wouldn't want anyone to die.

"You made the right choice," she repeated.

"You can say that now, but what if he'd shot you?"

"He didn't. He made some choices too. I think he might have made them before he jumped."

"What do you mean?"

"I think he knew he couldn't get away. That it was hopeless. He meant what he said, that it would have been easier for him if you had killed him. But I also believe he didn't think you would. And that he was glad of it."

"That's where you're wrong. He only admired strength."

"In the end, he saw that your conscience, the way you live your life, is your strength."

"Don't give him credit for anything. The man was a monster, Mary Beth," he said, defeat in his voice.

Suddenly she understood why he hadn't told her.

"You're nothing like him."

"I have the ability to kill a man with a single shot at a thousand yards. I'm even better than he was."

"But you chose to make a life outside of that ability. You chose something at the opposite end of death. You chose hope."

"It's his blood that flows through me."

"But it's Doña Elena who molded you."

The words hung in the silence around them.

"Are you willing to take a chance that I'm not like him?" he asked so quietly that Mary Beth had to strain to hear him.

"I won't be taking a chance. He would not acknowledge his own son, yet you have claimed your brother's as your own. You are nothing like him. You're Nicholas Romero." She'd been afraid from the moment she realized that she had fallen in love with him, afraid because it was such a risk on her part. But in reality it wasn't. "You're the man I love."

That stopped him. Very gently he reached out and cupped her cheek. "I'm obstinate, very hardheaded. When I make up my mind—'' He laughed a genuine laugh, running his hand over the tangled mess of her hair and down to her cheek again. ''I am no different than you. You are the most determined person I have ever met.''

She smiled. It felt so good to smile. She put her hand over his on her cheek. ''We will have to compromise, agree on some things.''

''I love you, Mary Beth.''

He said the words with such conviction, tears stung her eyes.

''We agree to love each other. No compromises with that. Ever. All else is negotiable.'' He took her hand and kissed the back. ''But,'' he said, his eyes dark, ''the truth can never come out.''

''I understand.''

He clasped her hand tightly. ''Be sure, *niña*. My life and my name are a lie, but they are what I am.''

''No.'' She shook her head, her voice trembling. ''Your life has made you into a man who is honest and good.''

The blue of his eyes bored into her. ''I may never tell Alex the truth. He may forever believe he is a Romero.''

She thought about that. Thought what the truth could do to the child, to the man he would become. ''You will decide. You and Laura.''

''You are sure?''

''Yes.'' She understood the need for these secrets.

He kissed her, a sweet gentle kiss that had her hugging him tightly. But when he pulled away, there was more than gentleness in his expression.

''Did you sleep? Are you tired?''

She laughed. ''I'm not *that* tired.''

''Mary Beth Williams, I love you,'' he said with a smile that lit up his face. ''I can show you.'' He glanced around the room, his gaze resting on the bed before he pulled her close.

''You think?'' she teased.

"I'm sure I can manage some demonstration of my devotion." But instead of taking her to bed, he pulled her into his lap as he sat down on a nearby upholstered chair.

She looped her arms around his neck and kissed him lightly on the lips. "I was hoping for a bit more than this."

Drawing her face down to his, he kissed her, his mouth open and hot. He felt so good, so strong. So right. He lifted the back of her nightshirt and ran his hands up and down her back. She tried to get closer, wanting, needing him. But he broke the kiss and rested his forehead against her, his breathing fast.

"Why are you stopping?" she asked.

He laughed, hugging her close. "Because I want it all." He released her, urging her to sit straighter and look down at him. When she did, he asked, "Will you marry me? Will you have my children?"

Without hesitation, with love and trust in her heart, she said, "Yes," and leaned down to kiss him.

Several intense moments later, Nick had managed to strip her of her nightshirt.

Then she remembered something. Something she'd forgotten to mention. Against his lips, she asked, "How do you feel about the possibility of children in pairs?"

"Pairs?" He blinked, his eyes heavy with passion. "I don't—" He stopped himself. "When is your birthday?"

She told him, wondering if he'd remember when she'd told him the date of Mark's birthday.

"That's your brother's birthday," he said.

"I'm eleven minutes older," she bragged, as she always had.

"*Dios mío.* Twins."

She smiled tentatively, worried. "Is that so awful?"

He began laughing, his eyes alive with light and joy. "Not awful at all, *querida.* Perfect. They can come in threes. We can handle anything together."

* * * * *

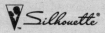

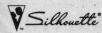

INTIMATE MOMENTS™

The first story in a new page-turning
miniseries by bestselling author

LINDA TURNER

Deadly Exposure

(Intimate Moments #1304)

She had unknowingly
photographed a killer
and now she was going
to pay. But Lily Fitzgerald's
only protection from the
man who threatened her
life was the man who
threatened her heart....

Available July 2004 at your favorite retail outlet

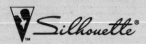

COMING NEXT MONTH

INTIMATE MOMENTS

#1303 RETRIBUTION—Ruth Langan
Devil's Cove

Had journalist Adam Morgan uncovered one too many secrets to stay alive? After witnessing a terrorist in action, he'd escaped to Devil's Cove to heal his battered body. He never expected to find solace in the arms of talented artist Sidney Brennan. Then the cold-blooded killer closed in on Adam's location. Could Adam protect Sidney against a madman bent on murder?

#1304 DEADLY EXPOSURE—Linda Turner
Turning Points

A picture is worth a thousand words, but the killer Lily Fitzgerald had unknowingly photographed only used four: *You're going to die.* Lily didn't want to depend on anyone for help—especially not pulse-stopping, green-eyed cop Tony Giovani. But now her only protection from the man who threatened her life was the man who threatened her heart.

#1305 IMMOVABLE OBJECTS—Marie Ferrarella
Family Secrets: The Next Generation

The secrets Elizabeth Caldwell harbored could turn sexy billionaire Cole Williams's hair gray. Although she'd kept her life as a vigilante secret, the skills she'd mastered were exactly the talents Cole needed to find his priceless statue and steal it back from his enemy's hands. When they uncovered its whereabouts, Cole wasn't prepared to let her go, but would learning the truth about her past tear them apart—or bring them closer together?

#1306 DANGEROUS DECEPTION—Kylie Brant
The Tremaine Tradition

Private investigator Tori Corbett was determined to help James Tremaine discover the truth behind his parents' fatal "accident," but working up-close-and-personal with the sexy tycoon was like playing with fire. And now there was evidence linking Tori's own father to the crime....

#1307 A GENTLEMAN AND A SOLDIER—Cindy Dees

Ten years ago, military specialist Mac Conlon broke Dr. Susan Monroe's heart…right before she nearly lost her life to an assassin's bullet. Now the murderer was determined to finish the job, and Mac was the only man she trusted to protect her from danger. Mac just hoped he could remain coolheaded enough in her enticing presence to do what he'd been trained to do: keep them both alive. Because Mac refused to lose Susan a second time.

#1308 THE MAKEOVER MISSION—Mary Buckham

"You look like a queen" sounded heavenly to small-town librarian Jane Richards—until Major Lucas McConneghy blindfolded her and whisked her away to an island kingdom. To safeguard the country's stability, he needed her to pretend to *be* the queen. But even with danger lurking in every palace corridor, Lucas's protection proved to be a greater threat to her heart than the assassin bent on ending the monarchy.

SIMCNM0604